Henry Glassford Bell

Life of Mary Queen of Scots
Volume 1

Henry Glassford Bell

Life of Mary Queen of Scots
Volume 1

1st Edition | ISBN: 978-3-75238-358-4

Place of Publication: Frankfurt am Main, Germany

Year of Publication: 2020

Outlook Verlag GmbH, Germany.

Reproduction of the original.

LIFE

OF

MARY QUEEN OF SCOTS.

BY

HENRY GLASSFORD BELL

VOL. I.

PREFACE.

A new work on the subject of Mary Queen of Scots runs an eminent risk of being considered a work of supererogation. No period of British history has been more elaborately illustrated than that of her life and reign. She ascended the Scottish throne at a time replete with interest; when the country had awakened from the lethargy of ages, and when the gray dawn of civilization, heralding the full sunshine of coming years, threw its light and shade on many a bold and prominent figure, standing confessed in rugged grandeur as the darkness gradually rolled away. It was a time when national and individual character were alike strongly marked,—a time when Knox preached, Buchanan wrote, Murray plotted, and Bothwell murdered. The mailed feudal barons,—the unshrinking Reformers, founders of the Presbyterian Church, and mailed in mind, if not in body,—the discomfited, but the still rich and haughty ecclesiastics of the Romish faith, the contemporaries and followers of the stern Cardinal Beaton,—all start forth so vividly before the mind's eye, that they seem subjects better suited for the inspired pencil of a Salvator Rosa, than for the soberer pen of History. Mary herself, with her beauty and her misfortunes, shining among the rest like the creation of a softer age and clime, fills up the picture, and rivets the interest. She becomes the centre round which the others revolve; and their importance is measured only by the influence they exercised over her fate, and the share they had in that strange concatenation of circumstances, which, as if in mockery of the nobility of her birth, and the splendour of her expectations, rendered her life miserable, and her death ignominious.

There is little wonder if such a theme, though in itself inexhaustible, should have exhausted the energies of many. Yet the leading events of Mary's reign still give rise to frequent doubts and discussions; and the question regarding her character, which has so long agitated and divided the literary world, remains undetermined. It is indeed only they who have time and inclination to dismantle the shelves of a library, and pore over many a contradictory volume,—examine many a perplexing hypothesis,—and endeavour to reconcile many an inconsistent and distracting statement,—who are entitled to pronounce upon her guilt or innocence.

Not that it is meant to be asserted, that unpublished manuscripts and documents, calculated to throw new light upon the subject, slumber in the archives of Government, or among the collections of the learned, which have hitherto escaped the notice of the antiquarian and the scholar. On the contrary, there is every reason to believe, that all the papers of value which exist, have already been found, and given to the world. After the voluminous publications of Anderson, Jebb, Goodall, Haynes, Hardwicke, Strype, Sadler, and Murdin, it is by no means probable, that future historians will discover additional materials to guide them in their narrative of facts. But few are disposed to wade through works like these; and they who are, find, that though they indicate the ground on which the superstructure of truth may be raised, they at the same time, from the diffuseness and often contradictory nature of their contents, afford every excuse to those who wander into error. The consequence is, that almost no two writers have given exactly the same account of the principal occurrences of Mary's life. And it is this fact which would lead to the belief, that there is still an opening for an author, who would endeavour, with impartiality, candour, and decision, to draw the due line of distinction between the prejudices of the one side, and the prepossessions of the other,—who would expose the wilful misrepresentations of party-spirit, and correct the involuntary errors of ignorance,—who would aim at being scrupulously just, but not unnecessarily severe—steadily consistent, but not tamely indifferent—boldly independent, but not unphilosophically violent.

It seems to be a principle of our common nature, to be ever anxious to wage an honourable warfare against doubt; and no one is more likely to fix the attention, than he who undertakes to prove what has been previously disputed. It is this principle which has attached so much interest to the life of the Queen of Scots, and induced so many writers (and some of no mean note) to investigate her character both as a sovereign and a woman; and the consequence has been, that one half have undertaken to put her criminality beyond a doubt, and the other as confidently pledged themselves to establish her innocence. It may seem a bold, but it is a conscientious opinion, that no single author, whether an accuser or a defender, has been entirely successful. To arrive at a satisfactory conclusion, the works of several must be consulted; and, even after all, the mind is often left tossing amidst a sea of difficulties. The talents of many who have broken a lance in the Marian controversy, are undoubted; but, if we attend for a moment to its progress, the reasons why it is still involved in obscurity may probably be discovered.

The ablest literary man in Scotland, contemporary with Mary, was George Buchanan; the Earl of Murray was his patron, and Secretary Cecil his admirer. The first publication regarding the Queen, came from his pen; it was written with consummate ability, but with a dishonest, though not unnatural leaning to the side which was the strongest at the time, and which his own interests and views of personal and family aggrandizement pointed out as the most profitable. The eloquence of his style, and the confidence of his statements, gave a bias to public opinion, which feebler spirits laboured in vain to counteract.—Less powerful as an author, but not less virulent as an enemy, Knox next appeared in the lists, and, unfurling the banner of what was then considered religion, converted every doubt into conviction, by appealing to the bigotry and the superstition of the uninformed multitude. Yet Knox was probably conscientious, if the term can be applied with propriety to one who did not believe that the Church of Rome possessed a single virtuous member. —In opposition to the productions of these authors, is the "Defence of Mary's Honour," by Lesley, Bishop of Ross, an able but somewhat declamatory work, and as liable to suspicion as the others, because written by an avowed partisan and active servant of the Queen. A crowd of inferior compositions followed, useful sometimes for the facts they contain, but all so strongly tinctured with party zeal, that little reliance is to be placed on their accuracy. Among these may be enumerated the works of Blackwood and Caussin, who wrote in French,—of Conæus, Strada, and Turner, (the last under the assumed name of Barnestaple,) who wrote in Latin,—and of Antonio de Herrera, who wrote in Spanish.

The calamities which, after the lapse of a century, again overtook the house of Stuart, recalled attention to the discussions concerning Mary; and though time had softened the asperity of the disputants, the question was once more destined to become connected with party prejudices. From the publication of Crawford's "Memoirs," in 1705, down to the appearance of Chalmers's "Life of Mary," in 1818, the history of the Queen of Scots has continued one of those standard subjects which has given birth to a new work, at least every five years. A few of the more important may be mentioned. In 1725, Jebb published his own life of Mary, and his collection, in two volumes folio, of works which had previously appeared both for and against her. The former production is of little value, but the latter is exceedingly useful, and indeed no one can write with fairness concerning Mary, without consulting it. Lives of the Queen by Heywood and Freebairn, shortly succeeded, both of whom were anxious to vindicate her, but in their anxiety, overshot the mark. In 1728, Anderson's "Collections" were presented to the public, containing many papers of interest and value, which are not to be found elsewhere. But they are often disingenuously garbled, that Mary may be made to appear in an unfavourable light; and a more recent author informs us, that they were, in consequence, "sold as waste paper, leaving the editor ruined in his character, and injured in his prospects."

In Scotland, the Rebellion of 1715, powerfully revived the animosities which had never lain entirely dormant since the establishment of a new dynasty, in 1688; and the transition from Charles to his ancestor Mary, was easy and natural. The second Rebellion in 1745, did not diminish the interest taken in the Queen of Scots, nor the ardor with which the question of her wrongs or crimes was agitated. In 1754, Mr Goodall, librarian to the Faculty of Advocates, made a valuable addition to the works already extant on the subject, in his "Examination" of the letters attributed to Mary. His habits of laborious research, combined with no inconsiderable powers of reasoning, enabled him not only to bring together many original papers, not before published, but to found on these much acute argument, and deduce from them many sound conclusions. Goodall's work will never be popular, because it is full of ancient documents, which one is more willing to refer to than to read; but, as may be remarked of Jebb and Anderson, he who means to write of Mary, should not commence until he has also carefully perused the "Examination."

Four years posterior to Goodall's two volumes, appeared Robertson's "History of Scotland." Of course, the leading events of Mary's reign were narrated at length, but too much with the stiff frigidity which Robertson imagined constituted historical dignity, and which was continually betraying a greater anxiety about the manner than the matter. Accordingly, what his style gained in constraint, his subject lost in interest. No one has said so much of Queen Mary, to so little definite purpose, as Robertson;—no one has so entirely failed in making us either hate or love her. Besides, he thought her guilty, on the authority of Buchanan, and has consequently thrown a false gloss over her character from beginning to end. He was supported in his opinions, it is true, by the historian Hume, but the latter having devoted most of his attention to the History of England, cannot be supposed to have been very deeply versed in the affairs of Scotland; and in so far as these are concerned, his authority is not of the highest weight. Yet, from the reputation which these two writers have acquired, and deservedly, upon other grounds, they have done more mischief to Mary than perhaps any of her calumniators, the multitude being too often inclined to forget, when once thoroughly *juratus in verba magistri*, that he who distinguishes himself in one department, may be, and commonly is, deficient in another.—In 1760, the credit both of Robertson and Hume was a good deal shaken, by Tytler's "Enquiry" into the evidence against Mary. This work is neither historical nor biographical, but argumentative and controversial. It is founded upon Goodall, to whom Tytler confesses his obligations, but the reasonings are much more lucidly and popularly arranged; and though not so complete or so full of research as it might have been, it is, upon the whole, the ablest and most convincing production which has yet appeared on the side of the Queen of Scots.

Of the five works of greatest consequence which have appeared since Tytler's, only one has ventured to tread in the footsteps of Buchanan. The first in order of date is the French "Histoire d'Elizabeth," in five volumes, by Mademoiselle de Keralio, who devotes a large portion of her book to Mary, and, with a degree of talent that does honour to the sex to which she belongs, vindicates the Scottish Queen from the obloquy which her rival, Elizabeth, had too great a share in casting upon her.—Nearly about the same time, was published Dr Gilbert Stuart's "History of Scotland." It came out at an unfortunate period, for Robertson had pre-occupied the field; and it was hardly to be expected, that a writer of inferior note would dispossess him of it. But Dr Stuart's History, though too much neglected, is in many essential particulars, superior to Robertson's, not perhaps in so far as regards precision of style, but in research, accuracy, and impartiality. It would be wrong to say, that Stuart has committed no mistakes, but they are certainly fewer and less glaring than those of his predecessor.—Towards the end of the last century, Whittaker stood forth as a champion of the Queen of Scots, and threw into the literary arena four closely printed volumes. They bear the stamp of great industry and enthusiasm; but his materials are not well digested, and his violence often weakens his argument. The praise of ardor, but not of judgment, belongs to Whittaker; he seems to have forgotten, that there may be bigotry in a good as well as in a bad cause; in his anxiety to maintain the truth, he often plunges into error, and in his indignation at the virulence of others, he not unfrequently becomes still more virulent himself. Had he abridged his work by one-third, it would have gained in force what it lost in declamation, and would not have been less conclusive, because less confused and verbose.—Whittaker was followed early in the present century by Mr Malcolm Laing, who, with a far clearer head, if not with a sounder heart, has, in his "Preliminary Dissertation," to his "History of Scotland," done much more against Mary than Whittaker has done for her. Calm, collected, and well-informed, he proceeds, as might be expected from an adept in the profession to which he belonged, from one step of evidence to another, linking the whole so well together that it is at first sight extremely difficult to discover a flaw in the chain. Yet flaws there are, and serious ones; indeed, Mr Laing's book is altogether a piece of special pleading, not of unprejudiced history. His ingenuity, however, is great; and his arguments carry with them such an air of sincerity, that they are apt to be believed almost before the judgment acknowledges them to be true. It is to be feared, that he is powerful only to be dangerous,—that he dazzles only to mislead.—The author whose two large quarto, or three thick octavo volumes, brings up the rear of this goodly array, is Mr George Chalmers. There was never a more careful compiler,—a more pains-taking investigator of public and private records, deeds, and registers,—a more zealous stickler for the accuracy of dates, the fidelity of witnesses, and the authenticity of facts. His work, diffuse, tedious, and ill-arranged though it be, full of perpetual repetitions, and abounding in erroneous theories, (for it is one talent to ascertain truth, and another to draw inferences), is nevertheless a valuable accession to the stock of knowledge previously possessed on this subject. His proofs are too disjointed to be conclusive, and his reasonings too feeble to be convincing; but the materials are better than the workmanship, and might be moulded by a more skilful hand into a shape of much beauty and excellence.

Such is an impartial view of the chief works extant upon Mary Queen of Scots; and it would appear in consequence, that something is still wanting to complete the catalogue. Three causes may be stated in particular, why so many persons of acknowledged ability should have devoted their time and talents to the investigation without exhausting it.

First, Several of the works we have named are Histories; and these, professing as they do, to describe the character of a nation rather than of an individual, cannot be supposed to descend to those minutiæ, or to enter into those personal details necessary for presenting the vivid portraits in which biography delights. History is more conversant with the genus or the species; and is addressed more to the judgment than to the feelings. There is in it a spirit of generalization, which, though it expands the mind, seldom touches the heart. Its views of human nature are on a comprehensive scale; it traces the course of empires, and marks the progress of nations. If, in the great flood of events, it singles out a few crowned and conspicuous heads, making them the beacons by which to guide its way, it associates itself with them only so long as they continue to exercise an influence over the destiny of others. It is alike ignorant and careless of those circumstances which make private life happy or miserable, and which exercise an influence over the fate of those who have determined that of so many others. Neither Hume, nor Robertson, nor Stuart, nor Keralio, therefore, have said all of Mary that they might have said;—they wrote history—not biography.

Second, Many of the productions we have named, are purely controversial, consisting almost entirely of arguments founded upon facts, not of facts upon which to found arguments. Among these may be particularly included, Tytler, Whittaker, and Laing, works which do not so much aim at illustrating the life and character of Mary, as of settling the abstract question of her guilt or innocence. They present, therefore, only such detached portions of her history as bear upon the question of which they treat. To become intimately acquainted with Mary, we must have recourse to other authors; to form an estimate of her moral character these might suffice, were it fair to be guided on that subject by the opinions of others.

Third, In most of the works, in which historical research is fully blended with argumentative deductions, erroneous theories have been broached, which, failing to make good their object, either excite suspicion, or lead into error. Thus, Goodall and Chalmers have laid it down as a principle, that in order to exculpate Mary, it was necessary to accuse her brother, the Earl of Murray, of all sorts of crimes. By representing Bothwell, as an inferior tool in his hands, they have involved themselves in improbabilities, and have weakened the strength of a good cause by a mistaken mode of treatment. Indeed this remark applies with a greater or less degree of force, to all the vindications of Queen Mary which have appeared. Why transfer the burden of Darnley's murder from Bothwell, the actual perpetrator of the deed, to one who may have been accessory to it, but certainly more remotely? Why confirm the suspicion against her they wish to defend, by unjustly accusing another, whom they cannot prove to be criminal? If Goodall and Chalmers have done this, their learning is comparatively useless, and their labour has been nearly lost.

If the author of the following "Life of Mary Queen of Scots," has been able in any measure, to execute his own wishes, he would trust, that by a careful collation of all the works to which he has referred; he has succeeded, in separating much of the ore from the dross, and in giving a freshness, perhaps in one or two instances, an air of originality to his production. He has affected neither the insipidity of neutrality, nor the bigotry of party zeal. His desire was to concentrate all that could be known of Mary, in the hope that a light might thus be thrown on the obscurer parts of his subject, sufficient to re-animate the most indifferent, and satisfy the most scrupulous. He commenced his readings with an unbiassed mind, and was not aware at the outset, to what conviction they would bring him. But if a conscientious desire to disseminate truth be estimable, it is hoped that this desire will be found to characterize these Memoirs. Little more need be added. The biography of a Queen, who lived two hundred and fifty years ago, cannot be like the biography of a contemporary or immediate predecessor; but the inherent interest of the subject, will excuse many deficiencies. Omissions may, perhaps, be pardoned, if there are no misrepresentations; and the absence of minute cavilling and trifling distinctions, may not be complained of, if the narrative leads, by a lucid arrangement, to satisfactory general deductions. Fidelity is at all times preferable to brilliancy, and a sound conclusion to a plausible hypothesis.

INTRODUCTION.

During the reigns of James IV. and James V., Scotland emerged from barbarism into comparative civilization. Shut out, as it had previously been, from almost any intercourse with the rest of Europe, both by the peculiarities of its situation, and its incessant wars with England, it had long slumbered in all the ignorance and darkness of those remote countries, which even Roman greatness, before its dissolution, found it impossible to enclose and retain within the fortunate pale of its conquests. The refinement, which must always more or less attend upon the person of a king, and shelter itself in the stronghold of his court, was little felt in Scotland. Though attached, from long custom, to the monarchical form of government, the sturdy feudal barons, each possessing a kind of separate principality of his own, took good care that their sovereign's superior influence should be more nominal than real. Distracted too by perpetual jealousies among themselves, it was only upon rare occasions that the nobles would assemble peaceably together, to aid the king by their counsel, and strengthen his authority by their unanimity. Hence, there was no standard of national manners,—no means of fixing and consolidating the wavering and turbulent character of the people. Each clan attached itself to its own hereditary chieftain; and, whatever his prejudices or follies might be, was implicitly subservient to them. The feuds and personal animosities which existed among the leaders, were thus invariably transmitted to the very humblest of their retainers, and a state of society was the consequence, pregnant with civil discord and confusion, which, on the slightest impulse, broke out into anarchy and bloodshed.

Many reasons have been assigned why the evils of the feudal system should have been more severely felt in Scotland than elsewhere. The leading causes, as given by the best historians, seem to be,—the geographical nature of the country, which made its baronial fastnesses almost impregnable;—the want of large towns, by which the vassals of different barons were prevented from mingling together, and rubbing off, in the collision, the prepossessions they mutually entertained against each other;—the division of the inhabitants, not only into the followers of different chiefs but into clans, which resembled so many great families, among all whose branches a relationship existed, and who looked with jealousy upon the increasing strength or wealth of any other clan;—the smallness of the number of Scottish nobles, a circumstance materially contributing to enhance the weight and dignity of each;—the frequent recourse which these barons had, for the purpose of overawing the crown, to leagues of mutual defence with their equals, or bonds of reciprocal protection and assistance with their inferiors;—the unceasing wars which raged between England and Scotland, and which were the perpetual means of proving to the Scottish king, that the very possession of his crown depended upon the fidelity and obedience of his nobles, whose good-will it was therefore necessary to conciliate upon all occasions, by granting them whatever they chose to demand; and, lastly—the long minorities to which the misfortunes of its kings exposed the country at an early period of its history, when the vigour and consistency, commonly attendant upon the acts of one mind, were required more than any thing else, but instead of which, the contradictory measures of contending nobles, or of regents hastily elected, and as hastily displaced, were sure to produce an unnatural stagnation in the government, from which it could be redeemed only by still more unnatural convulsions.

The necessary consequences of these political grievances were, of course, felt in every corner of the country. It is difficult to form any accurate estimate, or to draw any very minute picture of the state of manners and nicer ramifications of society at so remote a period. But it may be stated generally, that the great mass of the population was involved in poverty, and sunk in the grossest ignorance. The Catholic system of faith and worship, in its very worst form, combined with the national superstitions so prevalent among the vulgar, not only to exclude every idea of rational religion, but to produce the very lowest state of mental degradation. Commerce was comparatively unknown,—agriculture but imperfectly understood. If the wants of the passing hour were supplied, however sparely, the enslaved vassal was contented,—almost the only happiness of his life consisting in that animal gratification afforded him by the sports of the chase, or the bloodier diversion of the field of battle. Education was neglected and despised even by the wealthy, few of whom were able to read, and almost none to write. As for the middle and lower orders, fragments of rude traditionary songs constituted their entire learning, and the savage war-dance, inspired by the barbarous music of their native hills, their principal amusement. At the same time, it is not to be supposed that virtue and intelligence were extinct among them. There must be many exceptions to all general rules, and however unfavourable the circumstances under which they were placed for calling into activity the higher attributes of man's nature, it is not to be denied, that their chronicles record, even in the lowest ranks, many bright examples of patience, perseverance, unsinking fortitude, and fidelity founded upon generous and exalted attachment.

It has been said, that under the reigns of the Fourth and Fifth James, the moral and political aspect of the Scotch horizon began to brighten. This is to be attributed partly to the beneficial changes which the progress of time was effecting throughout Europe, and which gradually extended themselves to

Scotland,—and partly to the personal character of these two monarchs. France, Germany, and England, had made considerable strides out of the gloom of the dark ages, even before the appearance of Francis I., Charles V., and Henry VIII. James IV., naturally of a chivalric and ardent disposition, was extremely anxious to advance his own country in the scale of nations; and whilst, by the urbanity of his manners, he succeeded in winning the affections of his nobles, he contrived also to find a place in the hearts of his inferior subjects, even beside that allotted to their own hereditary chieftain,—an achievement which few of his predecessors had been able to accomplish. The unfortunate battle of Flodden, is a melancholy record both of the vigour of James's reign, and of the national advantages which his romantic spirit induced him to risk in pursuit of the worthless phantom of military renown.

James V. had much of the ardour of his father, combined with a somewhat greater share of prudence. He it was who first made any successful inroads upon the exorbitant powers of his nobility; and though, upon more occasions than one, he was made to pay dearly for his determination to vindicate the regal authority, he was, nevertheless, true to his purpose to the very last. There seem to be three features in the reign of this prince which particularly deserve attention. The first is, the more extensive intercourse than had hitherto subsisted, which he established between Scotland and foreign nations,—particularly with France. The inexhaustible ambition of Charles V., which aimed at universal empire, and which probably would have accomplished its design had he not met with a rival so formidable as Francis I., was the means of convincing the other states of Europe, that the only security for their separate independence was the preservation of a balance of power. Italy was thus roused into activity, and England, under Henry VIII., took an active share in the important events of the age. To the continental powers, against whom that monarch's strength was directed, it became a matter of no small moment to secure the assistance of Scotland. Both Francis and Charles, therefore, paid their court to James, who, finding it necessary to become the ally of one or other, prudently rejected the empty honours offered him by the Emperor, and continued faithful to France. He went himself to Paris in 1536, where he married Magdalene, daughter of Francis. She died however soon after his return home; but determined not to lose the advantages resulting from a French alliance, he again married, in the following year, Mary of Lorraine, daughter to the Duke of Guise, and the young widow of the Duke of Longueville. Following the example of their king, most of the Scotch nobility visited France, and as many as could afford it, sent their sons thither to be educated; whilst on the other hand, numerous French adventurers landed in Scotland, bringing along with them some of the French arts and luxuries. Thus the manners of the Scotch, gradually began to lose a little of that unbending severity, which had hitherto rendered them so repulsive.

The second peculiarity in the reign of James V., is the countenance and support he bestowed upon the clergy. This he did, not from any motives of bigotry, but solely as a matter of sound policy. He saw that he could not stand alone against his nobles, and he was therefore anxious to raise into an engine of power, a body of men whose interests he thus identified with his own. It is remarkable, that even in the most flourishing days of Catholicism, when the Pope's ecclesiastical authority extended itself everywhere, Scotland alone was overlooked. The king was there always the head of the church, in so far as regarded all ecclesiastical appointments, and the patronage of his bishoprics and abbeys was no slight privilege to the Scottish monarch, denied as it was to other kings of more extensive temporal jurisdiction. James converted into benefices, several of the forfeited estates of his rebellious nobles, and raised the clergy to a pitch of authority they had never before possessed in Scotland. He acted upon principle, and perhaps judiciously; but he was not aware, that by thus surrounding his priests with wealth and luxury, he was paving the way for their utter destruction, and a new and better order of things.

It will be useful to observe, as the third characteristic of this reign, the encouragement James gave to the arts and sciences. For the first time, education began to take some form and system. He gave stability to the universities, and was careful to select for them the best teachers. He was fond of drawing to his court men of learning and genius. He was himself a poet of considerable ability. He had likewise devoted much of his attention to architecture—his fondness for which elegant study was testified, by his anxiety to repair, or rebuild, most of the royal palaces. He established also on a permanent footing, the Court of Session, or College of Justice; and though his reign, as a whole, was not a happy one, it probably redounded more to the advantage of his country than that of any of his predecessors.

At his death, which took place in 1542, at the early age of 30, accelerated by the distress of mind occasioned by the voluntary defeats which his refractory nobles allowed themselves to sustain, both at Falla and Solway Moss, Scotland speedily fell into a state of confusion and civil war. The events which followed are indissolubly connected with the subject of these Memoirs, and are related at length in the succeeding pages.

CHAPTER I.

SCOTLAND AND ITS TROUBLES DURING MARY'S INFANCY.

James V. left, as an inheritance to his kingdom, an expensive and destructive war with England. He likewise left what, under such circumstances, was a very questionable advantage, a treasury well stored with gold, and a coinage in good condition, produced from the mines which he had worked in Scotland. The foreign relations of the country demanded the utmost attention; but the long minority necessarily ensuing, as Mary, his only surviving lawful child, was but a few days old when James died, awakened hopes and wishes in the ambitious which superseded all other considerations. For a time England was forgotten; and the prize of the Regency became a bone of civil contention and discord.

There were three persons who aspired to that office, and the pretensions of each had their supporters, as interest or reason might dictate. The first was the Queen-Dowager, a lady who inherited many of the peculiar virtues, as well as some of the failings, of the illustrious house of Guise, to which she belonged. She possessed a bold and masculine understanding, a perseverance to overcome difficulties, and a fortitude to bear up against misfortunes, not often met with among her sex. She was indeed superior to most of the weaknesses of the female character; and having, from her earliest years, deeply studied the science of government, she felt herself, so far as mere political tactics and diplomatic acquirements were concerned, able to cope with the craftiest of the Scotch nobility. Besides, her intimate connexion with the French court, coupled with the interest she might naturally be supposed to take in the affairs of a country over which her husband had reigned, and which was her daughter's inheritance, seemed to give her a claim of the strongest kind.

The second aspirant was Cardinal David Beaton, at that time the undoubted head of the Catholic party in Scotland. He was a man whose abilities all allowed, and who, had he been less tinctured with severity, and less addicted to the exclusive principles of the Church of Rome, might probably have filled with *éclat* the very highest rank in the State. He endeavoured to strengthen his title to the Regency, by producing the will of James V. in his favour. But as this will was dated only a short while before the King's death, it was suspected that the Prelate had himself written it, and obtained the King's signature, at a time when his bodily weakness had impaired his mental faculties. Beaton was, moreover, from his violence and rigour, particularly obnoxious to all those who favoured the Reformation.

James Hamilton, Earl of Arran, and next heir to the throne, was the third candidate, and the person upon whom the choice of the people ultimately fell. In more settled times, this choice might possibly have been judicious; but Arran was of far too weak and irresolute a character to be able to regulate the government with that decision and firmness which the existing emergency required. He had few opinions of his own, and was continually driven hither and thither by the contradictory counsels of those who surrounded him. He had joined, however, the reformed religion; and this, together with the inoffensive softness of his disposition, made him, in the eyes of many, only the more fit to govern.

The annexation of Scotland to the crown of England, either by conquest or the more amicable means of marriage, had for many years been the object nearest the heart of Henry VIII. and several of his predecessors. That his father, in particular, Henry VII., had given some thought to this subject, is evident from the answer he made to such of his Privy Council as were unwilling that he should give his daughter Margaret in marriage to James IV., on the ground that the English Crown might, through that marriage, devolve to a King of Scotland. "Whereunto the King made answer, and said, 'What then? for if any such thing should happen (which God forbid), yet I see our kingdom should take no harm thereby, because England should not be added unto Scotland, but Scotland unto England, as to the far most noble head of the whole island; for so much as it is always so, that the lesser is wont, for honour's sake, to be adjoined to that which is far the greater.'"[1] How correct Henry VII. was in his opinion, the accession of James VI. sufficiently proved.

Henry VIII., though aiming at the same object as his father, thought it more natural that Scotland should accept of an English, than England of a Scottish King. Immediately, therefore, after the birth of Mary, he determined upon straining every nerve to secure her for his son Edward. For this purpose, he concluded a temporary peace with the Regent Arran, and sent back into Scotland the numerous prisoners who had surrendered themselves at Solway Moss, upon an understanding that they should do all they could to second his views with their countrymen. His first proposals, however, were so extravagant, that the Scottish Parliament would not listen to them for a moment. He demanded not only that the young Queen should be sent into England, to be educated under his own superintendance, but that he himself, as her future father-in-law, should be allowed an active share in the government of Scotland. Having subsequently consented to depart considerably from the haughty tone in which these terms were dictated, a treaty of marriage was agreed upon at the instigation of Arran, whom Henry had won to his interests, in which it was promised, that Mary should be sent into England at the age of ten, and that six persons of rank should, in the mean time, be delivered as hostages for the fulfilment of this promise.

It may easily be conceived, that whatever the Regent, together with some of the reformed nobility and their partisans, might think of this treaty, the Queen Mother and Cardinal Beaton, who had for the present formed a coalition, could not be very well satisfied with it. Henry, with all the hasty violence of his nature, had, in a fit of spleen, espoused the reformed opinions; and if Mary became the wife of his son, it was evident that all the interests both of the House of Guise and of the Catholic religion in Scotland, would suffer a fatal blow. By their forcible representations of the inevitable ruin which they alleged this alliance would bring upon Scotland, converting it into a mere province of their ancient and inveterate enemies, and obliging it to renounce forever the friendship of their constant allies the French, they succeeded in effecting a change in public opinion; and the result was, that Arran found himself at length obliged to yield to their superior influence, to deliver up to the Cardinal and Mary of Lorraine the young Queen, and refuse to ratify the engagements he had entered into with Henry. The Cardinal now carried every thing before him, having converted or intimidated almost all his enemies. The Earl of Lennox alone, a nobleman whose pretensions were greater than his power, could not forgive Beaton for having used him merely as a cat's paw in his intrigues to gain the ascendency over Arran. Lennox had himself aspired at the Regency, alleging that his title, as presumptive heir to the Crown, was a more legitimate one than that of the House of Hamilton, to which Arran belonged. But the still more ambitious Cardinal flattered only to deceive him; and when Lennox considered his success certain, he found himself farther from the object of his wishes than ever.

Seeing every other hope vain, Lennox set on foot a secret correspondence with Henry, promising that monarch his best support, should he determine upon avenging the insult he had sustained, through the vacillating conduct of the Scotch. Henry gladly availed himself of the offer, and sent a considerable force under the Earl of Hartford to the North, by sea, which, having landed at Leith, and plundered that place, as well as the neighbouring city of Edinburgh, again took its departure for England, without attempting to penetrate further into the country. This was an unprofitable and ill-advised expedition, for it only tended to exasperate the minds of the Scotch, without being of any service to Henry. The Earl of Huntly well remarked concerning it, that even although he might have had no objections to the proposed match, he had a most especial dislike to the manner of wooing.

The Earl of Lennox now found himself deserted in the midst of his former friends, and went prudently into voluntary exile, by retiring into England. Here Henry, in reward of his former services, gave him his niece, the Lady Margaret Douglas, in marriage. She was the daughter, by the second marriage, of Henry's sister, the Lady Margaret, wife of James IV., who, after the King's death, espoused Archibald Earl of Angus. By this alliance, Lennox, though it was impossible for him to foresee such a result, became the father of Henry Darnley, and a long line of Kings.

Shortly afterwards, an event well known in Scottish history, and which was accomplished by means only too frequently resorted to in those unsettled times, facilitated the conclusion of a short peace with England. Cardinal Beaton, elevated by his success, and anxious, now that all more immediate danger was removed, to re-establish on a firmer basis the tottering authority of the Romish Church, determined upon striking awe into the people, by some memorable examples of severity towards heretics. About the end of the year 1545, he made a progress through several parts of his diocess, accompanied by the Earl of Argyle, who was then Lord Justice General, and other official persons, for the purpose of trying and punishing offenders against the laws of the Church. At Perth, several of the lieges were found guilty of arguing or disputing concerning the sense of the Holy Scriptures, in opposition to an Act of Parliament, which forbade any such freedom of speech, and five men and one woman were condemned to die. Great intercession was made for them, but in vain; the men were hanged, and the woman was drowned. Still farther to intimidate the Reformers, a yet more memorable instance of religious persecution and cruelty was presented to them a few months afterwards. George Wishart was at this time one of the most learned and zealous of all the supporters of the new doctrines in Scotland. He had been educated at the University of Cambridge, and had, in his youth, officiated as one of the masters of the grammar school at Montrose. His talents and perseverance rendered him particularly obnoxious to the Cardinal, who, having contrived to make him his prisoner, carried him to his castle at St Andrews. An Ecclesiastical Court was there assembled, at which Wishart was sentenced to be burnt. It may give us a clearer idea of the spirit of the times, to know, that on the day on which this sentence was to be put in execution, Beaton issued a proclamation, forbidding any one, under pain of church censure, to offer up prayers for so notorious a heretic. When Wishart was brought to the stake, and after the fire had been kindled, and was already beginning to take effect, it is said that he turned his eyes towards a window in the castle overlaid with tapestry, at which the Cardinal was sitting, viewing with complacency the unfortunate man's suffering, and exclaimed,—"He who, from yonder high place, beholdeth me with such pride, shall, within few days, be in as much shame as now he is seen proudly to rest himself." These words, though they met with little attention at the time, were spoken of afterwards as an evident and most remarkable prophecy.

It was not long after this martyrdom, that Cardinal Beaton was present at the marriage of one of his own illegitimate daughters, to whom he gave a dowry of 4000 merks, and whose nuptials were solemnized with great magnificence. Probably he conceived, that the more heretics he burned, the more unblushingly he might confess his own sins against both religion and common morality.

On the prelate's return to St Andrew's, Norman Lesly, a young man of strong passions, and eldest Son to the Earl of Rothes, came to him to demand some favour, which the Cardinal thought proper to refuse. The particulars of the quarrel are not precisely known, but it must have been of a serious kind; for Lesly, taking advantage of the popular feeling which then existed against the Cardinal, determined upon seeking his own revenge by the assassination of Beaton. He associated with himself several accomplices, who undertook to second him in this design. Early on the morning of the 29th of May 1546, having entered the castle by the gate, which was open to admit some workmen who were repairing the fortifications, he and his assistants proceeded to the door of the Cardinal's chamber, at which they knocked. Beaton asked,—"Who is there?"—Norman answered,—"My name is Lesly,"—adding, that the door must be opened to him, and those that were with him. Beaton now began to fear the worst, and attempted to secure the door. But Lesly called for fire to burn it, upon which the Cardinal, seeing all resistance useless, permitted them to enter. They found him sitting on a chair, pale and agitated; and as they approached him he exclaimed,—"I am a Priest —ye will not slay me!" Lesly, however, losing all command of his temper, struck him more than once, and would have proceeded to further indignities, had not James Melville, one of the assassins, "a man," says Knox, "of nature most gentle and most modest," drawn his sword, and presenting the point to the Cardinal, advised him to repent of his sins, informing him, at the same time, that no hatred he bore his person, but simply his love of true religion induced him to take part against one whom he looked upon as an enemy to the gospel. So saying, and without waiting for an answer, he stabbed him twice or thrice through the body. When his friends and servants collected without, the conspirators lifted up the deceased Prelate, and showed him to them from the very window at which he had sat at the day of Wishart's execution. Beaton, at the time of his death, was fifty-two. He had long been one of the leading men in Scotland, and had enjoyed the favour of the French King, as well as that of his own sovereign James V. Some attempt was made by the Regent to punish his murderers, but they finally escaped into France.[2]

There is good reason to believe that Henry VIII. secretly encouraged Lesly and his associates in this dishonest enterprise. But, if such be the case, that monarch did not live long enough to reap the fruits of its success. He died only a few months later than the Cardinal; and, about the same time, his cotemporary, Francis I., was succeeded on his throne by his son Henry II. These changes did not materially affect the relative situation of Scotland. They may, perhaps, have opened up still higher hopes to the Queen Dowager, and the French party; but, in England, the Duke of Somerset, who had been appointed Lord Protector during the minority of Edward VI., was determined upon following out the plans of the late monarch, and compelling the Scotch to agree to the alliance which he had proposed.

In prosecution of his designs, he marched a powerful army into Scotland, and the result was the unfortunate battle of Pinkie. The Earl of Arran, whose exertions to rescue the country from this new aggression, were warmly seconded by the people, collected a force sufficiently numerous to enable him to meet and offer battle to Somerset. The English camp was in the neighbourhood of Prestonpans, and the Scotch took up very advantageous ground about Musselburgh and Inveresk. Military discipline was at that time but little understood in this country; and the reckless impetuosity of the Scotch infantry was usually attended either with immediate success, or, by throwing the whole battle into confusion, with irretrievable and signal defeat. The weapons to which they principally trusted, were, in the first place, the pike, with which, upon joining with the enemy, all the fore-rank, standing shoulder to shoulder together, thrust straight forwards, those who stood in the second rank putting their pikes over the shoulders of their comrades before them. The length of these pikes or spears was eighteen feet six inches. They seem to have been used principally on the first onset, and were probably speedily relinquished for the more efficient exercise of the sword, which was broad and thin, and of excellent temper. It was employed to cut or slice with, not to thrust; and, in defence against any similar weapon of the enemy, a large handkerchief was wrapt twice or thrice about the neck, and a buckler invariably carried on the left arm.[3]

For some days the two armies continued in sight of each other, without coming to any general engagement. The hourly anxiety which prevailed at Edinburgh regarding the result, may be easily imagined. To inspire the soldiers with the greater courage, it was enacted by Government, that the heirs of those who fell upon this occasion in defence of their country, should for five years be free from Government taxes, and the usual assessments levied by landlords. At length, on Saturday the 10th of September 1547, the Scotch, misled by a motion in the English army, which they conceived indicated a design to retreat, rashly left their superior situation, and crossing the mouth of the Esk at Musselburgh, gave the Protector battle in the fields of Pinkie, an adjoining country seat. They were thus so exposed, that the English fleet, which lay in the bay, was enabled, by firing upon their flank to do them much mischief. The Earl of Angus, who was leading the van-guard, found himself suddenly assailed by a flight of arrows, a raking fire from a regiment or two of foreign fusileers, and a discharge of cannon which unexpectedly opened upon him. Unable to advance, he attempted to change his position for a more advantageous one. The main body imagined he was falling back upon them in confusion; and to heighten their panic, a vigorous charge, which was at this moment made by the English cavalry, decided the fortune of the day. After a feeble resistance the Scotch fled towards Dalkeith, Edinburgh, and Leith, and being hotly pursued by their enemies, all the three roads were strewed with the dead and dying. In this battle the Earl of Arran lost upwards of 8000 men; among whom were Lord Fleming, together with many other Scotch noblemen and gentlemen.

The English army advanced immediately upon Leith, which they took and pillaged; and would have entered Edinburgh, had they not found it impossible to make themselves masters of the Castle. The fleet ravaged the towns and villages on the coasts of the Forth, and proceeded as far north as the River Tay, seizing on whatever shipping they could meet with in the harbours by which they passed.

Far, however, from obtaining by these violent measures, the ultimate object of his desires, Somerset found himself farther from his point than ever. The Scotch, enraged against England, threw themselves into the arms of France; and the Protector, understanding that affairs in the south had fallen into confusion, in his absence, was obliged to return home, leaving strong garrisons in Haddington, and one or other places, which he had captured. The Earl of Arran, and Mary of Guise, sent immediate intelligence to Henry II., of all that had taken place; and, sanctioned by the Scottish Parliament, offered to conclude a treaty of marriage between his infant son, the Dauphin Francis, and the young Scottish Queen. They, moreover, agreed to send Mary into France, to be educated at the French Court, until such time as the nuptials could be solemnized. This proposal was every way acceptable to Henry, who, like his father Francis, perfectly understood the importance of a close alliance with Scotland, as the most efficient means for preventing the English from invading his own dominions. He sent over an army of 6000 men, to the aid of the Regent; and in the same vessels, which brought these troops, Mary was conveyed from Dumbarton into France. Henry also, with much sound policy, in order to strengthen his interests in Scotland, bestowed, about this time, upon the Earl of Arran, the title of the Duke of Chatelherault, together with a pension of some value. During a period of two years, a continual series of skirmishings were carried on between the Scotch, supported by their French allies, and the English; but without any results of much consequence on either side. In 1550, a general peace was concluded; and the marriage of the Scottish Queen was never afterwards made the ground of war between the two countries.

From this period, till Mary's return to her own country, the attention of Scotland was entirely engrossed with its own affairs, and the various important events connected with the rise, progress, and establishment of the Reformation. As these effected no slight change in the political aspect of the country, and exercised a material influence over Mary's future destiny, it will be proper to give some account of them in this place; and these details being previously gone through, the narrative, in so far as regards Queen Mary, will thus be preserved unbroken.

CHAPTER II.

SCOTLAND AND THE SCOTTISH REFORMERS, UNDER THE REGENCY OF THE QUEEN-DOWAGER.

It was in the year 1517, that Luther first stated his objections to the validity of the indulgences granted so liberally by Pope Leo X. From this year, those who love to trace causes to their origin, date the epoch of the Reformation. It was not, however, till a considerably later period, that the new doctrines took any deep root in Scotland. In 1552, the Duke of Chatelherault, wearied with the fatigues of Government, and provoked at the opposition he was continually meeting with, resigned the regency in favour of the Queen-mother. Mary of Guise, by a visit she had shortly before paid to the French Court, had paved the way for this accession of power. Her brothers, the Duke of Guise and Cardinal of Lorraine, were far from being satisfied with the state of parties in Scotland. Chatelherault, they knew to be of a weak and fluctuating disposition; and it seemed to them necessary, both for the preservation of the ancient religion, and to secure the allegiance of the country to their niece, the young Queen, that a stronger hand, guided by a sounder head, should hold the reigns of the State. Upon their sister's fidelity they knew they could depend; and it was principally through the influence of French gold and French intrigue, that she was placed in the regency.

The inhabitants of Scotland were at this time divided into two great classes,—those who were still staunch to the Church of Rome, and those who were determined on effecting a reformation. At the head of the former was John Hamilton, Archbishop of St Andrews, who, upon the murder of Cardinal Beaton, had obtained that appointment through the Duke of Chatelherault, whose natural brother he was. He was greatly the Duke's superior in courage and sagacity, and was deeply imbued with the prelatical spirit of ambition then so prevalent. The resignation of the regency provoked him exceedingly, the more especially as Mary, to strengthen her own authority, found it necessary at first to treat the Reformers mildly. He was consoled, however, by the death of Edward VI. in 1553, and the accession of the young King's eldest sister Mary to the English throne,—as bigoted and determined a Catholic as ever lived.

The man who had placed himself at the head of the Reformers, and who, although young, had already given Hamilton and his party good cause to tremble at his increasing authority, was James Stuart, the eldest of Mary's three illegitimate brothers,—and one who occupies a most important station in the history of his country. His father made him, when only seven years old, Prior or Commendator of St Andrews, an office which entitled him, though a layman, to the full income arising from that rich benefice. It was soon discovered, however, that he had views far beyond so comparatively humble a rank. Even when a boy, it was his ambition to collect around him associates who were devoted to his service and desires. He went over with Mary to France in 1548, but remained there only a very short time; and, at the age of twenty-one, he was already looked up to by the Scottish Reformers as their chief. His knowledge was extensive, and considerably in advance of the times in which he lived. His personal bravery was undoubted, and his skill in arms so great, that few of his military enterprises were unsuccessful. His passions, if they were strong, seem also to have been deep, and entirely under his own command. Whatever may be thought of the secret motives which actuated him, he was seldom betrayed into any symptoms of apparent violence. He thus contrived to hold a steady course, amidst all the turbulence and convulsions of the age in which he lived; whilst the external decorum and propriety of his manners, so different from the ill-concealed dissoluteness of many of his cotemporaries, endeared him the more to the stern followers of Luther. It is curious to observe the very opposite views which different historians have taken of his character, more especially when they come to speak of him as the Earl of Murray and the Regent of Scotland. It would be improper and unnecessary to anticipate these discussions at present, since it is hoped the reader will be able to form his own estimate upon this subject, from the facts he will find recorded in these Memoirs.

It must be evident, that with two such men, each at the head of his own party, the country was not likely to continue long in a state of quietness. The Queen Regent soon found it necessary, at the instigation of the French Court, to associate herself with the Archbishop of St Andrews,—in opposition to which coalition, a bond was drawn up in 1557, by some of the principal Reformers, in which they announced their resolution to form an independent congregation of their own, and to separate themselves entirely from the "congregation of Satan, with all the superstitious abomination and idolatry thereof." Articles, or Heads of a Reformation, were soon afterwards published, in which it was principally insisted, that on Sunday and other festival days, the Common-Prayer should be read openly in the parish churches, along with the lessons of the Old and New Testaments; and that preaching and interpretation of the Scriptures in private houses should be allowed.

In the following year, one of the first outrages which the Reformers committed in Scotland, took place in Edinburgh. On occasion of the annual procession through the city, in honour of the tutelar Saint—St Giles, the image of that illustrious personage, which ought to have been carried by some of the priests, was amissing,—the godly having, beforehand, according to John Knox, first drowned the idol in the North Loch, and then burned it. It was therefore necessary to borrow a smaller saint from the Gray-Friars, in order that this "great solemnity and manifest abomination" might proceed. Upon the day appointed, priests, friars, canons, and "rotten Papists," assembled, with tabors, trumpets, banners, and bagpipes. At this sight, the hearts of the brethren were wondrously inflamed; and they resolved, that this second dragon should suffer the fate of the first. They broke in upon the procession; and though the Catholics made some slight resistance at first, they were soon obliged to surrender the image into the hands of the Philistines, who, taking it by the heels, and knocking, or, as the reformed historian says, *dadding* its head upon the pavement, soon reduced it to fragments, only regretting, that "the young St Giles" had not been so difficult to kill as his father. The priests, alarmed for their personal safety, sought shelter as quickly as possible, and gave Knox an opportunity of indulging in some of that austere mirth which is peculiarly remarkable, because so foreign to his general style. "Then might have been seen," says he, "so sudden a fray as seldom has been seen among that sort of men within this realm; for down goes the cross, off go the surplices, round caps, and cornets with the crowns. The Gray-Friars gaped, the Black-Friars blew, and the priests panted and fled, and happy was he that first got the house; for such a sudden fray came never among the generation of Antichrist within this realm before." The magistrates had some difficulty in prevailing upon the mob to disperse, after they had kept possession of the streets for several hours; and the rioters escaped without punishment; for "the brethren assembled themselves in such sort in companies, singing psalms, and praising God, that the proudest of the enemies were astounded."[4]

The Commissioners who, about this time, were sent into France, and the motives of their embassy, will be spoken of afterwards. But the remarkable circumstance, that four of them died when about to return home,—one at Paris, and three at Dieppe,—had a considerable influence in exciting the populace to still greater hatred against the French party,—it being commonly suspected that they had come by their death unfairly. The Congregation now rose in their demands; and among other things, insisted that "the wicked and scandalous lives" of churchmen should be reformed, according to the rules contained in the New Testament, the writings of the ancient fathers, and the laws of Justinian the Emperor. For a while, the Queen Regent temporized; but finding it impossible to preserve the favour of both parties, she yielded at length to the solicitations of the Archbishop of St Andrews, and determined to resist the Reformers vigorously. In 1559, she summoned all the ministers of the Congregation, to appear before her at Stirling. This citation was complied with, but not exactly in the manner that the Queen wished; for the ministers came not as culprits, but as men proud of their principles, and accompanied by a vast multitude of those who were of the same mode of thinking. The Queen, who was at Stirling, did not venture to proceed to Perth; and the request she made, that the numbers there assembled should depart, leaving their ministers to be examined by the Government, having been refused, she proceeded to the harsh and decisive measure of declaring them all rebels.

The consternation which this direct announcement of hostilities occasioned among them, was still at its height, when the great champion of the Scottish Reformation, John Knox, arrived at Perth. This celebrated divine had already suffered much for "the good cause;" and though his zeal and devotion to it were well known, it was not till latterly that he had entertained much hope of its final triumph in his native country. He had spent the greater part of his life in imprisonment or exile; he had undergone many privations, and submitted to many trials. But these were the daily food of the Reformers; and, whilst they only served to strengthen them in the obduracy of their belief, they had the additional effect of infusing a morose acerbity into dispositions not naturally of the softest kind. Knox had returned only a few days before from Geneva, where he had been solacing his solitude by writing and publishing that celebrated work, which he was pleased to entitle, "The first blast of the trumpet against the monstrous regiment of women." This treatise, directed principally against Mary of England, not forgetting Mary Queen of Scots and her mother of Guise, rather overshot its own purpose, by bringing the Reformer into disrepute with Elizabeth, who came to the crown soon after its appearance. To pacify that Queen, for it appears even Knox could temporize occasionally, he gave up his original intention of blowing his trumpet thrice, and his first blast was his last.[5]

The day after the ministers and their friends, had been declared rebels, Knox delivered at Perth what Keith terms "that thundering Sermon against Idolatry." The tumult which ensued at the conclusion of this discourse, has been attributed by some historians to accident; but Keith's suspicion, that Knox had a direct intention to excite it, seems well founded, when we consider the ferment in which the minds of his audience were at the time, and the peculiar style in which he addressed them. Buchanan is of the same opinion, though he would naturally have leant to the other conclusion. He says that Knox, "in that ticklish posture of affairs, made such a pathetic sermon to the multitude who were gathered together, that he set their minds, which were already fired, all in a flame." If, in addition to this, the usual

24

manner of Knox's eloquence be considered, it will hardly be questioned but that the outrage of that day was of his doing. His vehemence in the pulpit was at all times tremendous; indeed, in so far as the effect he produced upon his hearers was concerned, he seems to have trusted almost as much to the display of his physical as of his mental energies. Many years after the period now alluded to, when he was in his old age, and very weak, Melville tells us, that he saw him every Sunday go slowly and feebly, with fur about his neck, a staff in his hand, and a servant supporting him, from his own house, to the parish church in St Andrews. There, after being lifted into the pulpit, his limbs for some time were so feeble, that they could hardly support him; but ere he had done with his sermon, he became so active and vigorous, that he was like "to ding the pulpit in blads, and flie out of it."[6] What he must have been, therefore, in his best days, may be more easily imagined than described.

On the present occasion, after Knox had preached, and some of the congregation had retired, it appears that some "godly men" remained in the church. A priest had the imprudence to venture in among them, and to commence saying mass. A young man called out that such idolatry was intolerable, upon which it is said that the priest struck him. The young man retorted, by throwing a stone, which injured one of the pictures. The affair soon became general. The enraged people fell upon the altars and images, and in a short time nothing was left undemolished but the bare walls of the church. The Reformers throughout the city, hearing of these proceedings, speedily collected, and attacking the monasteries of the Gray and Black Friars, along with the costly edifice of the Carthusian Monks, left not a vestige of what they considered idolatrous and profane worship in any of them. The example thus set at Perth was speedily followed almost everywhere throughout the country.

These outrages greatly incensed the Queen Regent, and were looked upon with horror by the Catholics in general. To this day, the loss of many a fine building, through the zeal of the early Reformers, is a common subject of regret and complaint. It is to be remembered, however, that no revolution can be effected without paying a price for it. If the Reformation was a benefit, how could the Catholic superstition be more successfully attacked, than by knocking down those gorgeous temples, which were of themselves sufficient to render invincible the pride and inveterate bigotry of its votaries? The saying of John Knox, though a homely, was a true one,—"Pull down their nests, and the rooks will fly away." It is not improbable, as M'Crie conjectures, that had these buildings been allowed to remain in their former splendour, the Popish clergy might have long continued to indulge hopes, and to make efforts, to be restored to them. Victories over an enemy are celebrated with public rejoicings, notwithstanding the thousands of our fellow-countrymen who may have fallen in the contest. Why should the far more important victory, over those who had so long held in thraldom the human mind, be robbed of its due praise, because some statues were mangled, some pictures torn, and some venerable towers overthrown?[7]

With as little delay as possible, the Queen Regent appeared with an army before Perth, and made herself mistress of the town. The Reformers, however, were not to be intimidated; and their strength having, by this time, much increased, it was deemed prudent by the Regent not to push matters to an extremity. Both parties agreed to disband their forces, and to refer the controversy to the next Parliament. As was to be expected, this temporary truce was not of long duration. Incessant mutual recrimination and aggression, soon induced both sides to concentrate their forces once more. Perth was re-taken by the Reformers, who shortly afterwards marched into Edinburgh. After remaining there for some time, they were surprised by a sudden march which the Queen made upon them from Dunbar, and were compelled to fall back upon Stirling.

A belief was at this time prevalent at the court of France, that the Prior of St Andrews, who was the principal military leader of the Congregation, had views of a treasonable nature even upon the crown itself, and that he hoped the flaw in his legitimacy might be forgotten, in consideration of his godly exertions in support of the true faith. A new reinforcement of French soldiers arrived at Leith, which they fortified; and the French ambassador was commanded to inform the Prior, that the King, his master, would rather spend the crown of France, than not be revenged of the seditious persons in Scotland.

The civil war now raged with increased bitterness, and with various success, but without any decisive advantage on either side for some time. The Reformers applied for assistance to Queen Elizabeth, who favoured their cause for various reasons, and would, no doubt, much rather have seen Murray in possession of the Scottish crown, than her own personal rival, Mary. The Congregation having found it impossible, by their own efforts, to drive the French out of Leith, Elizabeth, in the beginning of the year 1560, fitted out a powerful fleet, which, to the astonishment of the Queen Regent and her French allies, sailed up the Firth of Forth, and anchored in the Roads, before even the purpose for which it had come was known. A treaty was soon afterwards concluded at Berwick between the Lords of the Congregation and Elizabeth's Commissioner, the Duke of Norfolk, by which it was agreed, on the part of the former, that no alliance should ever be entered into by them with France; and on that of the latter, that an English army should march into Scotland early in spring, for the purpose of aiding in the expulsion of the

French troops.

This army came at the time appointed, and was soon joined by the forces of the Reformers. The allies marched directly for Leith, which they invested without loss of time. The siege was conducted with great spirit, but the town was very resolutely defended by the French. So much determination was displayed upon both sides, that it is difficult to say how the matter might have ended, had not the death of the Queen Regent, which took place at this juncture, changed materially the whole aspect of affairs. She had been ill for some time, and during her sickness resided in the Castle of Edinburgh. Perceiving that her end was approaching, she requested an interview with some of the leaders of the Congregation. The Duke of Chatelherault, the Prior of St Andrews, or the Lord James, as he was commonly called, and others, waited upon her in her sick-chamber. She expressed to them her sincere grief for the troubles which existed in the country, and advised that both the English and French troops should be sent home. She entreated that they would reverence and obey their native and lawful sovereign, her daughter Mary. She told them how deeply attached she was to Scotland and its interests, although by birth a Frenchwoman; and at the conclusion, she burst into tears, kissing the nobles one by one, and asking pardon of all whom she had in any way offended. The day after this interview, Mary of Guise died. Her many excellent qualities were long remembered in Scotland; for even those who could not love, respected her. In private life, if this term can be used with propriety when speaking of a Queen, she appears to have been most deservedly esteemed. She set an example to all her maids of honour, of piety, modesty, and becoming gravity of deportment; she was exceedingly charitable to the poor; and had she fallen upon better days, her life would have been a happier one for herself, and her memory more generally prized by posterity. Her body was carried over to France, and buried in the Benedictine Monastery at Rheims.[8]

Very soon after the death of the Queen Regent, Commissioners arrived both from France and England, with full powers to conclude a treaty of peace between the three countries. By the loss of their sister, the Princes of Lorraine had been deprived of their chief support in Scotland, and, being actively engaged in schemes of ambition nearer home, they found it necessary to conciliate, as they best could, the predominating party there. The important treaty of Edinburgh, which will be mentioned frequently hereafter, was concluded on the 14th of June 1560. It was signed on the part of France by the two plenipotentiaries, Monluc, Bishop of Valence, and the Sieur Derandon, reckoned two of the best diplomatists of the day; and, on the part of England, by Wotton, Dean of Canterbury, and Elizabeth's prime minister, Cecil, one of the ablest men of that or any age. The interests of the Congregation were intrusted principally to the Lord James. In consequence of this treaty, the French troops were immediately withdrawn. The fortifications of Leith and Dunbar were destroyed, and a Parliament was held, whose acts were to be considered as valid as if it had been called by the express commands of the Queen. In that Parliament, the adherents of the Congregation were found greatly to out-number their adversaries. An act of oblivion and indemnity was passed for all that had taken place within the two preceding years; and, for the first time, the Catholics, awed into silence, submitted to every thing which the Reformers proposed. A new Confession of Faith was sanctioned; the jurisdiction of the Ecclesiastical Courts was abolished; and the exercise of worship, according to the rites of the Romish Church, was prohibited under severe penalties—a third act of disobedience being declared capital.

Thus, the Reformation finally triumphed in Scotland. Though as yet only in its infancy, and still exposed to many perils, it was nevertheless established on a comparatively firm and constitutional basis. The Catholics, it is true, aware of the school in which Mary had been educated, were far from having given up all hope of retrieving their circumstances; and they waited for her return with the utmost impatience and anxiety. But they ought to have known, that whatever might have been Mary's wishes, their reign was over in Scotland. A Sovereign may coerce the bodies, but he can never possess a despotic sway over the minds of his subjects. The people had now begun to think for themselves; and a belief in the mere mummeries of a fantastic system of Christianity, and of the efficacy of miracles performed by blocks of wood and stone, was never again to form a portion of their faith. A brief account of one of the last, and not least ludicrous attempts which the Popish clergy made to support their sinking cause, will form a not improper conclusion to this chapter.

There was a chapel in the neighbourhood of Musselburgh, dedicated to the Lady of Loretto, which, from the character of superior sanctity it had acquired, had long been the favourite resort of religious devotees. In this chapel, a body of the Catholic priests undertook to put their religion to the test, by performing a miracle. They fixed upon a young man, who was well known as a common blind beggar, in the streets of Edinburgh, and engaged to restore to him, in the presence of the assembled people, the perfect use of his eyesight. A day was named, on which they calculated they might depend on this wonderful interposition of divine power in their behalf. From motives of curiosity, a great crowd was attracted at the appointed time to the chapel. The blind man made his appearance on a scaffold, erected for the occasion. The priests approached the altar, and, after praying very devoutly, and performing other religious ceremonies, he who had previously been stone blind, opened his eyes, and declared he saw all things plainly. Having humbly and gratefully thanked his benefactors, the priests, he was permitted to mingle among the astonished people, and receive their charity.

Unfortunately, however, for the success of this deception, a gentleman from Fife, of the name of Colville, determined to penetrate, if possible, a little further into the mystery. He prevailed upon the subject of the recent experiment to accompany him to his lodgings in Edinburgh. As soon as they were alone, he locked the chamber-door, and either by bribes or threats, contrived to win from him the whole secret. It turned out, that in his boyhood, this tool, in the hands of the designing, had been employed as a herd by the nuns of the Convent of Sciennes, then in the neighbourhood of Edinburgh. It was remarked by the sisterhood, that he had an extraordinary facility in "flyping up the lid of his eyes, and casting up the white." Some of the neighbouring priests, hearing accidentally of this talent, imagined that it might be applied to good account. They accordingly took him from Sciennes to the monastery near Musselburgh, where they kept him till he had made himself an adept in this mode of counterfeiting blindness, and till his personal appearance was so much changed, that the few who had been acquainted with him before, would not be able to recognise him. They then sent him into Edinburgh to beg publicly, and make himself familiarly known to the inhabitants, as a common blind mendicant. So far every thing had gone smoothly, and the scene at the Chapel of Loretto might have had effect on the minds of the vulgar, had Colville's activity not discovered the gross imposture. Colville, who belonged to the Congregation, instantly took the most effectual means to make known the deceit. He insisted upon the blind man's appearing with him next day, at the Cross of Edinburgh, where the latter repeated all he had previously told Colville, and confessed the iniquity of his own conduct, as well as that of the priests. To shelter him from their revenge, Colville immediately afterwards carried him off to Fife; and the story, with all its details, being speedily disseminated, exposed the Catholic clergy to more contempt than ever.[9]

CHAPTER III.

MARY'S BIRTH, AND SUBSEQUENT RESIDENCE AT THE FRENCH COURT, WITH A SKETCH OF THE STATE OF SOCIETY AND MANNERS IN FRANCE, DURING THE SIXTEENTH CENTURY.

Mary Stuart, Queen of Scots, was the third child of James V. and his wife, Mary of Guise. That lady had born him previously two sons, both of whom died in infancy. Mary came into the world on the 7th of December 1542, in the Palace of Linlithgow.[10] She was only seven days old when she lost her father, who at the time of her birth lay sick in the Palace of Falkland. James died, as he had lived, with a kingly and gallant spirit. In the language of Pitscottie, he turned him upon his back, and looked and beheld all his nobles and lords about him, and, giving a little smile of laughter, kissed his hand, and offered it to them. When they had pressed it to their lips for the last time, he tossed up his arms, and yielded his spirit to God. James was considered one of the most handsome men of his day. He was above the middle stature; his hair flowed luxuriantly over his shoulders in natural ringlets, and was of a dark yellow or auburn colour; his eyes were gray, and very penetrating; his voice was sweet toned; and the general expression of his countenance uncommonly prepossessing. He inherited a vigorous constitution, and kept it sound and healthy by constant exercise, and by refraining from all excesses in eating or drinking. He was buried in the Royal Vault in the Chapel of Holyrood House, where his embalmed body, in a state of entire preservation, was still to be seen in the time of the historian Keith.

The young Queen was crowned by Cardinal Beaton at Stirling, on the 9th of September 1543. Her mother, who watched over her with the most careful anxiety, had been told a report prevailed that the infant was sickly, and not likely to live. To disprove this calumny, she desired Janet Sinclair, Mary's nurse, to unswaddle her in the presence of the English Ambassador, who wrote to his own court that she was as goodly a child as he had seen of her age.

Soon after her birth, the Parliament nominated Commissioners, to whom they intrusted the charge of the Queen's person, leaving all her other interests to the care of her mother. The two first years of her life, Mary spent at Linlithgow, where it appears she had the small-pox, a point of some importance, as one of her historians remarks, in the biography of a beauty and a queen.[11] The disease must have been of a particularly gentle kind, having left behind no visible traces. During the greater part of the years 1545, 46 and 47, she resided at Stirling Castle, in the keeping of Lords Erskine and Livingstone. Here she received the first rudiments of education from two ecclesiastics, who were appointed her preceptors, more, however, as matter of form, than from any use they could be of to her at so early an age. When the internal disturbances of the country rendered even Stirling Castle a somewhat dangerous residence, Mary was removed to Inchmahome, a sequestered island in the Lake of Monteith. That she might not be too lonely, and that a spirit of generous emulation might present her with an additional motive for the prosecution of her studies, the Queen Dowager selected four young ladies of rank as her companions and playmates. They were each about her daughter's age, and either from chance, or because the conceit seemed natural, they all bore the same surname. The four Maries were, Mary Beaton, a niece of Cardinal Beaton, Mary Fleming, daughter of Lord Fleming, Mary Livingstone, whose father was one of the young Queen's guardians, and Mary Seaton, daughter of Lord Seaton.

Mary having remained upwards of two years in this island, those who had, at the time, the disposal of her future destiny, thought it expedient, for reasons which have been already explained, that she should be removed to France. She was accordingly, in the fifth year of her age, taken to Dumbarton, where she was delivered to the French Admiral, whose vessels were waiting to receive her, and attended by the Lords Erskine and Livingstone, her three natural brothers, and her four Maries, she left Scotland.

The thirteen happiest years of Mary's life were spent in France. Towards the end of July 1548, she sailed from Dumbarton, and, after a tempestuous voyage, landed at Brest on the 14th of August. She was there received, by Henry II.'s orders, with all the honours due to her rank and royal destiny. She travelled, with her retinue, by easy stages, to the palace at St Germain En Laye; and to mark the respect that was paid to her, the prison-gates of every town she came to were thrown open, and the prisoners set free. Shortly after her arrival, she was sent, along with the King's own daughters, to one of the first convents in France, where young ladies of distinction were instructed in the elementary branches of education.

The natural quickness of her capacity, and the early acuteness of her mind, now began to manifest themselves. She made rapid progress in acquiring that species of knowledge suited to her years, and her lively imagination went even the length of attaching a more than ordinary interest to the calm and secluded life of a nunnery. It was whispered, that she had already expressed a wish to separate herself forever from the world; and it is not improbable, that had this wish been allowed to foster itself silently in her bosom, Mary might ultimately have taken the veil, in which case her life would have been a blank in history. But these views were not consistent with the more ambitious projects entertained by Henry and her uncles of Lorraine. As soon as they were informed of the bent which her mind appeared to be taking, she was again removed from the convent to the palace. To reconcile her to parting with the vestal sisters, Henry, whose conduct towards her was always marked by affection and delicacy, selected, from all the noble Scotch families then residing in France, a certain number to constitute her future household. The tears which Mary shed, however, upon leaving the nunnery, proved the warmth of her young heart; and that her feelings were not of merely momentary duration, is evinced by the frequent visits she subsequently paid this asylum of her childhood,—and by the altar-piece she embroidered with her own hands for the chapel of the convent.

In no country of Europe was education better understood than it then was in France. Francis I., who remodelled, upon a magnificent scale, the University of Paris, only followed the example which had already been set him by Louis XII. The youth of all countries flocked to the French schools. The liberal principles which induced the government to maintain, at its own expense, professors, who lectured to as many students as chose to hear them, was amply repaid by the beneficial consequences arising from the great influx of strangers. A competent knowledge of Latin, Greek, Hebrew, Mathematics, Moral Philosophy and Medicine, could be acquired in France for literally nothing. Nor was it necessary, that he who sought for the blessings of education, should profess any particular system of religious faith. The German Protestant, and the Spanish Catholic, were allowed, in these noble institutions, to take their seat side by side. Henry supported the church as an engine of state, whilst he detested the arrogant pretensions and empty insolence of many of the clergy, and was determined that they should not interfere with the more enlightened views which he himself entertained. In this, he only followed the opinions of his illustrious father, Francis, who used to remark, that monks were better at teaching linnets to whistle, playing at dice, tippling, and gormandizing, than in doing good either to religion or morality.

The host of authors, and men of genius, who flourished in France about this period, was another cause of its literary eminence. "Learning," says Miss Benger, "far from being the badge of singularity, had become the attribute of a superior station." "There was," observes the ingenious Pasquier, "a glorious crusade against ignorance." Many of the names then celebrated have since, it is true, passed into oblivion, but the multitude who cultivated letters, show the spirit of the times. Beza, Seve, Pelletier and others, led the van in the severer departments of intellect; whilst Bellay, Ronsard and Jodelle, showed the way, to a host of followers, in the cultivation of poetry, and the softer arts of composition.

Nor must the great statesmen and warriors, whose presence lent a lustre to the court, be forgotten in this view of the existing pre-eminence of France. The two Houses of Bourbon and Guise, had each given birth to many names destined for immortality. The present chiefs of Bourbon were Anthony, Duke of Navarre, and Louis, known in the history of the world as the first Prince of Condé. There were six brothers of the Guises, of whom the two most illustrious were Francis Duke of Guise, and Charles Cardinal of Lorraine. But they all held the very highest offices in the church or state; one was a Cardinal, and another a Grand Prior; a third, the Duke d'Aumale, commanded the army then in Italy; and the fourth, the Marquis d'Elbeuf, was intrusted with the charge of the French troops in Scotland. But he who held the balance of power between all these contending interests, was the great Montmorency, Constable of France. He had, by this time, become a veteran in the service of the French monarchs. Louis XII. had acknowledged his virtues, and Francis I. looked to him for advice and aid in every emergency. Henry felt almost a filial affection and reverence for so distinguished a statesman and patriot; and Diana de Poictiers herself, the fascinating widow of the Duke de Valentinois, frequently found that she possessed less influence with the monarch than the venerable and unostentatious Montmorency. The minister was at all times surrounded by a formidable phalanx of friends and supporters. Of these his own sons were not the least considerable; and his nephews, the two Colignys, need only to be mentioned, to awaken recollections of some of the most remarkable events of French history.

Neither must we omit to mention the two ladies who held the highest places in the French Court. The sister and the wife of Henry II. resembled each other but faintly, yet both secured the admiration of the country. The Princess Margaret had established herself by her patronage of every liberal art, and her universal beneficence, in the hearts of the whole people. Her religion did not degenerate into bigotry, and her charity, whilst it was at all times efficient, was without parade. She became afterwards the Duchess of Savoy; but till past the meridian of life, she continued constantly at her brother's Court,—a bright example of all that was virtuous and attractive in female character. To her, France was indebted for discovering and fostering the talents of its great Chancellor Michel L'Hopital; and the honourable name by which she was universally known was that of Minerva. The King's wife, Catherine de Medicis, was more respected for her talents than loved for her virtues. But as yet, the ambition of her nature had not betrayed itself, and little occasion had been afforded for the exercise of those arts of dissimulation, or the exposure of that proneness to envy and resentment, which at a later period became so apparent. She was still in the bloom of youth, and maintained a high character, not without much show of reason.

Such being the general aspect of the country and the Court, it cannot fail to become evident, that so far from being a just cause of regret, nothing could have redounded more to Mary's advantage than her education and residence in France. If bigotry prevailed among the clergy, it was not countenanced at the Court, for Henry cared little about religion, and his sister Margaret was suspected of leaning to the Reformed opinions. If Parisian manners were known to be too deeply tinctured with licentiousness, the palace of Catherine must be excepted from the charge; for even the deportment of Diana herself was grave and decorous, and for his sister's sake, the King dared not have countenanced any of those grosser immoralities in which Henry VIII. of England so openly indulged. The Cardinal of Lorraine, who was at the head of the Parisian University, quickly discovering Mary's capabilities, directed her studies with the most watchful anxiety. She was still attended by the two preceptors who had accompanied her from Scotland, and before she was ten years old, had made good progress in the French, Latin, and Italian languages. French was all her life as familiar to her as her native tongue; and she wrote it with a degree of elegance which no one could surpass. Her acquaintance with Latin was not of that superficial kind but too common in the present day. This language was then regarded as almost the only one on whose stability any reliance could be placed. It was consequently deemed indispensable, that all who aspired at any eminence in literature, should be able to compose in it fluently. Mary's teacher was the celebrated George Buchanan, who was then in France, and who, whatever other praise he may be entitled to, was unquestionably one of the best scholars of his time. The young Queen's attention was likewise directed to Rhetoric, by Fauchet, author of a treatise on that subject which he dedicated to his pupil,—to history by Pasquier,—and to the delightful study of poetry, for which her genius was best suited, and for which she retained a predilection all her life, by Ronsard.

Nor must it be imagined that Mary's childhood was exclusively devoted to these more scholastic pursuits. She and her young companions, the Scotch Maries and the daughters of Henry, were frequently present at those magnificent galas and fêtes, in which the King himself so much delighted, and which were so particularly in unison with the taste of the times, though no where conducted with so much elegance and grace, as at the French Court. The summer tournaments and fêtes champêtres, and the winter festivals and masquerades, were attended by all the beauty and chivalry of the land. In these amusements, Mary, as she grew up, took a lively and innocent pleasure. The woods and gardens also of Fontainbleau, afforded a delightful variation from the artificial splendours of Paris. In summer, sailing on the lakes, or fishing in the ponds; and in winter, a construction of fortresses on the ice,—a mimic battle of snow-balls,—or skating, became royal pastimes. Mary's gait and air, naturally dignified and noble, acquired an additional charm from the attention she paid to dancing and riding. The favourite dance at the time was the Spanish minuet, which Mary frequently performed with her young consort, to the admiration of the whole court. In the livelier gailliarde, she was unequalled, as was confessed, even by the beautiful Anne of Este, who, in a pas des deux, acknowledged that she was eclipsed by Mary.

The activity of her body indeed, kept, upon all occasions, full pace with that of her mind. She was particularly fond of hunting; and she and her maids of honour were frequently seen following the stag through the ancestral forests of France. Her attachment to this amusement, which continued all her life, exposed her, on several occasions, to some danger. So early as the year 1559, when hunting in France, some part of her dress was caught by the bough of a tree, and she was cast off her horse when galloping at full speed. Many of the ladies and gentlemen in her train passed by without observing her, and some so near as actually to tread on her riding-dress. As soon as the accident was discovered, she was raised from the ground; but, though the shock had been considerable, she had too manly a spirit to complain, and, readjusting her hair, which had fallen into confusion, she again mounted her horse, and rode home smiling at the accident.[12]

Another, but more sedentary amusement with Mary, was the composition of devices. To excel in these, required some wit and judgment. A device was the skilful coupling of a few expressive words with any engraved figure or picture. It was an art intimately connected with the science of heraldry, and seems to have suggested the modern seal and motto. The composition of these devices was, as it is somewhere called, only "an elegant species of trifling;" but it had something intellectual in it, which the best informed ladies of the French court liked. An old author, who writes upon this subject, elevates it to a degree of importance rather amusing. "It delights the eye," he says, "it captivates the imagination, it is also profitable and useful; and therefore surpasseth all other arts, and also painting, since this only represents the body and exquisite features of the face, whereas a device exposes the rare ideas and gallant sentiments of its author; it also excels poetry, in as much as it joineth profit with pleasure, since none merit the title of devices unless they at once please by their grace, and yield profit by their doctrine."

Mary's partialities were commonly lasting, and when in very different circumstances, she frequently loved to return to this amusement of her childhood. Some of the emblems she invented, betray much elegance and sensibility of mind. On the death of her husband Francis, she took for her device a little branch of the liquorice-tree, whose root only is sweet, all the rest of the plant being bitter, and the motto was, *Dulce meum terra tegit*. On her cloth of state was embroidered the sentence, *En ma fin est mon commencement*; "a riddle," says Haynes, "I understand not;" but which evidently meant to inculcate a lesson of humility, and to remind her that life, with all its grandeur, was the mere prologue to eternity. The French historian, Mezeray, mentions also that Mary had a medal struck, on which was represented a vessel in a storm, with its masts broken and falling, illustrated by the motto, *Nunquam nisi rectam*; indicating a determination rather to perish than deviate from the path of integrity.[13] When she was in England, she embroidered for the Duke of Norfolk a hand with a sword in it, cutting vines, with the motto *Virescit vulnere virtus*. In these and similar fancies, she embodied strong and often original thoughts with much delicacy.

In the midst of these occupations and amusements, Mary was not allowed to forget her native country. Frequent visits were paid her from Scotland, by those personally attached to herself or her family. In 1550, her mother, Mary of Guise, came over to see her, accompanied by several of the nobility. The Queen-dowager, a woman of strong affections, was so delighted with the improvement she discovered in her daughter's mind and person, that she burst into tears of joy; and her Scottish attendants were hardly less affected by the sight of their future Sovereign. Henry, with his young charge, was at Rouen, when the Queen-dowager arrived. To testify his respect for her, he ordered a triumph to be prepared, which consisted of one of those grotesque allegorical exhibitions then so much in vogue; and, shortly afterwards, the two Queens made a public entry into Paris. Mary of Guise had there an opportunity likewise of seeing her son by her first husband, the Duke de Longueville, Mary's half-brother, but who seems to have spent his life in retirement, as history scarcely notices him. It may well be conceived, that the widow of James V. returned even to the regency of Scotland with reluctance, since she purchased the gratification of her ambition by a final separation from her children.[14]

It was about the same time that Mary first saw Sir James Melville, who was then only a few years older than herself, and who was sent over in the train of the Bishop of Monluc, when he returned after signing the Treaty of Edinburgh, to be one of Mary's pages of honour. Sir James was afterwards frequently employed by the Queen as her foreign ambassador, and his name will appear more than once in the sequel. We have spoken of him here for the purpose of introducing an amusing anecdote, which he gives us in his own Memoirs, and which illustrates the state of manners at that period. Upon landing at Brest, the Bishop proceeded direct to Paris. But Sir James, who was young, and could hardly have endured the fatigue of this mode of travelling, was intrusted to the care of two Scotch gentlemen, who had come over in the same ship. Their first step was to purchase three little "naigies," on which they proposed riding to Paris, any thing in the shape of a *diligence* being out of the question. To ensure greater safety on the journey, three others joined the party,—two Frenchmen, and a young Spaniard, who was on his way to the College at Paris. On the evening of the first day, they arrived at the town of Landerneau, where all the six were lodged in one room, containing three beds. The two Frenchmen slept together in one, the two Scotsmen in another, and Melville and the Spaniard in the third. The company on the whole does not appear to have been of the most respectable kind; for, as Melville lay awake, he heard "the twa Scotchmen devising how they were directed to let him want naething; therefore, said they, we will pay for his ordinair all the way, and shall count up twice as meikle to his master when we come to Paris, and sae shall win our ain expenses." The two Frenchmen, on their part, thinking that nobody in the room understood French, said to each other, "These strangers are all young, and know not the fashion of the hostelries; therefore we shall deal and reckon with the hosts at every repast, and shall cause the strangers pay more than the custom is, and that way shall we save our expenses." At all this Melville, as he tells us, could not refrain from "laughing in his mind," and determined to be upon his guard. "Yet the twa Scotch young men," he adds in his antique phraseology, "would not consent that I should pay for myself, hoping still to beguile the Bishop, but the Spaniart and I writ up every day's compt." The Frenchmen being foiled in their swindling intentions, had recourse to a still bolder manœuvre. One day, as the party were riding through a wood, two other Frenchmen, who had joined them a short time before, suddenly leapt off their horses, and, drawing their swords, demanded that the others should deliver up their purses. Melville and his Scotch friends, however, were not to be thus intimidated. They also drew their swords, and prepared for resistance; on seeing which, the Frenchmen affected to make a joke of the whole affair, saying that they merely wanted to try the courage of the Scotchmen, in case they should have been attacked by robbers. "But the twa last loons," says Melville, "left us at the next lodging; and the twa Scotch scholars never obtenit payment frae the Bishop for their pretendit fraud." Sir James arrived in safety at Paris, having taken thirteen days to ride from Brest to the capital.[15]

Thus diversified by intercourse with her friends and with her books, by study and recreation, Mary's early life passed rapidly away. It has been already seen, that whatever could have tended to corrupt the mind or manners was carefully removed from the young Queen. As soon as Mary entered upon her teens, she and her companions, the two young princesses, Henry's daughters, spent several hours every day in the private apartment of Catherine de Medicis, whose conversation, as well as that of the foreign ambassadors and other persons of distinction who paid their respects to her, they had thus an opportunity of hearing. Conæus mentions, that Mary was soon observed to avail herself, with great earnestness, of these opportunities of acquiring knowledge; and it has been hinted, that the superior intelligence she evinced, in comparison with Catherine's own daughters, was the first cause of exciting that Queen's jealousy. It was perhaps at some of these conferences that Mary imperceptibly imbibed, from her future mother-in-law, and her not unfrequent visitor, Nostradamus, a slight portion of that tendency to superstitious belief then so prevalent. One of the most remarkable characters about Henry's court, was Nicolas Cretin, or Nostradamus, as he was more commonly called, who combined in his own person the three somewhat incongruous professions of physician, astrologer, and philosopher. He asserted, that he was not only perfectly acquainted with the laws of planetary influence, but that, by the inspiration of divine power, he could predict the events of futurity. The style of his prophecies was in general sufficiently obscure; yet such was the reverence paid to learning in those days (and Nostradamus was a very library of learning), that he was courted and consulted even by the first statesmen in France. Mary had far too lively a fancy to escape the infection; and the force of this early bias continued to be felt by her more or less all her life.

CHAPTER IV.

MARY'S MARRIAGE, PERSONAL APPEARANCE, AND POPULARITY.

The time now approached when Henry began to think of confirming the French authority in Scotland, by consummating the contract of marriage which had so long existed between Francis and Mary. This was not, however, to be done without considerable opposition from several quarters. The Constable Montmorency, and the House of Bourbon, already trembled at the growing influence of the Guises, plainly foreseeing, that as soon as the niece of the Duke and Cardinal of Lorraine became wife to the Dauphin, and consequently, upon Henry's death, Queen of France, their own influence would be at an end. It is not improbable that Montmorency aimed at marrying one of his own sons to Mary. At all events, he endeavoured to persuade Henry that he might find a more advantageous alliance for Francis. The Guises, however, were not thus to be overreached; and the King more willingly listened to their powerful representations in favour of the match, as it had long been a favourite scheme with himself. It would be uncharitable to ascribe to the agency of any of those who opposed it, an attempt which was made some time before by a person of the name of Stuart, a Scottish archer in the King's guards, to poison Mary. Stuart being detected, was tried, condemned, and executed, but made no confession which could lead to any discovery of his motives. It is most likely that he had embraced the reformed religion, and was actuated by a fanatical desire to save his country from the dominion of a Catholic princess.

Francis, the young Dauphin, who was much about Mary's own age, was far inferior to her, both in personal appearance and mental endowments. He was of a very weakly constitution; and the energies of his mind seem to have been repressed by the feebleness of his body. But if unable to boast of any distinguishing virtues, he was undegraded by the practice of any vice. He was amiable, timid, affectionate, and shy. He was aware of his want of physical strength, and feared lest the more robust should make it a subject of ridicule. He appears to have loved Mary with the tenderest affection, being probably anxious to atone to her, by every mark of devotion, for the sacrifice he must have seen she was making in surrendering herself to him, in all the lustre of her charms. Yet there is good reason to believe that Mary really loved Francis. They had been playmates from infancy; they had prosecuted all their studies together; and though Francis cared little for the pleasures of society, and rather shunned than encouraged those who wished to pay their court to him, Mary was aware that, for this very reason, he was only the more sincere in his passion for her. It was not in Mary's nature to be indifferent to those who evinced affection for her; and if her fondness for Francis were mingled with pity, it has long been asserted, that "pity is akin to love".

On the 24th of April 1558, the nuptials took place. In December the preceding year, a letter from Henry had been laid before the Scotch Parliament, requesting that some persons of rank should be sent over from Scotland as Commissioners to witness the marriage; and in compliance with this desire, the Lord James, Prior of St Andrews, and eight other persons of distinction, arrived at the French Court in March 1558.[16] Their instructions commanded them to guard against French encroachments, upon the rights and privileges of Scottish subjects; and, that no doubt might remain regarding the right of succession to the Scottish throne, they were to obtain from the King of France a ratification of his former promise, to aid and support the Duke of Chatelherault in his claims upon the crown, in case Mary died without issue. They were also to require a declaration to a similar effect from the Queen and Dauphin. All these demands were at once complied with.

It has been alleged, however, that a very gross deceit was practised, upon this occasion, by the French Court. It is said, that though, to satisfy the Scotch Commissioners, all their requests were ostensibly granted, Henry took secret measures to render these grants entirely inefficacious. Mary, it is asserted, on the 4th of April, signed three papers, in the first of which she made over the kingdom of Scotland in free gift to the King of France, to be enjoyed by him and his heirs, should she die without children; in the second, (lest it might not be deemed expedient to insist upon the first,) she assigned to the King of France the possession of Scotland, after her decease without children, till he should be reimbursed of a million pieces of gold, or any greater sum which he should be found to have expended on her during her residence in France; and, in the third, she protested, that whatever declarations she might subscribe, in compliance with the desire of the Scotch Parliament, touching the lineal succession of her crown, the genuine sense of her mind was contained only in the two preceding papers.[17] If this dishonourable transaction really took place, whilst it cannot involve Mary, a young and inexperienced girl of fifteen, in any serious blame, it certainly reflects the highest discredit both upon Henry and his advisers of the house of Guise. There is good reason, however, to believe, that these instruments, though they unquestionably exist, are forgeries. It was not an uncommon trick in those times, for the Reformers to stir up jealousy against a Catholic sovereign, by alleging, that he had promised away his country to some well known papist. The Prince of Condé, in December 1568, was not aware of the authenticity of any such papers; for, if he had been, he would undoubtedly have mentioned them when he asked Elizabeth's assistance to establish the Protestant religion in France. On the contrary, he trumps up a ridiculous story, to which no one has ever given any credit, that Mary had ceded her right to the crown of England, in behalf of the King of France's brother, Henry Duke of Anjou. After Mary's death, it was confidently reported, and with equal falsehood, that by her testament she had left England to the King of Spain, unless her son became a Roman Catholic. There is, besides, internal evidence of a striking nature, that these deeds were forgeries. For its discovery, we are indebted to the industry and research of Goodall.[18]

Some of the provisions in the marriage-contract between Francis and Mary, are sufficiently remarkable to deserve being recorded. The jointure assigned by it to the Queen, provided her husband died King of France, is 60,000 livres, or a greater sum, if a greater had ever been given to a Queen of France. If her husband died only Dauphin, the jointure was to be 30,000 livres. The eldest son of the marriage was to be King of France and Scotland; and if there were no sons, the eldest daughter was to be Queen of Scotland only, with a portion of 400,000 crowns, as a daughter of France,—every younger daughter being allowed 300,000 crowns. Should her husband die, Mary was to be at liberty either to remain in France or return to Scotland, with an assurance that her jointure would be always duly paid her. The Dauphin was to bear the name and title of King of Scotland, and enjoy all the privileges of the crown-matrimonial.

The marriage, for which so many preparations had thus been made, was solemnized in the church of Notre Dame, the ceremony being performed by the Cardinal of Bourbon, Archbishop of Rouen. Upon this occasion, the festivities were graced by the presence of all the most illustrious personages of the Court of France; and when Francis, taking a ring from his finger, presented it to the Archbishop, who, pronouncing the benediction, placed it on the young Queen's finger, the vaulted roof of the Cathedral rung with congratulations, and the multitude without rent the air with joyful shouts. The spectacle was altogether one of the most imposing which, even in that age of spectacles, had been seen in Paris. The procession, upon leaving the church, proceeded to the palace of the Archbishop, where a magnificent collation was prepared,—largess, as it moved along, being proclaimed among the people, in the name of the King and Queen of Scots. In the afternoon, the royal party returned to the palace of the Tournelles—Catherine de Medicis and Mary sitting together in the same palanquin, and a Cardinal walking on each side. Henry and Francis followed on horseback, with a long line of princes and princesses in their train. The chronicler of these nuptials is unable to conceal his rapture, when he describes the manner in which the palace had been prepared for their reception. Its whole appearance, he tells us, was "light and beautiful as Elysium." During supper, which was served upon a marble table in the great hall, the King's band of "one hundred gentlemen" poured forth delicious strains of music. The members of Parliament attended in their robes; and the princes of the blood performed the duty of servitors—the Duke of Guise acting as master of the ceremonies. The banquet being concluded, a series of the most magnificent masks and mummeries, prepared for the occasion, was introduced. In the pageant, twelve artificial horses, of admirable mechanism, covered with cloth of gold, and ridden by the young heirs of noble houses, attracted deserved attention. They were succeeded by six galleys, which sailed into the hall, each rich as Cleopatra's barge, and bearing on its deck two seats, the one filled by a young cavalier, who, as he advanced, carried off from among the spectators, and gently placed in the vacant chair, the lady of his love. A splendid tournament concluded these rejoicings.

During the whole of these solemnities, every eye was fixed on the youthful Mary; and, inspired by those feelings which beauty seldom fails to excite, every heart offered up prayers for her future welfare and happiness. She was now at that age when feminine loveliness is perhaps most attractive. It is not to be supposed, indeed, that in her sixteenth year, her charms had ripened into that full-blown maturity which they afterwards attained; but they were, on this account, only the more fascinating. Some have conjectured that Mary's beauty has been extolled far beyond its real merits; and it cannot be denied that many vague and erroneous notions exist regarding it. But that her countenance possessed in a pre-eminent degree the something which constitutes beauty, is sufficiently attested by the unanimous declaration of all cotemporary writers. It is only, however, by carefully gathering together hints scattered here and there, that any accurate idea can be formed of the lineaments of a countenance which has so long ceased to exist, unless in the fancy of the enthusiast. Generally speaking, Mary's features were more Grecian than Roman, though without the insipidity that would have attached to them, had they been exactly regular. Her nose exceeded a little the Grecian proportion in length. Her hair was very nearly of the same colour as James V.'s—dark yellow, or auburn, and, like his, clustered in luxuriant ringlets. Her eyes,—which some writers, misled by the thousand blundering portraits of her scattered everywhere, conceive to have been gray, or blue, or hazel,— were of a chestnut colour,—darker, yet matching well with her auburn hair. Her brow was high, open, and prominent. Her lips were full and expressive, as the lips of the Stuarts generally were; and she had a small dimple in her chin. Her complexion was clear, and very fair, without a great deal of colour in her cheeks. Her mother was a woman of large stature, and Mary was also above the common size. Her person was finely proportioned, and her carriage exceedingly graceful and dignified.[19]

In this description of Mary's personal appearance, we have placed a good deal of reliance on the research and accuracy of Chalmers. It will be observed, that our account differs, in many essential particulars, from that of Robertson, who says—"Mary's hair was black, though, according to the fashion of that age, she frequently wore borrowed locks, and of different colours. Her eyes were a dark gray; her complexion was exquisitely fine; and her hands and arms remarkably delicate, both as to shape and colour. Her stature was of an height that rose to the majestic." Where Robertson discovered that Mary's hair was black, or her eyes gray, he does not mention. That her eyes were *not* black, we have the direct testimony of Beal, Clerk to the Privy Council of England, who was ordered by Cecil to be present at the death of the Scottish Queen, and who describes her as having "chestnut-coloured eyes." As to her hair, and her other features, though Melville, in his Memoirs, certainly seems to imply that the former was auburn, yet, as he does not expressly say so, we suspect correct conclusions can be arrived at only by a reference to the best authenticated portraits which have been preserved of Mary. This, however, is far from being a criterion by which opinions should be rashly formed. There are few persons in the whole range of history, likenesses of whom have been more eagerly sought after; and, in proportion to the anxiety manifested to secure originals, has been the temptation to mislead and deceive. Almost all the paintings said to be originals of Mary Queen of Scots, are the impositions of picture-dealers. When the demand for these paintings became general, it was not at all unusual to despatch emissaries over the Continent to pick up every picture, the costume and general appearance of which in the least resembled the Scottish Queen. During Mary's life, and for some time after her death, the fame of her beauty, and the interest attached to her fortunes, induced numerous ladies of rank, who flattered themselves that they were like her, to have portraits painted in the style then well understood by the phrase *à la Mary Stuart*. There was, in particular, a celebrated Continental beauty of those days—a Countess of Mansfeldt—(we speak on the authority of a living artist of celebrity), who resembled Mary in many particulars, and all whose portraits (nor were they few in number) when they afterwards came into the hands of the picture-dealers, were affirmed to be Maries. Thus, in the lapse of years, the truth became so involved in uncertainty, that even Robertson, allowing himself to be too hastily misled, has lent his name to the dissemination of error.

Horace Walpole, after having made extensive inquiries on this subject, has recorded, that he never could ascertain the authenticity and originality of any portrait of Mary, except of that in the possession of the Earl of Morton, which was painted when she was at Lochleven. Chalmers, in order to come as near the truth as possible, employed Mr Pailou, an artist of ability, to compare the picture belonging to the Earl of Morton, with two or three other undoubted originals which have been discovered since Walpole wrote. Pailou commenced by sketching the outline of his picture from Lord Morton's original. He then proceeded to the examination of three genuine portraits of Mary, one in the Church of St Andrew in Antwerp, another in the Scotch College at Douay, and a third in the Scotch College at Paris. Neither did he forget the profile heads of Mary struck upon her coins, nor the marble figure representing her on her tomb in Henry VII's Chapel, which Walpole thought a correct likeness. Mr Pailou thus made Lord Morton's picture the basis of his own, but, as he advanced, constantly referred to the others, "till he got the whole adjusted and coloured." Though we cannot exactly approve of thus cooking up a picture from various different sources, and should be inclined to think, that too much was left by such a mode of procedure to the arbitrary taste of the artist, we nevertheless feel satisfied that Mr Pailou has hit upon a tolerably accurate likeness. His picture, engraved by Scriven, forms the frontispiece to the second volume of Chalmers's work. The brow, eyes, mouth, and chin, he has given with great success. But the painting is far from being without faults;—the face is a good deal too round and plump, the nose is made slightly aquiline—a decided mistake,—and the neck is much too short, at least so it appears in the engraving.

The portrait of Mary, which forms the frontispiece to the present volume, and on which we place greater reliance than on any with which we are acquainted, is an engraving executed expressly for this work, from an original picture of much merit.[20] It was painted when Mary was in France, by an Italian artist of eminence, who flourished as her cotemporary in the sixteenth century, and whose name is on the canvas. It would have been impossible to say at what precise age it represented Mary, though, from the juvenility of the countenance, it might have been concluded that it was taken a year or two before she became Dauphiness, had not the painter fortunately obviated the difficulty, by inserting immediately after his own signature the date, which is 1556, when she was just fourteen. It is upon this picture that we have chiefly founded our description of Mary's personal appearance. What gives us the greater confidence in its authenticity and accuracy, is, that it very exactly corresponds with two other portraits, believed on good grounds to be originals. This is a strong circumstance, for it is a very common and just remark, that almost no two likenesses of Mary agree. The paintings to which we allude are, first, one at the seat of Logie Almond, which represents Mary at the same age, but in a religious habit. It gives precisely the same view of the left side of the face as the engraving in this volume does of the right. From the style and other circumstances, it is very probable, that both pictures were painted by the same artist. The second is in the possession of his Grace the Duke of Hamilton, and is in one of the private apartments at Hamilton palace. It represents Mary at a somewhat more advanced period of life, but the features are quite the same. There is still a third picture, said to be an original, in the collection of the Marquis of Salisbury, at Hatfield House, and which has been engraved for Miss Benger's Memoirs, which very closely resembles our own. To be yet more assured, we have carefully examined the heads upon Mary's gold and silver coins. Some of these are inaccurate, but they have all a general resemblance to each other. A silver coin, of 1561, and the gold real stamped in 1562, agree minutely with our picture,—a circumstance which cannot but be considered a strong corroboration of its truth. It is unnecessary to make any apology to the reader for having entered thus minutely upon a subject of so much general interest.[21]

With regard to the asseverations of cotemporary writers, as to the effects which Mary's beauty produced, many of them are almost too extravagant to be believed. They prove, nevertheless, that, whatever beauty may be, whether a mere fortunate arrangement of material atoms, or a light suffused upon the face, from the secret and etherial mind, it was a gift which Nature had lavishly bestowed on Mary. A year or two previous to her marriage, when walking in a religious procession, through the streets of Paris, with a lighted torch in her hand, a woman among the crowd was so struck with her appearance, that she could not help stopping her to ask,—"Are you not indeed an angel?" Brantome, with more questionable sincerity, compares her, at the age of fifteen, to the sun at mid-day. He tells us also, that the brother of Francis, afterwards Charles IX., never saw even a picture of Mary, without lingering to gaze upon it, declaring passionately, that he looked upon Francis as the happiest man on earth, to possess a creature of so much loveliness. Nay, Brantome even goes the length of asserting, that no man ever saw Mary who did not lose his heart to her. He is pleased, likewise, with some naïveté, to pay her several high compliments at the expense of her native country. It appears that Mary, amidst all the gaieties of the French Court, had not forgot her early residence at Inchmahome, in the quiet lake of Monteith. Actuated by these recollections and other motives, she delighted to testify her regard for Scotland in various ways; and, among others, by frequently wearing in public the graceful Highland costume. The rich and national Stuart tartan became her exceedingly; and Brantome, who seems to have been greatly puzzled by the novelty of the dress, is nevertheless forced to declare, that when arrayed after "the barbarous fashion of the savages of her country, she appeared a goddess in a mortal body, and in a most outré and astonishing garb." Mary herself, was so fond of this costume, that she wore it in one of the portraits which were taken of her in France. If she appeared so beautiful thus "habillée à la sauvage," exclaims Brantome, "what must she not be in her rich and lovely robes made à la Française, ou l'Espagnole, or with a bonnet à l'Italienne; or in her flowing white dress, contending in vain with the whiteness of her skin!" Even when she sung, and accompanied herself upon the lute, Brantome found occasion to discover a new beauty,—"her soft snowy hand and fingers, fairer than Aurora's." "Ah royaume d'Escosse!" he touchingly adds, "Je croy que, maintenant, vos jours sont encore bien plus courts qu'ils n'estoient, et vos nuits plus longues, puisque vous avez perdu cette Princesse qui vos illuminoit!" The historian, Castelnau, in like manner, pronounces Mary "the most beautiful and accomplished of her sex;" and Mezeray tells us, that "Nature had bestowed upon her every thing that is necessary to form a complete beauty;" adding, that "by the study of the liberal arts and sciences, especially painting, music, and poetry, she had so embellished her natural good qualities, that she appeared to be the most amiable Princess in Christendom." On the occasion of her marriage, not only were the brains of all the jewellers, embroiderers, and tailors of Paris put in requisition, but a whole host of French poets felt themselves suddenly inspired. Epithalamiums poured in from all quarters, spiced with flattery of all kinds, few of which have been borne down the stream of time so honourably for their author's abilities as that of Buchanan, who, having long struggled with poverty, had at last risen to independence, under the patronage of Cardinal Lorraine. This poem is well known, but is not more complimentary than that of Joachim du

Bellay, who, after comparing Mary to Venus, concludes his song with these lines:—

> "Par une chaîne à sa langue attachée
> Hercule à soi les peuple attiroit;
> Mais celle ci tire ceux qu'elle voit
> Par une chaîne à ses beaux yeux attachée."

Homage, so general, cannot have been entirely misplaced, or very palpably exaggerated.

In Scotland, through the instigation of the Queen Regent, Mary's nuptials, which were far from being agreeable to a numerous party, were celebrated with probably less sincere, and certainly much more homely expressions of pleasure. Orders were sent to the different towns "to make fyres and processions general." Mons-Meg, the celebrated great gun of Edinburgh Castle, was fired once; and there is a charge of ten shillings in the treasurer's accounts of that year paid to certain persons for bringing up the cannon "to be schote, and for the finding and carrying of her bullet after she was schote frae Wardie Muir to the Castel of Edinburgh,"—a distance of about two miles. A play was also enacted, but of what kind it is difficult to say, at the expense of the city of Edinburgh.

CHAPTER V.

MARY THE QUEEN DAUPHINESS, THE QUEEN, AND THE QUEEN DOWAGER OF FRANCE.

Shortly after the espousals, Mary and her husband retired to one of their princely summer residences. Here she unostentatiously discharged the duties of a respectful and attentive wife, in a manner which gained for her the admiration of all who visited them. Delightful as society and amusements must at that age have been to her, she readily accommodated herself to the peculiar temper of Francis, and seemed willing, for his sake, to resign all the gaieties of the court.

But the intriguing and restless ambition of her uncles could not allow her to remain long quiet. About this time, Mary Tudor, who had succeeded Edward VI. on the English throne, died; and although the Parliament of that country had declared that the succession rested in her sister Elizabeth, it was thought proper to claim for Mary Stuart a prior right. The ground upon which they built this claim was the following. Henry VIII. married for his first wife Catharine of Arragon, widow of his brother Arthur, and by her he had one child, Mary. Pretending after having lived with her eighteen years, that his conscience rebuked him for making his brother's wife the partner of his bed, he procured a divorce from Catharine for the purpose of marrying Anne Boleyn, by whom he had also one daughter, Elizabeth. Growing tired of this new wife, she was sent to the scaffold to make way for Jane Seymour, by whom he had one son, Edward. Of this uxorious monarch's other three wives, it is unnecessary to speak. Henry had procured from the British Parliament a solemn act, declaring both his daughters illegitimate, and he left his crown to Edward VI., who accordingly succeeded him. Upon Edward's death, the Parliament, rescinding their former act, in order to save the nation from a civil war, called to the throne Henry's eldest daughter Mary,—not, however, without a protest being entered in behalf of the Scotch Queen by her guardians. Upon Mary's death, the opportunity again occurred of pressing the claims of the daughter of James V. The mother of that king, it will be remembered, who married his father James IV., was the eldest daughter of Henry VII., and sister, consequently, of Henry VIII. Henry was, therefore, Mary's maternal grand-uncle; and if his wives, Catharine and Anne Boleyn, were legally divorced, she had certainly a better right to the English Crown than any of their illegitimate offspring. Soon after the accession, however, of Edward VI., the Parliament, complying with the voice of the whole nation, had declared them legitimate; and as Elizabeth now quietly took possession of the throne, and could hardly by any chance have been dispossessed, it was, to say the least, extremely ill-advised to push Mary forward as a rival claimant.

For various reasons, however, this was the policy which the Guises chose to pursue. Nor did they proceed to assert her right with any particular delicacy or caution. Whenever the Dauphin and his Queen came into public, they were greeted as the King and Queen of England; and the English arms were engraved upon their plate, embroidered upon their scutcheons and banners, and painted on their furniture.[22] Mary's favourite device, also, at this time, was the two crowns of France and Scotland, with the motto, *Aliamque moratur*, meaning that of England. The prediction made by the Duke of Alva, on observing this piece of empty parade, was but too fatally fulfilled,—"That bearing of Mary Stuart's," said he, "will not be easily borne."

About this time Mary seems to have been attacked with the first serious illness which had overtaken her in France. It was not of that acute description which confined her to bed, but was a sort of general debility accompanied with a tendency to frequent fainting. It is mentioned in Forbes's State Papers, that on one occasion, to prevent her from swooning in church, her attendants were glad to bring her wine from the altar. There were some at the French Court who would have felt little grief had this illness ended fatally, considering how serious a blow Mary's death would have been to the too predominating influence of the House of Guise. In England, the news would have been particularly agreeable to Elizabeth, whose ambassador at Paris eagerly consoled her with the intelligence that Mary was not expected to be of long continuance. The natural strength of her constitution, however, soon restored her to her former health and spirits.

But it was destined that there was to be another and more unexpected death at the French Court. Henry II., while exhibiting his prowess at a tournament, on the occasion of the marriage of his daughter Elizabeth to Philip of Spain, in July 1559, received a wound in the head from the spear of his antagonist, the Count Montgomery, which, though apparently not of much consequence at first, occasioned his dissolution eight days afterwards. A considerable change immediately took place in the aspect of the Court. The stars of the Duchess de Valentinois, and of the Constable Montmorency, set at once; and that of Catharine de Medicis, though not entirely obscured, shone lower in the horizon. She was now only the second lady in France, Mary Stuart taking the precedence. The Guises reigned along with her, and the House of Bourbon trembled. Catharine, who could bear no superior, more especially one young enough to be her own daughter, could ill disguise her chagrin. As a guardian, however, of her late husband's younger sons, the presumptive heirs to the crown, she was entitled to maintain her place and authority in the Government. There is a curious little anecdote of her which shows how much the change in her situation was preying on her mind. As she was leaving the Palace of the Tournelles, to accompany Francis to the Louvre, where he was to appear as the new Sovereign, she fell into a reverie, and in traversing the gallery, took a wrong turn, and was entirely separated from her party before she discovered her mistake. She soon overtook them, however, and as they passed out, said to Mary,—"Pass on, Madam, it is now your turn to take precedence." Mary accepted the courtesy, but with becoming delicacy insisted that Catharine should enter the carriage first.[23] There is something more affecting in the change which Henry's death produced in the condition of the venerable Montmorency and his family. He whom three monarchs had loved and respected, who had given dignity to their counsels, and ensured success to their arms, was not considered worthy of remaining in the palace of the feeble and entrammelled Francis. With a princely retinue, he retired honourably to his mansion at Chantilly.

Mary was now at the very height of European grandeur. The Queen of two powerful countries—and the heir-presumptive of a third,—in the flower of her age,—and, from her superior mental endowments, much more worshipped, even in France, than her husband, she affords at this period of her history as striking an example as can be found of the concentration of all the blessings of fortune in one person. She stood unluckily on too high and glorious a pinnacle to be able to retain her position long, consistent with the *vices vitæ mortalium*. Whilst she conducted herself with a prudence and propriety altogether remarkable, considering her youth and the susceptibility of her nature, she began to be regarded with suspicion at once by France, England, and Scotland. In France, she was obliged to bear the blame of many instances of bigotry and over-severity in the government of her uncles;—in England, Elizabeth took every opportunity to load with opprobrium a sister Queen, whose descent, birth, station, and accomplishments, were so much superior to her own;—in Scotland, the Reformers, inspired by James Stuart, who, with ulterior views of his own, was contented to act as the tool of Elizabeth, laboured to make it be believed that Mary was an uncompromising and narrow-minded Catholic.

In September 1559, Francis was solemnly crowned at Rheims; and during the remainder of the season, he and Mary, attended by their nobles, made various progresses through the country. In December, Francis, whose health was evidently giving way, went, by the advice of his physicians, to Blois, celebrated for the mildness of its climate. It affords a very vivid idea of the ignorant superstition of the French peasantry to learn, that on his journey thither, every village through which he passed was deserted. An absurd story had been circulated, and was universally believed, that the nature of Francis's complaints were such, that they could only be cured by the royal patient bathing in the blood of young children. Francis himself, although probably not informed of the cause, observed with pain how he was every where shunned; and, notwithstanding the soothing tenderness of Mary, who accompanied him, is said to have exclaimed to the Cardinal Lorraine, "What have I done to be thus shunned and detested? They fly me; my people abhor me! It is not thus that the French used to receive their King."[24]

Misfortunes, it is said, never come singly. Whilst Mary was performing the part of an affectionate nurse to her husband, she sustained an irretrievable loss in the death of her mother, the Scottish Regent, in June 1560; and in the December following, her husband, Francis, died at Orleans, in the 17th year of his age, and the 17th month of his reign.[25] Feeling that his exhausted constitution was sinking rapidly, and that his death was at hand, almost the last words he spoke were to testify his affection for Mary, and his sense of her virtues. He earnestly beseeched his mother to treat her as her own daughter, and his brother to look upon her as a sister. He was a prince, says Conæus, in whom, had he lived, more merit would probably have been discovered than most people suspected.[26] The whole face of things in France was by this event instantly changed again. Francis the Little, as he was contemptuously termed by the French, in opposition to his father Francis the Great, was succeeded by his younger brother, Charles IX. He being still a minor, his mother, Catharine, contrived to get herself appointed his guardian, and thus became once more Queen of France, the nobility, as Chalmers remarks, being more inclined to relish a *real* minority, than an imaginary *majority*. Catharine's jealousy of Mary Stuart, of course extended itself, with greater justice, to her uncles of Guise. It was now their turn to make way for Montmorency; and the Cardinal of Lorraine, one of the most intriguing statesmen of the age, retired, in no very charitable mood of mind, to his archbishopric at Rheims, where, in a fit of spleen, he declared he would devote himself entirely to religion.

There is something exceedingly naïve and amusing in Sir James Melville's account of this "gret changement." "The Queen-mother," says he, "was blyth of the death of King Francis, her son, because she had na guiding of him, but only the Duke of Guise and the Cardinal, his brother, by raisoun that the Queen, our maistress, was their sister's dochter. Sa, the Queen-mother was content to be quit of the government of the house of Guise; and for their cause (sake) she had a great mislyking of our Queen." Of Montmorency, who, as soon as he heard of the illness of Francis, commenced his journey towards the Court, he says,—"The Constable, also chargit to come to the court, looked for na less, and seamed to be seak, making little journeies, caried in a horse-litter, drew time sae lang by the way, that the King, in the meantime, died. Then he lap on horsbak and cam freely to the Court and commandit, like a Constable, the men of war that gardit the Croun, by the Duke of Guise commandement, to pack them aff the toune. The Queen-mother was also very glaid of his coming, that by his autority and frendship with the King of Navarre, she mycht the better dryve the house of Guise to the door." Of Mary, who, it may well be supposed, felt this change more than any one, Melville says,—"Our Queen also, seeing her friends in disgrace, and knawing hirself no to be weil liked, left the Court, and was a sorrowful widow when I took my leave at hir, in a gentilman's house, four myle fra Orleans." To this "gentilman's house," or chateau, in the neighbourhood of Orleans, Mary had retired to shed in private those tears, which the death of her husband called forth. In losing Francis, she had lost the playmate of her childhood, the husband of her youth, and what, by many women, would be considered as serious a loss as either, the rank and title of Queen of France. It was here, probably, that she composed those verses to the memory of her deceased husband, which her biographers have so frequently copied, and which are so full of gentle and unaffected feeling.

Mary, however, was at this time a personage of too much importance in the politics and affairs of Europe, to be left long unmolested to the indulgence of that sincere, but commonly temporary, sorrow of a widow of eighteen. New suitors were even now beginning to form hopes of an alliance with her; and two of the earliest in the field were, Don Carlos of Spain, and the King of Navarre. But Mary was determined to listen to no proposals of a matrimonial nature, till she had arranged the plan of her future life. France was no longer for her the country it had once been. Her affectionate father-in-law Henry, and her amiable, though weak, husband Francis, both of whom commanded for her the first rank in the State, were dead; her mother would never visit her more, for her tomb had already been erected at Rheims, and her proud uncles had been banished from the Court. Mary had too high a spirit, and knew her own superiority too well, to brook for a moment the haughty control of Catharine de Medicis. She felt that not all the blood of all the merchants of Italy, could ever elevate the Queen-Dowager to an equality with one who, as it is said she herself once expressed it, drew her descent from a centinary line of Kings. Catharine felt this painfully, and the more so, that when Mary once more made her appearance at Court, she perceived, in the words of Miss Benger, that "the charms of her conversation, her graceful address, her captivating accomplishments, had raised the *woman* above the *Queen*."

In the mean time, by the Reformed party in Scotland, the news of the death of Francis was received with any thing but sorrow. Knox declared triumphantly that "his glory had perished, and that the pride of his stubborn heart had vanished into smoke." The Lord James, her natural brother, was immediately deputed by the Congregation to proceed to France, to ascertain whether the Queen intended returning to her native country, and if she did, to influence her as much as possible in favour of the true gospel and its friends. Nor were the Catholics inactive at this critical juncture. A meeting was held, at which were present the Archbishop of St Andrews, the Bishops of Aberdeen, Murray, and Ross, the Earls of Huntly, Athol, Crawfurd, and Sutherland, and many other persons of distinction, by whom it was determined to send as *their* ambassador to Mary, John Lesly, afterwards Bishop of Ross, and one of the Queen's staunchest friends, both during her life and after it. He was of course instructed to give her a very different account of the state of matters from that which the Lord James would do. He was to speak to her of the power and influence of the Catholic party; and to contrast their fidelity both to her and to her mother, with the rebellious proceedings of those who supported the covenant.

The Lord James went by the way of England, and Lesly sailed from Aberdeen for Holland. Both made good speed; and Lesly arrived at Vitry in Champagne, where Mary was then residing, only one day before the Prior of St Andrews. He lost no time in gaining admission to the Queen; and though there is little doubt that his views were more sincere and honourable than those of her brother, it is at the same time very questionable whether the advice he gave her was judicious; and it is probably fortunate that Mary's good sense and moderation led her to reject it. Lesly commenced with cautioning her against the crafty speeches which he knew the Lord James was about to make to her, assuring her that his principal object was to insinuate himself into her good graces, to obtain the chief management of affairs, and crush effectually the old religion. The Prior, Lesly assured her, was not so warm in the cause of the Reformers, from any conviction of its truth, as from his wish to make it a stepping-stone for his own ambition. For these reasons, he advised her to bring with her to Scotland an armed force, and to land at Aberdeen, or some northern port, where the Earl of Huntly and her other friends would join her with a numerous army, at the head of which she might advance towards Edinburgh, and defeat at once the machinations of her enemies. The Queen, in reply to all this, merely desired that Lesly should remain with her till she returned to Scotland, commanding him to write, in the mean time, to the Lords and Prelates who sent him, to inform them of her favourable sentiments towards them, and of her intention to come speedily home.[27]

The day after Lesly's audience, Mary's old friend the Lord James (for it will be remembered, that thirteen years before he had come to France with her, and he had in the interval paid her one or two visits) obtained an interview with his sister. He had every desire to retain the favourable place which he flattered himself he held in her estimation; and, though so rigid a Reformer among his Scottish friends, his conscience does not seem to have prevented him from paying all the court he could to his Catholic Sovereign. In the course of his conversation with her, he carefully avoided every subject which might have been disagreeable to Mary. He beseeched her to believe, that she would not find the remotest occasion for any foreign troops in Scotland, as the whole nation was prepared faithfully to obey her. This assurance was true, as it turned out; but it is not quite certain whether the Prior of St Andrews was thinking, at the time, so much of its truth, as of its being convenient, for various reasons, that Mary should have no standing force, at her command, in her own kingdom. Mary gave to her brother the same general sort of answer that she had previously given to Lesly. At the same time, she was secretly disposed to attribute greater weight to his arguments, and treat him with higher consideration, for a reason which Melville furnishes. It appears that the French noblemen, who, on the conclusion of peace with England had returned from Scotland, had all assured her, that she would find it most for her interest to associate in her councils the leaders of the Reformers,—particularly the Prior himself,—the Earl of Argyle, who had married her natural sister, the Lady Jane Stuart,—and Maitland of Lethington.

It is worthy of notice, that, affairs of state having been discussed, the Prior ventured to speak a word or two for his own interest. He requested that the Earldom of Murray might be conferred on him, and the Queen promised to attend to his request on her return to Scotland. Having thus prudently discharged his commission, the Lord James took his leave, visiting Elizabeth on his way home, as he had already done before passing over into France. About the same time, many of the Scotch nobility, in anticipation of her speedy return, came to pay their duty to the Queen, and, among them, was the celebrated Earl of Bothwell.[28]

CHAPTER VI.

MARY'S RETURN TO SCOTLAND, AND PREVIOUS NEGOTIATIONS WITH ELIZABETH.

Elizabeth being informed of Mary's intended movements, thought the opportunity a favourable one, for adjusting with her one or two of their mutual disagreements. Mary's refusal to ratify the celebrated treaty of Edinburgh, had particularly galled the English Queen. Most of the essential articles of that treaty had already been carried into effect; and as Francis and Mary had sent their ambassadors into Scotland with full powers, they were bound according to the ordinary laws of diplomacy, to agree to whatever concessions their plenipotentiaries made. But, as Robertson has remarked, Cecil "had proved greatly an overmatch for Monluc." In the sixth article, which was by far the most offensive to the Scottish Queen, he had got the French delegates to consent to a declaration, that Francis and Mary should abstain from using and bearing the title and arms of the kingdom of England, not only during the life of Elizabeth, but "*in all times coming.*" There was here so palpable a departure from all law and justice, that, if there was ever a case in which a sovereign was justified in refusing to sanction the blunders of his representatives, it was this. Robertson's observations on the point are forcible and correct. "The ratification of this article," says he, "would have been of the most fatal consequence to Mary. The Crown of England was an object worthy of her ambition. Her pretensions to it gave her great dignity and importance in the eyes of all Europe. By many, her title was esteemed preferable to that of Elizabeth. Among the English themselves, the Roman Catholics, who formed at that time a numerous and active party, openly espoused this opinion; and even the Protestants, who supported Elizabeth's throne, could not deny the Queen of Scots to be her immediate heir. A proper opportunity to avail herself of all these advantages, could not, in the course of things, be far distant, and many incidents might fall in to bring this opportunity nearer than was expected. In these circumstances, Mary, by ratifying the article in dispute, would have lost that rank which she had hitherto held among neighbouring princes; the zeal of her adherents must have gradually cooled; and she might have renounced, from that moment, all hopes of ever wearing the English crown."

Mary, therefore, cannot be, in fairness, blamed for her conduct regarding this treaty. But, as has been already said, she allowed herself to be persuaded to a very great imprudence, when she advanced, what she declared to be a present and existing claim on the English Crown. This was an aggravation of the offence, which Elizabeth could never pardon. She determined to retort upon Mary, as efficiently though not quite so directly. She found means to hint to her friends in Scotland, that it would not be disagreeable to her, were the Earl of Arran, eldest son of the Duke of Chatelherault, and, after his father, presumptive heir to the throne, to propose himself to her as a husband. This was accordingly done, and must have touched Mary very closely, especially as she had no children by her husband Francis. But as Elizabeth had never any serious intention of accepting of Arran's proposals, she was resolved upon taking another and much more unjustifiable method of harassing Mary.

Knowing that she possessed the command of the seas, the English Queen imagined that she had it in her power to prevent, if she chose, Mary's return to her own kingdom. Before granting her, therefore, as in common courtesy she was bound to do, a free passage, she determined on seizing the opportunity for again pressing the ratification of the treaty of Edinburgh. With this view, she desired Sir Nicolas Throckmorton, her ambassador at Paris, to wait on the Queen of Scots, ostensibly to congratulate her on her recovery from an attack of ague, but in reality to press this matter upon her attention. The audience which Mary granted to Throckmorton upon this occasion, together with another which she gave him a few weeks afterwards, introduce us to her, for the first time, acting for herself, in her public and important capacity of Queen of Scotland. All historians unite in expressing their admiration of the talented and dignified manner in which she conducted herself, though only in her nineteenth year. We have fortunately a full account of both conferences, furnished by Sir Nicolas Throckmorton himself, in his letters to the Queen of England.

The ambassador, on his first interview, having expressed Elizabeth's happiness at Mary's recovery, proceeded to renew the demand which had so frequently been made to her regarding the treaty of Edinburgh. Mary, in answer, said, that she begged to thank the Queen her good sister for her congratulations, and though she was not yet in perfect health, she thanked God for her evident convalescence. As to the treaty of Edinburgh, she begged to postpone giving any final answer in the affair until she had taken the advice of the nobles and estates of her own realm. "For though this matter," she said, "doth touch me principally, yet doth it also touch the nobles and estates of my realm; and, therefore, it is meet that I use their advice therein. Heretofore they have seemed to be grieved that I should do any thing without them, and now they would be more offended if I should proceed in this matter of myself without their advice." She added, that she intended to return home soon, and that she was about to send an ambassador to Elizabeth, to require of her the common favour of a free passage which princes usually ask of each other in such cases. In a spirit of conciliation and sound policy, she concluded with these words. "Though the terms wherein we have stood heretofore have been somewhat hard, yet I trust, that from henceforth we shall accord together as cousins and good neighbours. I mean to retire all the Frenchmen from Scotland who have given jealousy to the Queen my sister, and miscontent to my subjects; so that I will leave nothing undone to satisfy all parties, trusting the Queen my good sister will do the like, and that from henceforth none of my disobedient subjects shall find aid or support at her hands."—Seeing that Mary was not to be moved from the position she had taken regarding this treaty, Throckmorton went on to sound her upon the subject of religion. His object was to ascertain what course she intended to pursue towards the Scottish Reformers. Mary stated to him distinctly her views upon this important matter, and there was a consistency and moderation in them hardly to have been expected from the niece of the Cardinal of Lorraine, had we not been previously aware of the strength of her superior mind. "I will be plain with you," said she to the ambassador. "The religion which I profess I take to be most acceptable to God; and indeed, I neither know, nor desire to know, any other. Constancy becometh all people well, but none better than princes, and such as have rule over realms, and especially in matters of religion. I have been brought up in this religion, and who might credit me in any thing if I should show myself light in this case." "I am none of those," she added, "that will change their religion every year; *but I mean to constrain none of my subjects, though I could wish that they were all as I am; and I trust they shall have no support to constrain me.*" It will be seen, in the sequel, whether Mary ever deviated for a moment from the principles she here laid down. Throckmorton ventured to ask, if she did not think many errors had crept into her church, and whether she had ever seriously weighed the arguments in support of the Reformed opinions. "Though I be young, and not well learned," she replied modestly, "yet have I heard this matter oft disputed by my uncle,—my Lord Cardinal, with some that thought they could say somewhat in the matter; and I found no great reason to change my opinion. But I have oft heard him confess, that great errors have come into the church, and great disorder among the ministers and clergy, of which errors and disorders he wished there might be a reformation." Here this conference concluded.[29]

Elizabeth, as soon as she understood that Mary waited for the advice of her Privy Counsellors and her Parliament, before ratifying the treaty of Edinburgh, addressed a letter to the "States of Scotland," as she was pleased to term them, but, in point of fact, only to her old allies the Lords of the Congregation. The object of this letter was to convey, in haughty and even insolent terms, a threat that, unless they secured their Queen's assent to the treaty, they might cease to look for any aid or protection from her. In other words, its meaning was this:—Through my interference, you have been able to establish the new Gospel; your Queen you know to be a Catholic; and as it is not unlikely that she may associate in her councils your old enemies the Catholic nobility, it is in me you trust to enable you to rebel successfully against your lawful Sovereign. But I have no intention to give you my support for nothing; and unless your reformed consciences will permit of your insisting that Mary Stuart shall sign away her hereditary right of succession to the English throne, I shall henceforth have nothing more to do with you. No other interpretation can be put on such expressions as the following, couched in terms whose meaning sophistry itself could not hide. "In a matter so profitable to both the realms, we think it strange that your Queen hath no better advice; and therefore we do require ye all, being the States of that realm upon whom the burden resteth, to consider this matter deeply, and to make us answer whereunto we may trust. And if you shall think meet, she shall thus leave the peace imperfect, by breaking of her solemn promise, contrary to the order of all princes, we shall be well content to accept your answer, and shall be as careless to see the peace kept, as ye shall give us cause; and doubt not, by the grace of God, but whosoever of ye shall incline thereto, shall soonest repent. You must be content with our plain writing."

To this piece of "plain writing," the Reformers, probably at the instigation of the Lord James, sent a submissive and cringing answer. "Your Majesty," they say, "may be well assured, that in us shall be noted no blame, if that peace be not ratified to your Majesty's contentment."—"The benefit that we have received is so recent, that we cannot suddenly bury it in forgetfulness. We would desire your Majesty rather to be persuaded of us, that we, to our powers, will study to leave it in remembrance to our posterity." In other words,—Whatever our own Queen Mary may determine on doing, we shall remain steady to your interests, and would much rather quarrel with her than with you. To this state of mind had Elizabeth's machinations contrived to bring the majority of the young Queen's subjects.[30]

In the meantime, Mary had sent an ambassador into England to demand a safe conduct for her approaching voyage. This was expressly refused; and Throckmorton was again ordered to request an audience with Mary, to explain the motives of this refusal. "In this conference," observes Robertson, "Mary exerted all that dignity and vigour of mind of which she was so capable, and at no period of her life, were her abilities displayed to greater advantage." Throckmorton had recourse to the endless subject of the treaty of 1560, or, as it is more commonly called, the treaty of Edinburgh, as the apology his mistress offered for having, with studied disrespect, denied the suit made by Mary's ambassador, in the presence of a numerous audience,—a direct breach of courtly etiquette. Mary, before answering Throckmorton, commanded all her attendants to retire, and then said,—"I like not to have so many witnesses of my passions as the Queen, your mistress, was content to have, when she talked with M. D'Oysel. There is nothing that doth more grieve me, than that I did so forget myself, as to require of the Queen, your mistress, that favour, which I had no need to ask. I may pass well enough home into my own realm, I think, without her passport or license; for, though the late king, your master, used all the impeachment he could, both to stay me and catch me, when I came hither, yet you know, M. l'Ambassadeur, I came hither safely, and I may have as good means to help me home again, if I could employ my friends." "It seemeth," she added, with much truth, "that the Queen, your mistress, maketh more account of the amity of my disobedient subjects, than she doth of me, their sovereign, who am her equal in degree, though inferior in wisdom and experience, her nighest kinswoman, and her next neighbour." She then proceeded very forcibly to state, once more, her reasons for refusing to ratify the treaty. It had been made, she said, during the life of Francis II., who, as her lord and husband, was more responsible for it than she. Upon his death, she ceased to look for advice to the council of France, neither her uncles nor her own subjects, nor Elizabeth herself, thinking it meet, that she should be guided by any council but that of Scotland. There were none of her ministers with her; the matter was important; it touched both them and her; and she, therefore, considered it her duty to wait, till she should get the opinions of the wisest of them. As soon as she did, she undertook to send Elizabeth whatever answer might appear to be reasonable. "The Queen, your mistress," observed Mary, "saith that I am young; she might say that I were as foolish as young, if I would, in the state and country that I am in, proceed to such a matter, of myself, without any counsel; for that which was done by the King, my late lord and husband, must not be taken to be my act; and yet I will say, truly, unto ye, and as God favours me, I did never mean otherwise, unto the Queen, your mistress, than becometh me to my good sister and cousin, nor meant her any more harm than to myself. God forgive them that have otherwise persuaded her, if there be any such."

It may seem strange, that as the sixth article was the only one in the whole treaty of Edinburgh, which occasioned any disagreement, it was not proposed to make some alteration in it, which might have rendered it satisfactory to all parties. Mary would have had no objection to have given up all claim upon the Crown of England, during the lifetime of Elizabeth, and in favour of children born by her in lawful wedlock,—if, failing these children, her own right was acknowledged. There could have been little difficulty, one would have thought, in expressing the objectionable article accordingly. But this amendment would not by any means have suited the views of Elizabeth.[31]

To have acknowledged Mary's right of succession would have been at once to have pointed out to all the Catholics of Europe, the person to whom they were to pay their court, on account not only of her present influence, but of the much greater which awaited her. Besides, it might have had the appearance of leaving it doubtful, whether Elizabeth's possession of the throne was not conceded to her, more as a favour than as a right. This extreme jealousy on the part of the English Queen, originated in Mary having imprudently allowed herself to be persuaded to bear the arms of England, diversely quartered with her own, at the time Elizabeth was first called to the crown. At the interview we have been describing, Throckmorton, being silenced with regard to the ratification of the treaty, thought he might with propriety advert to this other subject of complaint.

"I refer it to your own judgment, Madam," said he, "if any thing can be more prejudicial to a prince, than to usurp the title and interest belonging to him." Mary's answer deserves particular attention. "M. L'Ambassadeur," said she, "I was then under the commandment of King Henry my father, and of the king my lord and husband; and whatsoever was then done by their order and commandments, the same was in like manner continued until both their deaths; *since which time, you know I neither bore the arms, or used the title of England.* Methinks," she added, "these my doings might ascertain the queen your mistress, that that which was done before, was done by commandment of them that had power over me; and also, in reason, she ought to be satisfied, seeing I (now) order my doings, as I tell ye." With this answer Throckmorton took his leave.[32]

Seeing that matters could not be more amicably adjusted, Mary prepared to return home, independent of Elizabeth's permission. Yet it was not without many a bitter regret that she thought of leaving all the fascinations of her adopted country, France. When left alone, she was frequently found in tears; and it is more than probable, that, as Miss Benger has expressed it, "there were moments when Mary recoiled with indescribable horror from the idea of living in Scotland—where her religion was insulted, and her sex contemned; where her mother had languished in misery, and her father sunk into an untimely grave." At last, however, the period arrived when it was necessary for her to bid a final adieu to the scenes and friends of her youth. She had delayed from month to month, as if conscious that, in leaving France, she was about to part with happiness. She had originally proposed going so early as the spring of 1561, but it was late in July before she left Paris; and as she lingered on the way, first at St Germains, and afterwards at Calais, August was well advanced before she set sail. The spring of this year, says Brantome poetically, was so backward, that it appeared as if it would never put on its robe of flowers; and thus gave an opportunity to the gallants of the Court to assert, that it wore so doleful a garb to testify its sorrow for the intended departure of Mary Stuart.[33] She was accompanied as far as St Germains by Catharine de Medicis, and nearly all the French Court. Her six uncles, Anne of Este, and many other ladies and gentlemen of distinction, proceeded on with her to Calais. The historians Castelnau and Brantome were both of the Queen's retinue, and accompanied her to Scotland. At Calais she found four vessels, one of which was fitted up for herself and friends, and a second for her escort; the two others were for the furniture she took with her.

Elizabeth, meanwhile, was not inattentive to the proceedings of the Scottish Queen. Through the agency of her minister, Cecil, she had been anxiously endeavouring to discover whether she would render herself particularly obnoxious either to Catharine de Medicis, or the leading men in Scotland, by making herself mistress of Mary's person on her passage homewards, and carrying her a prisoner into England. Her ambassador, Throckmorton, had given her good reason to believe that Catharine was not disposed to be particularly warm in Mary's defence.[34] As to Scotch interference, Camden expressly informs us, that the Lord James, when he passed through England on his return from France, warned Elizabeth of Mary's intended movements, and advised that she should be intercepted. This assertion, though its truth has been doubted, is rendered exceedingly probable by the contents of two letters, which have been preserved. The first is from Throckmorton, who assures Elizabeth that the Lord James deserves her most particular esteem;—"Your Majesty," he says, "may, in my opinion, make good account of his constancy towards you; and so he deserveth to be well entertained and made of by your Majesty, as one that may stand ye in no small stead for the advancement of your Majesty's desire. Since his being here (in France), he hath dealt so frankly and liberally with me, that I must believe he will so continue after his return home."[35] The other letter is from Maitland of Lethington, one of the ablest men among the Scotch Reformers, and the personal friend and co-adjutor of the Lord James, to Sir William Cecil. In this letter he says;—"I do also allow your opinion anent the Queen our Sovereign's journey towards Scotland, whose coming hither, if she be enemy to the religion, and so affected towards that realm as she yet appeareth, shall not fail to raise wonderful tragedies." He then proceeds to point out, that, as Elizabeth's object, for her own sake, must be to prevent the Catholics from gaining ground in Scotland, her best means of obtaining such an object, is to prevent a Queen from returning into the kingdom, who "shall so easily win to her party the whole Papists, and so many Protestants as be either addicted to the French faction, covetous, inconstant, uneasy, ignorant, or careless."—"So long as her Highness is absent," he adds, "in this case there is no peril; but you may judge what the presence of a prince being craftily counselled is able to bring to pass." "For my opinion," he concludes, "anent the continuance of amity betwixt these two realms, there is no danger of breach so long as the Queen is absent; but her presence may alter many things."[36]

To make assurance doubly sure, Cecil desired Randolph, the English resident in Scotland, to feel the pulse of the nobility. On the 9th of August 1561, only a few days before Mary sailed from France, Randolph wrote from Edinburgh an epistle to Cecil, in which he assures him that it will be a "stout adventure for a *sick crazed woman*," (a singular mode of designating Mary), to venture home to a country so little disposed to receive her. "I have shewn your Honour's letters," he says, "unto the Lord James, Lord Morton, Lord Lethington; *they wish, as your Honour doth, that she might be stayed yet for a space; and if it were not for their obedience sake, some of them care not tho' they never saw her face.*"—And again—"Whatsomever cometh of this, he (Lethington), findeth it ever best that she come not." Knox also, it seems, had been written to, and had expressed his resolution to resist to the last Mary's authority. "By such letters as ye have last received," says Randolph, "your Honour somewhat understandeth of Mr Knox himself, and also of others, what is determined,—he himself to abide the uttermost, and others never to leave him, until God hath taken his life."—"His daily prayer is, for the maintenance of unity with England, and that God will never suffer men to be so ungrate as by any persuasion to run headlong unto the destruction of them that have saved their lives, and restored their country to liberty."[37]

Elizabeth having thus felt her way, and being satisfied that she might with safety pursue her own inclinations, was determined not to rest contented with the mere refusal of passports. Throckmorton was ordered to ascertain exactly when and how Mary intended sailing. The Scottish Queen became aware of his drift, from some questions he put to her, and said to him cuttingly,—"I trust the wind will be so favourable, as I shall not need to come on the coast of England; and if I do, then M. l'Ambassadeur, the Queen, your mistress, shall have me in her hands to do her will of me; and if she be so hard-hearted as to desire my end, she may then do her pleasure, and make sacrifice of me. Peradventure, that casualty might be better for me than to live." Throckmorton, however, made good his point, and was able to inform Elizabeth that Mary would sail either from Havre-de-Grace or Calais, and that she would first proceed along the coast of Flanders, and then strike over to Scotland. For the greater certainty, he suggested the propriety of some spies being sent across to the French coast, who would give the earliest intelligence of her movements. Profiting by this and other information, all the best historians of the time agree in stating, that Elizabeth sent a squadron to sea with all expedition. It was only a thick and unexpected fog which prevented these vessels from falling in with that in which Mary sailed. The smaller craft which carried her furniture, they did meet with, and, believing them to be the prize they were in search of, they boarded and examined them. One ship they detained, in which was the Earl of Eglinton, and some of Mary's horses and mules, and, under the pretence of suspecting it of piracy, actually carried it into an English harbour. The affectation of "clearing the seas from pirates," as Cecil expresses it, was a mere after-thought, invented to do away with the suspicion which attached itself to this unsuccessful attempt. Its real purpose was openly talked of at the time. Sir Nicholas Bacon, Lord Keeper, in a speech he made at a meeting of the Privy Council in 1562, said frankly, —"Think ye that the Scottish Queen's suit, made in all friendly manner, to come through England at the time she left France, and the denial thereof, unless the treaty were ratified, is by them forgotten, or else your sending of your ships to sea at the time of her passage?" Camden, Holinshed, Spottiswoode, Stranguage, and Buchanan, all speak to the same effect; and Elizabeth's intentions, though frustrated, hardly admit of a doubt.[38]

On the 25th of August 1561, Mary sailed out of the harbour of Calais,—not without shedding, and seeing shed many tears. She did not, however, part with all the friends who had accompanied her to the coast. Three of her uncles,—the Duke d'Aumale, the Marquis D'Elbeuf, and the Grand Prior,— the Duke Danville, son to Montmorency, and afterwards Constable of France, one of the most ardent and sincere admirers that Mary perhaps ever had,—and many other persons of rank, among whom was the unfortunate poet Chatelard, who fluttered like a moth round the light in which he was to be consumed,—sailed with her for Scotland. Just as she left the harbour, an unfortunate accident happened to a vessel, which, by unskilful management, struck upon the bar, and was wrecked within a very short distance of her own galley. "This is a sad omen," she exclaimed, weeping. A gentle breeze sprang up; the sails were set, and the little squadron got under way, consisting, as has been said, of only four vessels, for Mary dreaded lest her subjects should suppose that she was coming home with any military force. The feelings of "la Reine Blanche," as the French termed her, from the white mourning she wore for Francis, were at all times exceedingly acute. On the present occasion, her grief amounted almost to despair. As long as the light of day continued, she stood immoveable on the vessel's deck, gazing with tearful eyes upon the French coast, and exclaiming incessantly,—"Farewell, France! farewell, my beloved country!" When night approached, and her friends beseeched her to retire to the cabin, she hid her face in her hands, and sobbed aloud. "The darkness which is now brooding over France," said she, "is like the darkness in my own heart." A little afterwards, she added,—"I am unlike the Carthaginian Dido, for she looked perpetually on the sea, when Æneas departed, whilst all my regards are for the land." Having caused a bed to be made for her on deck, she wept herself asleep, previously enjoining her attendants to waken her at the first peep of day, if the French coast was still visible. Her wishes were gratified; for during the night the wind died away, and the vessel made little progress. Mary rose with the dawn, and feasted her eyes once more with a sight of France. At sunrise, however, the breeze returned, and the galley beginning to make way, the land rapidly receded in the distance. Again her tears burst forth, and again she exclaimed,

—"Farewell, beloved France! I shall never, never, see you more." In the depth of her sorrow, she even wished that the English fleet, which she conjectured had been sent out to intercept her, would make its appearance, and render it necessary for her to seek for safety, by returning to the port from whence she had sailed. But no interruption of this kind occurred.[39]

It is more than likely, that it was during this voyage Mary composed the elegant and simple little song, so expressive of her genuine feelings on leaving France. Though familiarly known to every reader, we cannot deny ourselves the pleasure of inserting it here.

> Adieu, plaisant pays de France!
> O my patrie,
> La plus cherie;
> Qui a nourri ma jeune enfance.
> Adieu, France! adieu, mes beaux jours!
> La nef qui déjoint mes amours,
> N'à cy de moi que la moitié;
> Une parte te reste; elle est tienne;
> Je la fie à ton amitié,
> Pour que de l'autre il te souvienne![40]

Brantome, who sailed in the same vessel with Mary, and gives a particular account of all the events of this voyage, mentions, that the day before entering the Frith of Forth, so thick a mist came on, that it was impossible to see from the poop to the prow. By way of precaution, lest they should run foul of any other vessel, a lantern was lighted, and set at the bow. This gave Chatelard occasion to remark, that it was taking a very unnecessary piece of trouble, so long at least as Mary Stuart remained upon deck, and kept her eyes open. When the mist, at length, cleared away, they found their vessel in the midst of rocks, from which it required much skill and no little labour to get her clear. Mary declared, that so far as regarded her own feelings, she would not have looked upon shipwreck as a great calamity; but that she would not wish to see the lives of the friends who were with her endangered (among whom not the least dear were her four Maries), for all the kingdom of Scotland. She added, that as a bad omen had attended her departure so this thick fog seemed to be but an evil augury at her arrival. At length, the harbour of Leith appeared in sight, and Mary's eye rested, for the first time, upon Arthur Seat and the Castle of Edinburgh.

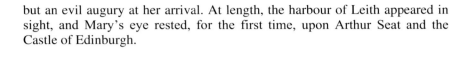

CHAPTER VII.

MARY'S ARRIVAL AT HOLYROOD, WITH SKETCHES OF HER PRINCIPAL NOBILITY.

Mary landed in Scotland with a mind full of anxiety and uncertainty. She came alone and unprotected, to assume the government of a country which had long been distinguished for its rebellious turbulence. The masculine spirit of her father had quailed before the storm. Her mother, whose intellectual energy she well knew, had in vain attempted to bring order out of confusion, and harassed and worn out, had at length surrendered her life in the struggle. For the last two years, it is true, the country had enjoyed, not peace and tranquillity, but a cessation from an actual state of warfare. Nevertheless, the seeds of discontent, and of mutual distrust and hatred, were as abundant as ever. Mary's religion was well known; and her confirmed devotion to it, was by one party magnified into bigotry, and pronounced criminal; whilst by another, it was feared she would show herself too lukewarm in revenging the insults which the ancient worship had sustained. Such being the state of things, how could a young, and comparatively inexperienced queen, just nineteen years of age, approach her kingdom otherwise than with fear and trembling?

Contrasted too with her former situation, that which she was now about to fill, appeared particularly formidable. In France, even during the life of her husband, and while at the very height of her power, few of the severer duties of government rested upon her. She had all the essential authority, without much of the responsibility of a sovereign. Francis consulted her upon every occasion, and followed her advice in almost every matter in which she chose to interfere; but it was to him, or her uncles of Guise, that the nation looked, when any of the state-machinery went wrong. It would be very different in Scotland. By whatever counsel she acted, the blame of all unpopular measures would be sure to rest with her. If she favoured the Protestants, the Catholics would renounce her; if she assisted the Catholics, the Protestants would again be found assembling at Perth, listening, with arms in their hands, to the sermons of John Knox, pulling down the remaining monasteries, and subscribing additional covenants. Is it surprising then, that she found it difficult to steer her course between the rocks of Scylla and the whirlpools of Charybdis? If misfortunes ultimately overtook her, the wonder unquestionably ought to be, not that they ever arrived, but that they should have been guarded against so long. Nothing but the wisest and most temperate policy, could have preserved quietness in a country so full of the elements of internal discord. Mary's system of government throughout all its ramifications, must have been such as no Queen of her age could have established, had there not been more than an empty compliment, in those lines of Buchanan, in which he addresses his Royal mistress as one

"Quae sortem antevenis meritis, virtutibus annos,
Sexum animis, morum nobilitate genus."

There is, besides, a natural feeling of loyalty, which, though it may be evanescent, hardly fails to be kindled in the breasts of the populace, at the sight of their native sovereign. The Scots, though they frequently were far from being contented with the measures pursued by their monarchs, have been always celebrated for their attachment to their persons. Mary, on her first landing, became aware of this truth. As soon as it was known that she intended returning from all the splendours of France, to the more homely comforts of the land of her birth, the people, flattered by the preference she was about to show them, abated somewhat of their previous asperity. They were the more pleased, that she came to them, not as the Queen of France, who might have regarded Scotland as only a province of her empire, but as their own exclusive and independent sovereign. They recollected that she had been at the disposal of the Estates of the country, from the time she was seven days old, and they almost felt as if she had been a child of their own rearing. They knew, also, that she had made a narrow escape in crossing the seas; and the confidence she evidently placed in them, by casting anchor in Leith Roads, with only two galleys, did not pass unnoticed. But she had arrived sooner than was expected; for, so little were they aware of her intended motions, that when her two ships were first observed in the Frith, from the Castle of Edinburgh, no suspicion was entertained that they carried the Queen and her suite. It was not, till a royal salute was fired in the Roads, that her arrival was positively known, and that the people began to flock in crowds to the shore.

On the 20th or 21st of August, 1561, the Queen landed at Leith. Here she was obliged to remain the whole day, as the preparations for her reception at Holyroodhouse were not completed. The multitude continued in the interval to collect at Leith, and on the roads leading to the Palace. On the road between Leith and Restalrig, and from thence to the Abbey, the different trades and corporations of Edinburgh were drawn up in order, lining the way with their banners and bands of music. Towards evening, horses were brought for the Queen and her attendants. When Mary saw them, accustomed as she had been to the noble and richly caparisoned steeds of the Parisian tournaments, she was struck both with the inferiority of their breed, and the poorness of their furnishings. She sighed, and could not help remarking the difference to some of her friends. "But they mean well," said she, "and we must be content." As she passed along, she was every where greeted with enthusiastic shouts of applause—the involuntary homage which the beauty of her countenance, the elegance of her person, and the graceful dignity of her bearing, could not fail to draw forth. Bonfires were lighted in all directions; and though illuminations were then but indifferently understood in Scotland, something of the kind seems to have been attempted. On her arrival at the Palace, all the musicians of Edinburgh collected below her windows, and in strains of most discordant music continued all night to testify their joy for her return. Some of the more rigid Reformers, willing to yield in their own way to the general feeling, assembled together in a knot, and sung psalms in her honour. Among the musical instruments, the bagpipes were preeminently distinguished, which, not exactly suiting the uncultivated taste of Brantome, he pathetically exclaims, "He! quelle musique! et quel repos pour sa nuit!"[41]

It is worth while remarking here, how Knox, in his History of the Reformation, betrays his chagrin at the affectionate manner in which Mary was received. "The very face of the heavens, at the time of her arrival," he says, "did manifestly speak what comfort was brought into this country with her, by sorrow, dolor, darkness, and all impiety; for in the memory of man that day of the year was never seen a more dolorous face of the heavens, than was at her arrival, which two days after did so continue; for, besides the surface wet, and the corruption of the air, the mist was so thick and dark, that scarce could any man espy another the length of two pair of butts. The sun was not seen to shine two days before, nor two days after. That forewarning gave God to us, but alas! the most part were blind."[42] Knox proceeds to reprobate, in the severest terms, the unhallowed amusements which Mary permitted at Holyroodhouse. "So soon as ever her French fillocks, fiddlers, and others of that band, got the house alone, there might be seen skipping not very comely for honest women. Her common talk was, in secret, that she saw nothing in Scotland but gravity, which was altogether repugnant to her nature, for she was brought up in joyeusitye." If Knox really believed in the omens he talks of, or thought the less of a young and beautiful woman for indulging in innocent recreation, his judgment is to be pitied. If he, in truth, did not give any credence to the one, and saw no sin in the other, his candour and sincerity cannot be very highly praised.

M'Crie, the able but too partial biographer of Knox, and the defender of all his errors and failings, speaking of Mary at this period, says;—"Nursed from her infancy in a blind attachment to the Roman Catholic religion, every means had been employed before she left France, to strengthen this prejudice, and to inspire her with aversion to the religion which had been embraced by her people. She was taught that it would be the great glory of her reign, to reduce her kingdom to the obedience of the Romish See, and to co-operate with the Popish Princes on the Continent in extirpating heresy. With these fixed prepossessions, Mary came into Scotland, and she adhered to them with singular pertinacity to the end of her life."[43] The whole of this statement is in the highest degree erroneous. We have seen that Mary was *not* nursed in a blind attachment to the Catholic religion—some of her best friends, and even one or two of her preceptors, being attached to the new opinions. We have seen, that so far from having any "prejudice" strengthened before she left France, she was expressly advised to give her support to the Reformers; and we have heard from her own lips, her mature determination to tolerate every species of worship throughout her kingdom. That she ever thought of "co-operating with the Popish Princes of the Continent, that she might reduce her kingdom to the obedience of the Romish See, and extirpate heresy," will be discovered immediately to be a particularly preposterous belief, when we find her intrusting the reins of Government to the leaders of the Reformed party. To this system of moderation, much beyond that of the age in which she lived, Mary adhered, "with singular pertinacity, to the end of her life." M'Crie, in proof of his gratuitous assertions, affirms, that she never examined the subjects of controversy between the Papists and Protestants. This also is incorrect, as he would have known, had he read that letter of Throckmorton's, in which, as has been seen, she informed the Ambassador of the frequent opportunities she had enjoyed of hearing the whole matter discussed in the presence of the Cardinal Lorraine; and the confession which that discussion extorted both from the Cardinal and herself, of the necessity of some reformation among the Catholics, though not to the extent to which the Protestants pushed it. M'Crie further objects, that Mary never went to hear Knox, or any of the Reformed divines, preach. Knox, from the invariable contempt with which he affected to treat Mary, no doubt particularly deserved such a compliment; and as to the other divines, by all of whom she was hated, what would have been the use of leaving her own chapel to listen to sermons which could not have altered the firm conviction of her mind, and which, consequently, it would have been hypocrisy to pretend to admire? We return from this digression.

The nobility, who now flocked to Holyrood from all parts of the country, constituted that portion of the inhabitants of Scotland, who, for many centuries, had exercised almost unlimited influence over their native sovereigns. Their mutual dissensions during the late long minority, had a good deal weakened their respective strength; and the progress of time was gradually softening the more repulsive features of the feudal system. But still the Scottish barons deemed themselves indispensable to the councils of their monarch, and entitled to deliver opinions, which they expected would be followed, on every affair of state. They collected at present, under the influence of a thousand contending interests and wishes. With some of the more distinguished figures in the group, it will be necessary to make the reader better acquainted.

Of the Lord James, who was now shortly to become the Earl of Murray, the title by which he is best known in Scottish history, a good deal has already been said. That he must secretly have regretted his sister's return to Scotland, may be safely concluded, from the facts formerly stated. He was too skilful a politician, however, to betray his disappointment. Had he openly ventured to oppose Mary, the result would have been at all events uncertain, and his own ruin might have been the ultimate consequence. He considered it more prudent to use every means in his power to conciliate her friendship; and wrought so successfully, that before long, he found himself the person of by far the most consequence in the kingdom. Mary, perhaps, trusted too implicitly to his advice, and left too much to his controul; yet it is difficult to see how she could have managed otherwise. It is but fair also to add, that for several years Murray continued to keep his ambition (which, under a show of moderation, was in truth enormous) within bounds. Nor does there appear to be any evidence sufficient to stamp Murray with that deeper treachery and blacker guilt, which some writers have laid to his charge. The time, however, is not yet arrived for considering his conduct in connexion with the darker events of Mary's reign. The leading fault of his administration is, that it was double-faced. In all matters of importance, he allowed himself to be guided as much by the wishes of Elizabeth, secretly communicated to him, as by those of his own Sovereign. He probably foresaw that, if he ever quarrelled with Mary, it would be through the assistance of the English Queen alone he could hope to retrieve his fortunes. This subservience to Elizabeth, among those in whom she confided, was, indeed, the leading misfortune of Mary's reign. Had her counsellors been unbiassed, and her subjects undistracted by English intrigue, her prudent conduct would have got the better of the internal dissensions in her kingdom, and she would have governed in peace, perhaps in happiness. But it was Elizabeth's jealous and narrow-minded policy, to prevent, if possible, this consummation. With infinite art, and, if the term is not debased by its application, with no little ability, she accomplished her wishes, principally through the agency of the ambitious and the self-interested, among Mary's ministers. One of these, the Earl of Murray, unquestionably was. At the time of which we are writing, he was in his thirty-first year, possessing considerable advantages both of face and person, but of reserved, austere, and rather forbidding manners. Murray's mother, who was the Lady Margaret Erskine, daughter of Lord Erskine, had married Sir Robert Douglas of Lochleven. He had also, as has been mentioned, several illegitimate brothers, particularly Lord John and Lord Robert, and one sister, Jane, who married the Earl of Argyle, and to whom Mary became very sincerely attached.

Associated with the Earl of Murray, both as a leader of the Reformers, and as a servant of Elizabeth, but not allowing his ambitious views to carry him quite so far as the Earl, was William Maitland of Lethington, Mary's Secretary of State. He was the eldest son of Sir Richard Maitland of Lethington, and was about five years older than Murray. He had been educated at the University of St Andrews, and had travelled a good deal on the Continent, where he studied civil law. John Knox, in his History, claims the honour of having converted Maitland to the Reformed opinions. Whether this be true or not, it is certain that, after having for some time co-operated with Mary of Guise, he finally deserted her, and continued to act with the Reformers, as Secretary of State, an office to which he had been appointed for life, in 1558. It has been already seen, that a close and confidential intercourse subsisted between him and Cecil; and that he too would have been glad, had Mary's return to Scotland been prevented. That Maitland possessed an acute and subtle genius, there can be no doubt; that he had cultivated his mind to good purpose, and understood the art of composition as well as any man of the age, is undeniable. That his manners were more polished than those of most of the Scottish nobility, is also true; but, that his talents were of that high and exquisite kind, which Robertson and some other historians have described, does not appear. During his political career, many instances occur, which seem to imply a vacillating and unsteady temperament, a fault which can hardly be forgiven in a statesman.

James Douglas, Earl of Morton, another associate of Murray, was one of the most powerful and least respectable of those who had embraced the Reformation. Restless, factious, crafty, avaricious and cruel, nothing could have saved him from general odium, but his pretended zeal for religion. This was a cloak for many sins; by flattering the vanity of Knox and the other gospel-ministers, he contrived to cover the hollowness of his character, and to patch up a reputation for sanctity. In consequence of the rebellion of the Earl of Angus, his uncle, during the reign of James V., Morton had been obliged to spend several years in England, where he lived in great poverty. But the only effect adversity had produced upon him, was a determination to be more rapacious when he recovered his power. His ambition was of a more contracted and selfish kind than Murray's, and he had not so cool a head, or so cautious a hand.

The Duke of Chatelherault, Mary's nearest relation, being advanced in years, had retired from public life. The Earl of Arran, his son, who, it will be remembered, had been induced to propose himself as a husband for Elizabeth, was of a weak and almost crazed intellect. Indeed it was not long before the increasing strength of the malady made it necessary to confine him. He came to Court, however, upon Mary's arrival, and having been unsuccessful with Elizabeth, chose to fall desperately in love with his own Queen. But Mary had always an aversion to him, originating no doubt in the want of delicacy towards her, which had characterized his negociations with Elizabeth, and confirmed by his own presuming and disagreeable manners. His father's natural brother, the Archbishop of St Andrews, is the only other member of the family worth mentioning. He was still staunch to the Roman Catholic party; but had of late seen the wisdom of remaining quiet, and though he became rather a favourite with Mary, it does not appear that he henceforth took a very active interest in public affairs.[44]

James Hepburne, Earl of Bothwell, though some of the leading features of his character had hardly shown themselves at the period of which we speak, merits nevertheless, from the part he subsequently acted, especial notice at present. He had succeeded his father in his titles and estates in the year 1556, when he was five or six and twenty years of age. He enjoyed not only large estates, but the hereditary offices of Lord High Admiral of Scotland, Sheriff of Berwick, Haddington and Edinburgh, and Baillie of Lauderdale. With the exception of the Duke of Chatelherault, he was the most powerful nobleman in the southern districts of Scotland. Soon after coming to his titles, he began to take an active share in public business. In addition to his other offices, he was appointed the Queen's Lieutenant on the Borders, and Keeper of Hermitage Castle, by the Queen Regent, to whom he always remained faithful, in opposition to the Lord James, and what was then termed the English faction. He went over to France on the death of Francis II. to pay his duty to Mary, and on his return to Scotland, was by her intrusted with the discharge of an important commission regarding the Government. Though all former differences were now supposed to have been forgotten, there was not, nor did there ever exist, a very cordial agreement between the Earls of Murray and Bothwell. They were both about the same age, but their dispositions were very different. Murray was self-possessed, full of foresight, prudent and wary. Bothwell was bold, reckless, and extravagant. His youth had been devoted to every species of dissipation; and even in manhood, he seemed more intent on pleasure than on business. This was a sort of life which Murray despised, and perhaps he calculated that Bothwell would never aim at any other. But, though guided by no steady principles, and devoted to licentiousness, Bothwell was nevertheless not the mere man of pleasure. He was all his life celebrated for daring and lawless exploits, and vanity or passion, were motives whose force he was never able to resist. Unlike Murray, who, when he had an end in view, made his advances towards it as cautiously as an Indian hunter, Bothwell dashed right through, as careless of the means by which he was to accomplish his object, as of the consequences that were to ensue. His manner was of that frank, open, and uncalculating kind, which frequently catches a superficial observer. They who did not study him more closely, were apt to imagine that he was merely a blustering, good-natured, violent, headstrong man, whose manners must inevitably have degenerated into vulgarity, had he not been nobly born, and accustomed to the society of his peers. But much more serious conclusions might have drawn by those who had penetration enough to see under the cloak of dissoluteness, in which he wrapped himself and his designs. With regard to his personal appearance, it does not seem to have been remarkably prepossessing. Brantome says, that he was one of the ugliest men he had ever seen, and that his planners were correspondently outré.[45] Buchanan, who must have known Bothwell well, and who draws his character with more accuracy than was to have been expected from so partial a writer, says, in his "Detection:"—"Was there in him any gift of eloquence, or grace of beauty, or virtue of mind, garnished with the benefits which we call of fortune? As for his eloquence and beauty, we need not make long tale of them, since both they that have seen him can well remember his countenance, his gait, and the whole form of his body, how gay it was; they that have heard him, are not ignorant of his rude utterance and blockishness." As to Bothwell's religious opinions, Buchanan remarks very truly, that wavering between the different factions, and despising either side, he counterfeited a love of both.[46] Such was the man of whom we shall have occasion to say so much in the course of these Memoirs.

In the Lords Ruthven and Lindsay, remained unaltered all the characteristics of the ruder feudal chiefs, rendered still more repulsive by their bigoted zeal in favour of the Reformed opinions. They were men of coarse and contracted minds, fit instigators to villany, or apt tools in the hands of those who were more willing to plan than to execute.

Opposed to all these nobles, was the great lay head of the Catholic party in Scotland, John, Earl of Huntly. His jurisdiction and influence extended over nearly the whole of the north of Scotland, from Aberdeen to Inverness. He was born in 1510, and had been a personal friend and favourite of James V. He ranked in Parliament as the Premier Earl of Scotland, and in 1546, was appointed Chancellor of the kingdom. He was always opposed to the English party, and had been taken prisoner at the battle of Pinkie, fighting against the claims of Edward VI., upon the infant Mary. He made his escape, in 1548, and as a reward for his services and sufferings, obtained, in the following year, a grant of the Earldom of Murray, which, however, he again resigned in 1554. He continued faithful to the Queen Regent till her death. Upon that occasion, we have seen that he and other nobles sent Lesley, with certain proposals, to Mary. He was an honourable man and a good subject, though the termination of his career was a most unfortunate one. The respect which his memory merits, is founded on the conviction, that he had too great a love for his country and sovereign ever to have consented to have made the one little better than tributary to England, or to have betrayed the other into the hands of her deadliest enemy.

Such were the men who were now to become Mary's associates and counsellors. The names of most of them occur as members of the Privy Council which she constituted shortly after her return. It consisted of the Duke of Chatelherault, the Earl of Huntly, the Earl of Argyle, the Earl of Bothwell, the Earl of Errol, Earl Marschall, the Earl of Athol, the Earl of Morton, the Earl of Montrose, the Earl of Glencairn, the Lord Erskine, and the Lord James Stuart. In this Council, the influence of the Lord James, backed as it was by a great majority of Protestant nobles, carried every thing before it.

Elizabeth, finding that Mary had arrived safely in her own country, and had been well received there, lost no time in changing her tone towards the Scottish queen. Her English resident in Scotland, was the celebrated Randolph, whom she kept as a sort of accredited spy at Mary's court. He has rendered himself notorious by the many letters he wrote to England upon Scottish affairs. He had an acute, inquisitive, and gossiping turn of mind. His style is lively and amusing; and though the office he had to perform is not to be envied, he seems to have entered on it *con amore*, and with little remorse of conscience. His epistles are mostly preserved, and are valuable from containing pictures of the state of manners in Scotland at the time, not to be found any where else, though not always to be depended on as accurate chronicles of fact. To Randolph, the Queen of England now wrote, desiring him to offer her best congratulations to Mary upon her safe arrival. She sent him also a letter which he was to deliver to Mary, in which she disclaimed ever having had the most distant intention of intercepting her on her voyage. Mary answered Elizabeth's letter with becoming cordiality. She, likewise, sent Secretary Maitland into England, to remain for some time as her resident at Elizabeth's Court. She was well aware for what purposes Randolph was ordered to continue in Edinburgh; and said, that as it seemed to be Elizabeth's wish that he should remain, she was content, but that she would have another in England as crafty as he. Maitland was certainly as crafty, but his craftiness was unfortunately too frequently directed against Mary herself.

CHAPTER VIII.

JOHN KNOX, THE REFORMERS, AND THE TURBULENT NOBLES.

Mary had been only a few days in Scotland when she was painfully reminded of the excited and dangerous state of feeling which then prevailed on the important subject of Religion. Her great and leading desire was to conciliate all parties, and to preserve, unbroken, the public peace. With this view she had issued proclamations, charging her subjects to conduct themselves quietly; and announcing her intention to make no alteration in the form of religion as existing in the country at her arrival. Notwithstanding these precautions, the first breach of civil order took place at the very Palace of Holyroodhouse. Mary had intimated her intention to attend the celebration of a solemn mass in her chapel, on Sunday the 24th of August, 1561, the first Sunday she spent in Scotland. The Reformers, as soon as they got the upper hand, had prohibited this service under severe penalties, and these principles of intolerance they were determined to maintain. Mary had not interfered with their mode of worship; but this was not enough;—they considered themselves called upon to interfere with hers. In anticipation of the mass, for which she had given orders, the godly, Knox tells us, met together and said,—"Shall that idol be suffered again to take place within this realm? It shall not." They even repented that they had not pulled down the chapel itself at the time they had demolished most of the other religious houses; for the sparing of any place where idols were worshipped was, in their opinion, "the preserving the accursed thing." When Sunday arrived, a crowd collected on the outside of the chapel; and Lord Lindsay, whose bigotry has been already mentioned, called out with fiery zeal,—"The idolatrous priests shall die the death, according to God's law." The Catholics were insulted as they entered the chapel, and the tumult increased so much, that they feared to commence the service. At length, the Lord James, whose superior discrimination taught him, that his party, by pushing things to this extremity, were doing their cause more harm than good, stationed himself at the door, and declared he would allow no evil-disposed person to enter. His influence with the godly was such, that they ventured not to proceed to violence against his will. He was a good deal blamed, however, by Knox for his conduct. When the service was concluded, Lord James's two brothers were obliged to conduct the priests home, as a protection to them from the insults of the people; and in the afternoon, crowds collected in the neighbourhood of the palace, who, by their disloyal language and turbulent proceedings, signified to the Queen their disapprobation, that she had dared to worship her God in the manner which seemed to herself most consistent, both with the revealed and natural law. Many of Mary's friends, who had accompanied her from France, were so disgusted with the whole of this scene, that they announced their intention of returning sooner than they might otherwise have done. "Would to God," exclaims Knox, "that altogether, with the mass, they had taken good-night of the realm for ever!"

On the following Sunday, Knox took the opportunity of preaching, what Keith might have termed, another "thundering sermon" against idolatry. In this discourse he declared, that one mass was more fearful to him than ten thousand armed enemies would be, landed in any part of the realm on purpose to suppress the whole religion. No one will deny, that the earlier Reformers of this and all other countries would, naturally and properly, look upon Popish rites with far greater abhorrence than is done by the strictest Protestants of more modern times. Nor is it wonderful that the ablest men among them, (and John Knox was one of those), should have given way so far to the feelings of the age, as to be unable to draw the exact line of distinction between the improvements of the new gospel, and the imperfections of the old. The faith which they established, was of a purer, simpler, and better kind than that from which they were converted. Yet, making all these allowances, there does seem to have been something unnecessarily overbearing and illiberal in the spirit which animated Knox and some of his followers. When contrasted with the mildness of Mary at least, and even with the greater moderation observed in some of the other countries of Europe, where the Reformation was making no less rapid progress, the anti-Catholic ardor of the good people of Scotland must be allowed to have over-stepped considerably the just limits of Christian forbearance. It is useful also to observe the inconsistencies which still existed in the Reformed faith. Whilst the Catholic religion was reprobated, Catholic customs springing out of that religion do not seem to have called forth any censure. On the very day on which Knox preached the sermon already mentioned, a great civic banquet was given by the city of Edinburgh to Mary's uncles, the Duke Danville, and other of her French friends; and, generally speaking, Sunday was, throughout the country, the favourite day for festivities of all kinds.

The mark of attention paid to her relations pleased Mary, but her pleasure was rendered imperfect, by perceiving how powerful and unlooked for an enemy both she and they had in John Knox. Aware of the liberal manner in which she had treated him and his party, she thought it hard that he should so unremittingly exert his influence to stir up men's minds against her. That this influence was of no insignificant kind, is attested by very sufficient evidence. Knox was not a mere polemical churchman. His friends and admirers intrusted to him their temporal as well as spiritual interests. He was often selected as an umpire in civil disputes of importance; and persons whom the Town-council had determined to punish for disorderly conduct, were continually requesting his intercession in their behalf. When differences fell out even among the nobility, he was not uncommonly employed to adjust them. He was besides, at that time, the only established clergyman in Edinburgh who taught the Reformed doctrines. There was a minister in the Canongate, and another in the neighbouring parish of St Cuthberts, but Knox was *the* minister of Edinburgh. He preached in the church of St Giles, which was capable of holding three thousand persons. To this numerous audience he held forth twice every Sunday, and thrice on other days during the week. He was regular too in his attendance at the meetings of the Synod and the General Assembly, and was frequently commissioned to travel through the country to disseminate gospel truth. In 1563, but not till then, a colleague was appointed to him.

Animated by a sincere desire to soften if possible our Reformer's austere temper, Mary requested that he might be brought into her presence two days after he had delivered his sermon against idolatry. Knox had no objection whatever to this interview. To have it granted him at all would show his friends the importance attached to his character and office; and from the manner in which he determined to carry himself through it, he hoped to strengthen his reputation for bold independence of sentiment, and undeviating adherence to his principles. This was so far well; but Knox unfortunately mingled rudeness with his courage, and stubbornness with his consistency.

Mary opened the conversation by expressing her surprise that he should have formed so very unfavourable an opinion of herself; and requested to know what could have induced him to commence his calumnies against her so far back as 1559, when he published his book upon the "monstrous government of women."[47] Knox answered, that learned men in all ages considered their judgments free, and that, if these judgments sometimes differed from the common judgment of mankind, they were not to blame. He then ventured to compare his "First Blast of the Trumpet" to Plato's work "On the Commonwealth," observing, with much self-complacency, that both these books contained many new sentiments. He added, that what he had written was directed most especially against Mary—"that wicked Jezabel of England." The Queen, perceiving that this was a mere subterfuge, said, "Ye speak of women in general." Knox confessed that he did so, but again went the length of assuring her, though the assurance seems to involve a contradiction, that he had said nothing "intended to trouble her estate."

Satisfied with this concession, Mary proceeded to ask, why he could not teach the people a new religion without exciting them to hold in contempt the authority of their Sovereign? Knox found it necessary to answer this question in a somewhat round-about manner. "If all the seed of Abraham," said he, "should have been of the religion of Pharaoh, what religion should there have been in the world? Or if all men, in the days of the Roman Emperors, should have been of the religion of the Roman Emperors, what religion should have been on the face of the earth? Daniel and his fellows were subject to Nebuchadnezzar and unto Darius, and yet they would not be of their religion." "Yea," replied Mary promptly, "but none of these men raised the sword against their princes." "Yet you cannot deny that they resisted," said Knox, refining a little too much; "for those who obey not the commandment given them, do in some sort resist." "But yet," said the Queen, perceiving the quibble, "they resisted not with the sword." The Reformer felt that he had been driven into a corner, and determined to get out of it at whatever cost. "God, Madam," said he, "had not given unto them the power and the means." "Think ye," asked Mary, "that subjects having the power may resist their princes?" "If princes exceed their bounds, Madam," said Knox, evidently departing from the point, "no doubt they may be resisted even by power." He proceeded to fortify this opinion with arguments of no very loyal kind; and Mary, overcome by a rudeness and presumption she had been little accustomed to, was for some time silent. Nay, Randolph, in one of his letters, affirms that he "knocked so hastily upon her heart that he made her weep." At length she said, "I perceive then that my subjects shall obey you, and not me, and will do what they please, and not what I command; and so must I be subject to them, and not they to me." Knox answered, that a subjection unto God and his Church was the greatest dignity that flesh could enjoy upon the face of the earth, for it would raise it to everlasting glory. "But you are not the Church that I will nourish," said Mary; "I will defend the Church of Rome, for it is, I think, the true Church of God." Knox's coarse and discourteous answer shows that he was alike ignorant of the delicacy with which, in this argument, he should have treated a *lady*, and of the respect a *queen* was entitled to demand. "Your *will*, Madam," said he, "is no reason; neither doth your thought make the Roman harlot to be the true and immaculate spouse of Jesus Christ. Wonder not, Madam, that I call Rome a harlot, for that Church is altogether polluted with all kinds of spiritual fornication, both in doctrine and manners." Whilst this speech must have deeply wounded the feelings of Mary, a sincere Catholic as she was, it cannot entitle the Reformer to any praise on the score of its bravery and independence. Knox knew that the whole country would, in a few days, be full of his conference with the Queen. By yielding to her, he had nothing to gain; and, as his reputation was his dearest possession, he hoped to increase it by an unmanly display of his determined zeal. Mary, perceiving what sort of a man she had to deal with, soon afterwards broke off the conversation.[48]

On the same day that the Queen gave Knox this audience, she made her first public entry into Edinburgh. She rode up the Canongate and High Street, to the Castle, where a banquet had been prepared for her. She was greeted, as she passed along, with every mark of respect and loyalty; and pains had been taken to give to the whole procession, as striking and splendid an air as possible. The Town had issued proclamations, requiring the citizens to appear in their best attire, and advising the young men to assume a uniform, that they might make "the convoy before the court more triumphant." When Mary left the castle after dinner, on her way back, a pageant which had been prepared was exhibited on the Castle Hill. The Reformers could not allow this opportunity to pass, without reminding her that she was now in a country where their authority was paramount. The greater part of this pageant, represented the terrible vengeance of God upon idolaters. It was even, at one time, intended to have had a priest burned in effigy; but the Earl of Huntly declared, he would not allow so gross an insult to be offered to his sovereign.

Soon after paying this compliment to the City of Edinburgh, Mary determined upon making a progress through the country, that she and her subjects might become better acquainted with each other. She made this progress upon horseback, accompanied by a pretty numerous train. There appears at the time to have been only one wheeled carriage in Scotland. It was a chariot, (as it is called in the treasurer's books), probably of a rude enough construction, which Margaret of England brought with her when she married James IV. Mary, no doubt, knew that it would have been rather adventurous to have attempted travelling on the Scotch roads of that day in so frail and uncertain a vehicle. It is not, however, to be supposed, that a Queen such as Mary, with her Lords and Ladies well-mounted around her, could pass through her native country without being the object of universal admiration, even without the aid of so wonderful a piece of mechanism as a coach or a chariot. Her first stage was to the palace at Linlithgow. Here she remained a day or two, and then proceeded to Stirling. On the night of her arrival there, she made a very narrow escape. As she lay in bed asleep, a candle, that was burning beside her, set fire to the curtains; and had the light and heat not speedily awakened her, when she immediately exerted her usual presence of mind, she might have been burned to death. The populace said at the time, that this was the fulfilment of a very old prophecy, that a Queen should be burned at Stirling. It was only the bed, however, not the Queen that was burned, so that the prophet must have made a slight mistake. On the Sunday she spent at Stirling, the Lord James, finding perhaps, that his former apparent defence of the mass, had hurt his reputation among the Reformers, corrected the error by behaving with singular impropriety in the Royal chapel. He was assisted by the Lord Justice General, the Earl of Argyle, in conjunction with whom he seems to have come to actual blows with the priests. This affair was considered good sport by many. "But there were others," says Randolph, alluding probably to Mary, "that shed a tear or two." "It was reserved," Chalmer's remarks, "for the *Prime Minister* and the *Justice General*, to make a riot in the house which had been dedicated to the service of God, and to obstruct the service in the Queen's presence."[49]

Leaving Stirling, Mary spent a night at Lesly Castle, the seat of the Earl of Rothes, a Catholic nobleman. On the 16th of September she entered Perth. She was everywhere welcomed with much apparent satisfaction; but in the midst of their demonstrations of affection, her subjects always took care to remind her that they were Presbyterians, and that she was a Papist. In the very pious town of Perth, pageants greeted her arrival somewhat similar to those which had been exhibited to her on the Castle Hill at Edinburgh. Mary was not a little affected by observing this constant determination to wound her feelings. In riding through the streets of Perth, she became suddenly faint, and was carried from her horse to her lodging. Her acute sensibility often produced similar effects upon her health, although the cause was not understood by the unrefined multitude. With St Andrews, the seat of the Commendatorship of the Lord James, she seems to have been most pleased, and remained there several days. She returned to Edinburgh by the end of September, passing, on the way, through Falkland, where her father had died. Knox was much distressed at the manifestation of the popular feeling in favour of Mary during this journey. He consoles himself by saying, that she polluted the towns through which she passed with her idolatry; and in allusion to the accident at Stirling, remarks, "Fire followed her very commonly on that journey."[50]

It was, perhaps, to counteract, in some degree, the impression which Mary's affability and beauty had made upon her subjects, that soon after her return to Edinburgh, a very singular proclamation was issued by the civil authorities of that town. It was couched in the following terms:—"October 2. 1561. On which day the Provost, Baillies, Council, and all the Deacons, perceiving the Priests, Monks, Friars, and others of the wicked rabble of the Anti-Christ the Pope, to resort to this town, contrary to the tenor of a previous proclamation; therefore ordain the said proclamation, charging all Monks, Friars, Priests, Nuns, Adulterers, Fornicators, and all such filthy persons, to remove themselves out of this town and bounds thereof, within twenty-four hours, under the pain of carting through the town, burning on the cheek, and perpetual banishment."[51] The insult offered to the Sovereign of the realm, by thus attempting to confound the professors of the old religion with the most depraved characters in the country, was too gross to be allowed to pass unnoticed. Mary did not bring these bigoted magistrates to trial,—she did not even imprison them, but with much mildness, though with no less firmness, she ordered the Town-Council instantly to deprive the Provost and Baillies of the offices they held, and to elect other better qualified persons in their stead. [52]

During the remainder of the year 1561, the only public affairs of consequence, were the appointment of the Lord James as the Queen's Lieutenant on the Borders, where he proceeded to hold courts, and endeavoured, by great severity and many capital punishments, to reduce the turbulent districts to something like order; and the renewal on the part of Queen Elizabeth of the old dispute concerning the treaty of Edinburgh. Mary, having now had the benefit of advice from her Council, without directly refusing what Elizabeth asked, gave her, in pretty plain terms, to understand, that she could never think of signing away her hereditary title and interest to the Crown of England. "We know," she says, in a letter she wrote to Elizabeth on the subject, "how near we are descended of the blood of England, and what devices have been attempted to make us, as it were, a stranger from it. We trust, being so nearly your cousin, you would be loth we should receive so manifest an injury, as entirely to be debarred from that title, which, in possibility, may fall to us."

Most of Mary's French friends had, by this time, returned home. Her uncle, the Marquis D'Elbeuf, however, remained all winter with her. In losing the Duke of Danville, Mary lost one of her warmest admirers; but it appears, that from his being already married, (though he could have obtained a divorce,) and from other considerations, Mary rejected his addresses. Many foreign princes were suing for the honour of her alliance, among whom were Don Carlos of Spain, the Archduke Charles of Austria, the King of Sweden, the Duke of Ferrara, and the Prince of Condé; but Mary did not yet see the necessity of an immediate marriage. Among her own subjects, there were two who ventured upon confessing their attachment, and nourishing some hopes that she might be brought to view it propitiously. These were the Earl of Arran, already mentioned, and Sir John Gordon, second son of the Earl of Huntly. The former of these Mary never liked; and though the latter far excelled him in accomplishments, both of body and mind, she does not seem to have given him encouragement either. Inspired by mutual jealousy, these noblemen, of course, detested each other; but Arran was the more factious and absurd. Having taken offence at some slights which he supposed had been offered him, he had retired to St Andrews, where he was believed, by those who knew his restless temperament, to be hatching sedition. Upon one occasion—a Sunday night in November—just before the Queen had retired to bed, a report was suddenly spread through the palace, that Arran had crossed the water at the head of a strong body of retainers, and was marching direct for Holyroodhouse, with the intention of carrying off the Queen to Dumbarton Castle, which was in the possession of his father, or to some other place of strength. This report, which gained credit, it was scarcely known how, excited the greatest alarm. Mary's friends collected round her with as much speed as possible; the gates were closed, and the Lords remained in arms within the court all night. Arran did not make his appearance, and the panic gradually subsided,—though the nobles determined to keep guard every night for some time. This is the foundation of the assertion made by some writers, that Mary kept a perpetual body guard, which, unfortunately, she never did during the whole of her reign. The Duke of Chatelherault, who came to Court soon after, alleged, that the rumour which had gained credence against his son, was only a manœuvre of his enemies; and though his son's conduct was, on all occasions, sufficiently outré, it is not unlikely that this allegation was true.

Another tumult, which soon afterwards occurred, shows how difficult it was, at this time, to preserve quietness and good order. It had been reported among the more dissolute nobles, that the daughter of a respectable merchant in Edinburgh, was the *chere amie* of the Earl of Arran. Bothwell, always at home in any affair of this kind, undertook to introduce the Marquis D'Elbeuf to the lady; Lord John, brother of the Commendator of St Andrews, was also of the party. They went to her house the first night in masks, and were admitted, and courteously entertained. Returning next evening, they were disappointed to find, that the object of their admiration refused to receive their visits any longer. They proceeded, therefore, to break open the doors, and to create much disturbance in the house and neighbourhood. Next day the Queen was informed of their disorderly conduct, and she rebuked them sharply. But Bothwell and the Lord John, animated partly by their dislike to the house of Hamilton, and partly by a turbulent spirit of contradiction, declared they would repeat their visit the very next night in despite of either friend or foe. Their intentions being understood, the servants of the Duke of Chatelherault and Arran thought themselves called upon to defend a lady whom their masters patronized. They assembled accordingly with jack and spear in the streets, determined to oppose force to force. Bothwell wished for nothing else, and collected his friends about him in his own lodgings. The opposite party, however, increased much more rapidly than his, and began to collect in a threatening manner before his house. The magistrates saw the necessity of interfering; the alarm-bell was rung, and despatches were sent off to Holyrood, to know what course was to be taken. The Earls of Argyle and Huntly, together with the Lord James, joined the civic authorities, and, proceeding out to the mob, made proclamation, that all men should instantly depart on pain of death. This had the desired effect; the streets gradually became quiet, and Bothwell gave up his wild scheme. Mary, next day, ordered both the Duke of Chatelherault and the Earl of Bothwell to appear before her. The first came accompanied by a crowd of Protestants, and the latter with an equal number of Catholics. But the Queen was not to be over-awed, and having investigated the matter, Bothwell was banished from Court for ten days.[53]

This was only the prelude to a still more serious difference, which took place between these untamed and irascible nobles. The Earl of Arran appeared before the Queen, and declared that a powerful conspiracy had been formed against the life of the Lord James, upon whom the title of Earl of Mar, as preliminary to that of Murray, had recently been conferred. This conspiracy, he said, had originated with himself and his father, who were beginning to tremble, lest the newly created Earl's influence with the Queen, might induce her to set aside the Hamilton succession, in favour of her illegitimate brother. That the Earl of Mar had really proposed some such arrangement, seems to be established on good authority.[54] The Earl of Huntly, together with Mar's old enemy, Bothwell, had been induced by the Hamiltons to join in this plot. The intention was, to shoot the Earl of Mar when hunting with the Queen, to obtain for the Hamiltons his authority in the government, and to give the Catholic party greater weight in the state. Huntly's eldest son, the Lord Gordon, was also implicated in Arran's confession. A few days before the whole of these plans were to be carried into execution, the weak and vacillating Arran, according to his own declaration, had been seized with remorse of conscience; and, actuated by his ancient friendship for Mar, and his love for the Queen, determined on disclosing every thing.

Historians seem to have been puzzled, what degree of dependence they should place upon the truth of this strange story, told by one who was already half crazed, and soon afterwards altogether insane. That there is good reason, however, for giving credit to his assertions, is evident, from the manner in which all contemporary writers speak, and the fact, that the Queen sent both him and Bothwell to prison. When the affair was further investigated, it was found to involve so many of the first nobility of the land, and among others, Arran's own father, Chaltelherault, whom he could never be expected publicly to accuse, that Mary resolved not to push matters to extremity against any one. She ordered the Duke of Chatelherault, however, to deliver up the Castle of Dumbarton; and, at the Earl of Mar's instigation, she kept Bothwell a prisoner, first in the Castle of St Andrews, and afterwards in that of Edinburgh, until he made his escape, and left the country for upwards of two years. It is remarkable, that this conspiracy should not have been hitherto dwelt upon at greater length, tending as it does to develope the secret motives by which the Earl of Mar was actuated in his subsequent feuds with the Earl of Huntly.[55] It is worth recollecting too, though the fact has not been previously noticed, that this was the *first* occasion on which Bothwell aimed at making himself master of the Queen's person. The design, though unsuccessful, shows the spirit which long continued to actuate him. Had Mary fallen into his hands at this period, it is not likely that she would ever have had it in her power to marry Darnley, and the whole complexion of her fate might have been changed.

In February 1562, Mary gave a series of splendid entertainments, on the occasion of the marriage of her favourite brother, James. He was then in the thirty-first year of his age, and chose for his wife Lady Agnes Keith, eldest daughter of the Earl of Marschal. The marriage was solemnized in the church of St Giles; and Knox took advantage of the occasion, to offer the Lord James a wholesome, but somewhat curiously expressed advice; "for," said the preacher to him, "unto this day has the kirk of God received comfort by you, and by your labours; in the which, if hereafter you shall be found fainter than you were before, it will be said that your wife has changed your nature." Knox and his friends were subsequently much scandalized by "the greatness of the banquetting, and the vanity thereof," which characterized the honeymoon. The issue of this marriage was three daughters, two of whom married Scotch noblemen, and the third died young.[56]

In August 1562, Mary commenced the progress into the North, which, in so far as some of her principal nobility were concerned, was attended with such very important consequences.

CHAPTER IX.

MARY'S EXPEDITION TO THE NORTH.

The Lord James, now Earl of Mar, had for some time felt, that so long as he was regarded with suspicion by the Hamiltons, and with ill-concealed hatred by the Earl of Huntly and the Gordons, his power could not be so stable, nor his influence so extensive, as he desired. If it is true that he had already proposed to Mary to set aside the succession of the Earl of Arran, it is equally true that she had refused his request. Foiled, therefore, in this, his more ambitious aim, he saw the necessity of limiting, in the meantime, to more moderate bounds, his views of personal preferment. With regard to the Hamiltons, he had succeeded in securing their banishment from court, and in making them objects of suspicion and dislike to the Queen. There was not indeed sufficient talent in the family ever to have made it formidable to him, had it not been that it was of the blood royal. Though not possessing this advantage, the Gordons were always looked upon by Mar as more dangerous rivals. He had long nursed a secret desire, at least to weaken, if not to crush altogether, the power of Huntly. In getting himself created Earl of Mar, he had made one step towards his object. The lands which went along with this title were part of the royal demesnes; but had for some time been held in fee by the Earls of Huntly. Her brother had prevailed upon Mary to recall them in his favour, and he was thus able to set himself down in the very heart of a country, which had hitherto acknowledged no master who did not belong to the house of Gordon. Huntly felt this encroachment bitterly; and it makes it the more probable, that he had secretly joined with Arran in his plot upon Mar; at any rate Mar gave him full credit for having done so. Their mutual animosity being thus exasperated, to the highest pitch, Huntly left the Court, and the Prime Minister waited anxiously for the first opportunity that might occur, to humble effectually the great leader of the Catholics.

In prosecution of his purpose, Mar now obtained a grant under the Privy Seal of the earldom of Murray. A grant under the Privy Seal constituted only an inchoate, not a complete title. To ratify the grant and make it legal, it was necessary to have the Great Seal also affixed to it. The Great Seal, however, was in the custody of Huntly, as Lord Chancellor; and as Mar well knew that the grant of this second earldom infringed upon Huntly's rights even more than the former, he saw the propriety of keeping it secret for some time. The earldom of Murray, which, with its lands and appurtenances, was bestowed upon Huntly in 1549, for his services in the war with England, had been again recalled by the Crown in 1554, when Huntly fell into the displeasure of the

Queen-Regent, in consequence of having refused to punish with fire and sword some Highland rebels. But in 1559, the title and lands were restored, not as a free grant, but as a lease during five years, to Huntly, his wife and heirs, on the condition of a yearly payment of 2500 merks Scots. Till 1564, therefore, Huntly was entitled to consider himself master of all the lands and revenues of this earldom. But in 1561, the title and lands were privately conferred upon the Earl of Mar. It is true, that he might have applied thus early only to prevent himself from being anticipated, and might not have intended to encroach on Huntly's rights before the legal period of his enjoying them had expired. The advantage, however, he so eagerly took of an incident that occurred in the month of June 1562, proves that Mar had never any intention to keep his title to the earldom of Murray locked up for three years. [57]

The father of James, Lord Ogilvy, had married one of the Earl of Huntly's sisters, who gave her some lands in liferent as her dowry. Upon her husband's death, considerations induced her to surrender the liferent to her brother, and the Earl then gave it to his son, Sir John Gordon. But Lord Ogilvy was displeased with his mother's conduct, and questioned its legality. The matter, however, was decided against him, though not before it had occasioned much bad blood between him and Sir John Gordon. These two noblemen unfortunately met on the streets of Edinburgh; and though Sir John had married Ogilvy's sister, all ties of relationship were disregarded, and an affray took place, in which both were assisted by their respective servants. It does not exactly appear who was the aggressor in this scuffle, but, from the circumstances which led to it, the probability is, that it was Ogilvy. Both noblemen were severely wounded; and the magistrates, enraged at their breach of the peace, committed them to prison.[58] Mary with her Court was at Stirling, but the Earl of Mar obtained permission to depart for Edinburgh, to examine into the whole affair. The son of the Earl of Huntly was now within his power, and he saw the advantages which might be made to accrue to himself in consequence. After examination, he ordered the Lord Ogilvy and his retainers to be set at liberty, but Sir John Gordon he sent to the common gaol. Sir John, not liking to trust himself in such hands, made his escape, after remaining in prison for about a month, and proceeded to his father's house in the North to recite to him his grievances.[59]

Such being the state of feeling subsisting between the Queen's prime minister and these great Northern chieftains, it can scarcely be allowed that Robertson expresses himself correctly when he says, "The Queen *happened* to set out on a progress into the northern parts of the kingdom." Her motions were at this time entirely regulated by the Earl of Mar, who, seeing the contempt which had been offered to her authority by the flight of his son, felt satisfied that

Mary could not pass through the extensive territories of Huntly, without either giving or receiving some additional cause of offence, which would in all probability lead to consequences favourable to Mar's ambition. Unless this hypothesis be adopted, no rational cause can be assigned why the Queen should have chosen this particular season for her visit to the North. From the recent suspicion which had attached to the Earl of Huntly, as one of Arran's colleagues in a conspiracy against her favourite minister, and the still more recent conduct of his son Sir John Gordon, she certainly could have no intention to pay that family the compliment of honouring them with her royal presence as a guest. North of Aberdeen, however, nearly the whole country was subservient to Huntly; and if Mary did not pass through it as a friend, she must as an enemy. This was the consideration that prompted the Earl of Mar to fix this year for the expedition. It was owing to negociations with Elizabeth, concerning a personal interview between the two Queens, that Mary was unable to set out till towards the middle of August.

The Queen left Edinburgh on horseback, as usual, attended by a very considerable train. Among others, four members of her Privy Council went with her,—the Earls of Argyle, Morton, Marschall, and Mar,—the three first of whom had no particular liking for Huntly, and were, besides, entirely under the direction of the last. Randolph also attended the Queen in this journey, and furnishes some details concerning it. On the 18th of August, 1562, she left Stirling; and, after a disagreeable and fatiguing journey, arrived at Old Aberdeen on the 27th. Here she remained for several days, and all the nobility in these parts came to pay their homage to her. Among the rest were the Earl and Countess of Huntly, who entreated her to honour them with a visit at Huntly Castle, informing her that they had endeavoured to make suitable preparations for her entertainment. Mary, at Mar's instigation of course, (for, as far as her own feelings were concerned, she must have looked with favour upon the first Catholic Peer of the realm), received them coldly. This was but a poor return for Huntly's long tried fidelity to herself and family; for, whatever quarrels he may have had with the nobility, he had always preserved inviolate his respect for the royal prerogative. His son, Sir John Gordon, also came to Aberdeen, and surrendered himself to the Queen, to be dealt with as her justice might direct. He was neither tried nor taken into custody; but, with more refined policy, he was ordered by Mar, and the rest of the Queen's Council, to proceed voluntarily to Stirling Castle, and there deliver himself, as a prisoner, to the keeper, Lord Erskine, Mar's uncle. It was, no doubt, foreseen that this order, so disproportioned in its severity to the offence which occasioned it, would not be complied with, nor was it wished that it should. Guided by similar advice, Mary refused to visit the residence of the Earl of Huntly,—a refusal which was pathetically lamented by Randolph, as it was "within three miles of her way, and the fairest house in this country." We learn from the same authority, that there was such a scarcity of accommodation, in Old Aberdeen, that Randolph, and Maitland the secretary, who had recently returned from England, were obliged to sleep together in the same bed. This is, perhaps, rendered the less remarkable, when we are informed that there were, at the University, only fifteen or sixteen scholars.

On the 1st of September, Mary left Aberdeen for Inverness; but, in the interval, the Earl of Mar, perceiving that there might be some occasion for their services, had collected a pretty strong body of men, who marched forward with the Queen and her train. In journeying northwards, she travelled by Rothiemay, Grange, Balvenie, and Elgin, passing very near the Earl of Huntly's castle. No entreaty would induce her to enter it; but she permitted the Earl of Argyle and Randolph to partake of its hospitality for two days. "The Earl of Huntly's house," says Randolph, "is the best furnished that I have seen in this country. His cheer is marvellous great; his mind then, such, as it appeared to us, *as ought to be, in any subject, to his sovereign.*" On the 8th of September, Mary went from Elgin to Tarnaway, the baronial residence of the earldom of Murray, and at that time in possession of a tenant of the Earl of Huntly. Information being there received that Sir John Gordon's friends and vassals, exasperated at the over-degree of rigour with which he was treated, were assembling in arms; and that Sir John, instead of going to Stirling, had joined the rebels, a proclamation was issued, charging him to surrender, by way of forfeit, into the Queen's hands, his houses and fortresses of Findlater and Auchindoune. This proclamation was expressed with a bitterness which must only have enraged the discontents the more. It required the surrender of these strongholds, with the avowed intention of breaking the power of the rebels, and in consideration of her Majesty having heard "the many grievous complaints of the poor people of this country, hearing them to be *herreit* (robbed) and oppressed by him and his accomplices, in times by-past; and fearing the like, or worse, should be done in time coming." The same proclamation described Sir John Gordon's wife as "Lady Findlater, his *pretended* spouse."[60]

Fearing that even all this might not be enough to induce Huntly to take such steps as might be plausibly construed into treason, Mar now, for the first time, produced his title to the Earldom of Murray, and assumed the name. The only meeting of council held north of Aberdeen was at Tarnaway, and at the first council after the Queen had returned to Aberdeen, we find Mar's name changed to that of Murray. Robertson, who has followed Buchanan's, or in other words Murray's own account of the transactions in the North, in referring Mar's assumption of the Earldom of Murray to a later date, forgets that it must have been sanctioned by Mary and her Council; and that the only opportunity for doing so, in the interval of their departure from, and return to Aberdeen, was at Tarnaway.[61]

This new insult upon himself and family was, as Murray expected, deeply felt by the Earl of Huntly. He began to suspect that it was intended to ruin him; and in this extremity, with evident reluctance, he prepared to defend himself. Mary, meanwhile, marched forward to Inverness. "On her arrival," says Robertson, "the commanding officer in the Castle, *by Huntly's orders*, shut the gates against her." The gates were shut, but certainly not by Huntly's orders; for as soon as he heard that the Castle had been summoned, he sent his express commands to the governor (who had acted upon his own responsibility) to surrender it. These commands, however, came too late; the Castle had been taken by storm, and the governor put to death. What right the Earl of Murray, or even the Queen herself, had to demand the surrender of the castle, which belonged hereditarily to Lord George Gordon, the Earl of Huntly's eldest son, does not appear. As Chalmers remarks, the whole proceeding seems to have been illegal and unwarrantable. Huntly, who was on his way to Inverness, to attempt an arrangement of these disputes, by a personal interview with the Queen, when he heard of the execution of the governor, returned to his castle.[62]

The Gordons were now fairly roused; and, collecting their followers, they determined to act resolutely, but not as aggressors. Mary was made to believe that she was in the midst of a hostile country; and though there was, in reality no intention to attack her, every means was taken to inspire her with fear, and to convince her of the treacherous designs of the Earl of Huntly. But Mary, had a courageous spirit, when it was necessary to exert it. "In all those garbrilles," says Randolph, "I never saw the Queen moved,—never dismayed; nor never thought I that stomach to be in her that I find. She repented nothing, but when the Lords and others at Inverness came in the morning from the watch; that she was not a man, to know what life it was to lie all night in the fields, or to walk upon the causeway with a jack and knapsack, a Glasgow buckler and a broadsword."

On the 15th of September, the Queen returned southwards. She had with her about two thousand men, and as she advanced, their number increased to 3000. She marched by Kilravock and Tarnaway, to Spynie Castle. Thence, she proceeded through the country of the Gordons, crossing the Spey at Fochabers, and going by the way of Cullen and Banff. Throughout the whole course of this march, Murray took care to make her believe that she was in danger of being attacked every moment. If there had been any enemy to fight with, "what desperate blows," says Randolph, "would not have been given, when every man should have fought in the sight of so noble a Queen, and so many fair ladies!" The only incidents which seem to have occurred, were summonses to surrender, given by sound of trumpet at Findlater House, and at Deckford, mansions of Sir John Gordon. The keepers of both refused; but they were not acting upon their master's authority. Having slept a night at the Laird of Banff's house, Mary returned, on the 22d of September, to Aberdeen. Her entry into the New Town, was celebrated by the inhabitants with every demonstration of respect. Spectacles, plays, and interludes were devised; a richly wrought silver cup, with 500 crowns in it, was presented to her; and wine, coals, and wax, were sent in great abundance to her lodgings.

But the Earl of Murray, was not yet satisfied that he had humbled the Gordons enough. It was true, that the lands of Sir John had been forfeited,—that the castle of Lord George had been captured,—and that the title and estates of the earldom of Murray had been wrested from Huntly. But Huntly's power still remained nearly as great as ever; and it seemed doubtful whether Murray would ever be able to seat himself quietly in his new possessions, situated as they were in the very heart of the Earl's domains. The privy council were therefore prevailed upon to come to the resolution that the Earl of Huntly, in the language of Randolph, "shall either submit himself, and deliver his disobedient son John, or utterly to use all force against him, *for the subversion of his house for ever.*" To enforce this determination, Murray levied soldiers, and sent into Lothian and Fife for officers in whom he could place confidence, particularly Lindsay and Grange. With what show of reason the unfortunate Huntly could be subjected to so severe a fate, it is difficult to say. He had come to offer his obedience and hospitality to the Queen, on her first arrival at Aberdeen;—he remained perfectly quiet during her journey through that part of the country which was subject to him;—he sent to her, after she returned to Aberdeen, the keys of the Houses of Findlater and Deckford, which she had summoned unsuccessfully on her march from Cullen to Banff; —and he delivered to her, out of his own castle, a field-piece which the Regent Arran had long ago given to him, and which Mary now demanded. He added, that "not only that, which was her own, but also his body and goods, were at her Grace's commands."[63] His wife, the Countess of Huntly, led Captain Hay, the person sent for the cannon, into the chapel at her castle, and placing herself at the altar, said to him,—"Good friend, you see here the envy that is borne unto my husband. Would he have forsaken God and his religion as those that are now about the Queen's grace, and have the whole guiding of her, have done, my husband had never been put at as now he is. God, and He that is upon this holy altar, whom I believe in, will, I am sure, preserve, and let our true meaning hearts be known; and as I have said unto you, so, I pray you, let it be said unto your mistress. My husband was ever obedient unto her, and so will die her faithful subject."[64]

That Mary should have given her sanction to these iniquitous proceedings, can only be accounted for by supposing, what was in truth the case, that she was kept in ignorance of every thing tending to exculpate Huntly, whilst various means were invented to inspire her with a belief, that he had conceived, and was intent upon executing a diabolical plot against herself and government. It was given out, that his object was to seize upon the Queen's person,—to marry her by force to his son Sir John Gordon,—and to cut off Murray, Morton, and Maitland, his principal enemies.[65] Influenced by these misrepresentations, which would have been smiled at in later times, but which, in those days, were taken more seriously, the Queen put the fate of Huntly into the hands of Murray. Soon after her return to Aberdeen, an expedition was secretly prepared against Huntly's castle. If resistance was offered, the troops sent for the purpose were to take it by force, and if admitted without opposition, they were to bring Huntly, a prisoner to Aberdeen. Intimation, however, of this enterprise and its object was conveyed to the Earl, and he contrived to baffle its success. His wife received the party with all hospitality; threw open her doors, and entreated that they would examine the whole premises, to ascertain whether they afforded any ground of suspicion. But Huntly himself, took care to be out of the way, having retired to Badenoch.[66]

Thus foiled again, Murray, on the 15th of October, called a Privy Council, at which he got it declared, that unless Huntly appeared on the following day before her Majesty, "to answer to such things as are to lay to his charge," he should be put to the horn for his contempt of her authority, and "his houses, strengths, and friends, taken from him."[67] However willing he might have been to have ventured thus into the lion's den, Huntly could not possibly have appeared within the time appointed. On the 17th of October, he was therefore denounced a rebel in terms of the previous proclamation, and his lands and titles declared forfeited.[68] Even yet, however, Huntly acted with forbearance. He sent his Countess to Aberdeen on the 20th, who requested admission to the Queen's presence, that she might make manifest her husband's innocence. So far from obtaining an audience, this lady, who was respected and loved over the whole country, was not allowed to come within two miles of the Court, and she returned home with a heavy heart. As a last proof of his fidelity, Huntly sent a messenger to Aberdeen, offering to enter into ward till his cause might be tried by the whole nobility. Even this offer was rejected; and, goaded into madness, the unfortunate Earl at length collected his followers round him, and, raising the standard of rebellion, not against the Queen, but against Murray, advanced suddenly upon Aberdeen.

This resolute proceeding excited considerable alarm at Court. Murray, however, had foreseen the probability of such a step being ultimately taken, and had been busy collecting forces sufficient to repel the attack. A number of the neighbouring nobility had joined him, who, not penetrating the prime minister's real motives, were not displeased to see so proud and powerful an earldom as that of Huntly likely to fall to pieces. On the 28th of October, Murray marched out of Aberdeen at the head of about 2000 men. He found Huntly advantageously stationed at Corrachie, a village about fifteen miles from Aberdeen. Huntly's force was much inferior to that of Murray, scarcely exceeding 500 men. Indeed, it seems doubtful, whether he had advanced so much for the purpose of fighting, as for the sake of giving greater weight to his demands, to be admitted into the presence of the Queen, who, he always maintained, had been misled by false council. Perceiving the approach, however, of his inveterate enemy Murray, and considering the superiority of his own position on the hill of Fare, he relinquished all idea of retreat, and determined, at any risk to accept the battle which was offered him. The contest was of short duration. The broadswords of the Highlanders, even had the numbers been more equal, would have been no match for the spears and regular discipline of Murray's Lowland troops. Their followers fled; but the Earl of Huntly and his two sons, Sir John Gordon and Adam, a youth of seventeen, disdaining to give ground, were taken prisoners. The Earl, who was advanced in life, was no sooner set upon horseback, to be carried triumphantly into Aberdeen, than the thoughts of the ruin which was now brought upon himself and his family overwhelmed him; and, without speaking a word, or receiving a blow, he fell dead from his horse.[69]

Sir John Gordon who was pronounced the author of all these troubles, having been marched into Aberdeen, was tried, condemned, and executed. He may have been an enemy of Murray's, but so far from being a traitor to the Queen, he was one of the most devoted admirers and attached subjects she ever had. Yet Murray took care to have it reported, that Sir John, before he was beheaded, confessed, that if his father had taken Aberdeen, he was determined to have "burned the Queen, and as many as were in the house with her."[70] So palpable a falsehood throws additional light upon the motives which instigated the prime minister throughout. With a refinement of cruelty, he insisted upon Mary giving her public countenance to his proceedings, by consenting to be present at Gordon's death. She was placed at a window, opposite to which the scaffold had been erected. Gordon, who was one of the handsomest men of his times, observed her, and fixing his eyes upon her, "gave her to understand by his looks," says Freebairn, "that her presence sweetened the death he was going to suffer only for loving her too well." He then fell upon his knees, and prepared to lay his head upon the block. Mary, totally unable to stand this scene, was already suffused in tears; and when she was informed that the unskilful official, instead of striking off the head, had only mangled the neck, she fainted away, and it was some time before she could be recovered.[71] Adam Gordon was indebted to his youth for saving him from his brother's fate. He lived to be, as his father had been, one of Mary's most faithful servants. Lord Gordon, the late Earl's eldest son, who was with his father-in-law, the Duke of Chatelherault, at Hamilton, was soon afterwards seized and committed to prison, Murray finding it convenient to declare him implicated in the Earl's guilt. Having remained under arrest for some months, he was tried and found guilty, but the execution of his sentence was left at the Queen's pleasure. She sent him to Dunbar Castle; and as Murray could not prevail upon her to sign the death-warrant, he had recourse to forgery; and had the keeper of the castle not discovered the deceit, the Lord Gordon's fate would have been sealed. Mary was content with keeping him prisoner, till a change in her administration restored him to favour, and to the forfeited estates and honours of his father.

One other incident connected with these tragical events is worth recording. Means having been taken for the preservation of Huntly's body, it was sent by sea to Leith, and lay for several months at Holyroodhouse. In the Parliament which met in May 1563, these melancholy remains were produced, to have sentence of forfeiture pronounced against them. To obviate if possible this additional calamity, the Countess of Huntly, widow of the deceased, appeared before the Parliament, and with the spirit of a Gordon requested to be heard in her late husband's defence. The request was refused; Huntly's castles and houses were rifled of their property, his friends and vassals fined, and many escheats granted to those who had assisted in crushing this once noble family. [72]

Murray having now no farther occasion for the Queen's presence at Aberdeen, the Court moved southwards on the 5th of November. On her way home, she visited Dunottar Castle, Montrose, Arbroath, Dundee, Stirling, and Linlithgow. She arrived at Edinburgh on the 22d, having been absent upwards of three months. It is much to be regretted, that she ever undertook this northern expedition. Though she had little or no share in its guilt, she had allowed herself to be made an effectual tool in the hands of Murray, who was now more powerful than any minister of Mary's ought to have been. He had forced the Earl of Bothwell into exile; he had brought the Duke of Chatelherault and Arran into disgrace; and having accomplished the death of the courageous Huntly, he had obtained for himself and friends the greater part of that nobleman's princely estates and titles. Besides, he was more popular among the Reformers than ever, for the destruction of the Gordon family had been long wished for by them. In short, though without the name, he was the King of Scotland, and his sister Mary was his subject.

CHAPTER X.

CHATELARD'S IMPRUDENT ATTACHMENT, AND KNOX'S PERSEVERING HATRED.

Mary returned from her Northern expedition towards the conclusion of the year 1562. The two following years, 1563 and 1564, undistinguished as they were by any political events of importance, were the quietest and happiest she spent in Scotland. Her moderation and urbanity had endeared her to her people; and, in her own well regulated mind, existed a spring of pure and abiding satisfaction. Nevertheless, vexations of various sorts mingled their bitterness in her cup of sweets. An occurrence which took place early in 1563, demands our attention first.

The poet Chatelard has been already mentioned as one of those who sailed in Mary's train, when she came from the continent. He had attached himself to the future Constable of France, the Duke Danville, and was a gentleman of good family and fortune, being by the mother's side the grand-nephew of the celebrated Chevalier Bayard. The manly beauty of his person was not unlike that of his ancestor; and, besides being well versed in all the more active accomplishments of the day, he had softened and refined his manners by an ardent cultivation of every species of belles-lettres. It was this latter circumstance that gained for him the occasional favourable notice of Mary. A poetess herself, as much by nature as by study, her heart warmed towards those who indulged in the same delightful art. Chatelard wrote both in French and Italian; and, finding that Mary deigned to read and admire his productions, he seems thenceforth to have made her the only theme of his enamoured and too presumptuous Muse. To the Queen this was no uncommon compliment. She received it, gracefully, and sometimes even amused herself with answering Chatelard's effusions. This condescension almost turned the young poet's brain. He had left Scotland with the Duke Danville, and Mary's other French friends, at the end of the year 1561; but he eagerly seized the opportunity afforded him, by the civil wars in France, to return before twelve months had elapsed. The Duke Danville sent him to Mary's court, there is every reason to believe, to press upon her attention once more his own pretensions to her hand. But Chatelard, in the indulgence of his mad passion, forgot the duty he owed his master; and, for every word he spoke in prose for the Duke, he spoke in verse twenty for himself. Mary, long accustomed to this species of adulation, and looking upon flattery as a part of a poet's profession, smiled at the more extravagant flights of his imagination, and forgot them as soon as heard. These smiles, however, were fatal to Chatelard. "They tempted him," says Brantome, "to aspire, like Phaeton, at ascending the chariot of the sun." In February 1563, he had the audacity to steal into the Queen's bedchamber, armed with sword and dagger, and attempted to conceal himself till Mary should retire to rest. He was discovered by her maids of honour; and Mary, though much enraged at his conduct, was unwilling, for a first offence, to surrender him to that punishment which she knew would be inflicted were it known to her Privy Council. She was contented with reprimanding him severely, and ordering him from her presence.

This leniency was thrown away upon the infatuated Chatelard. Only two nights afterwards, the Queen having, in the interval, left Edinburgh for St Andrews, he again committed the same offence. As she went to St Andrews by the circuitous route of the Queensferry, she slept the first night at Dumfermline, and the second at Burntisland. Here Chatelard insolently followed the Queen into her bedroom, without attempting any concealment, and assigned, as the motive for his conduct, his desire to clear himself from the blame she had formerly imputed to him. Mary commanded him to leave her immediately, but he refused; upon which she saw the necessity of calling for assistance. The Earl of Murray was at hand, and came instantly. The daring boldness of Chatelard's conduct could no longer be concealed; the proper legal authorities were sent for from Edinburgh; the poet was tried at St Andrews, and was condemned to death. He was executed on the 22d of February, and conducted himself bravely, but as a confirmed enthusiast, even on the scaffold. He would not avail himself of the spiritual advice of any minister or confessor; but having read Ronsard's Hymn on Death, he turned towards the place where he supposed the Queen was, and exclaimed in an unfaltering voice, "Farewell, loveliest and most cruel Princess whom the world contains!" He then, with the utmost composure, laid his head upon the block, and submitted, with all resignation, to his fate.[73]

Mary remained at St Andrews till the middle of April, when she removed to Loch Leven, where she had better opportunities of enjoying her favourite amusements of hunting and hawking. She went thither in considerable grief, occasioned by the news she had lately received from France, of the death of two of her uncles, the Duke of Guise, and the Grand Prior. The former had been barbarously assassinated at the siege of Orleans, by a Protestant bigot of the name of Poltrot; and the latter had been fatally wounded at the battle of Dreux. Alluding triumphantly to the murder of the Duke of Guise, Knox expressed himself in these words, "*God* has stricken that bloody tyrant." This enmity to the House of Guise, which Knox carried even beyond the grave, was now no novelty. Some months before, he had taken occasion to preach a severe sermon against Mary and her friends, in consequence of an entertainment she gave at Holyrood, upon receiving news of her uncles' successes in the French civil wars. Mary had, in consequence, sent for Knox a second time, when he repeated to her the principal part of his sermon, in a manner which made it appear not quite so obnoxious as she had been induced to believe. She had then the magnanimity to tell him, that though his words were sharp, she would not blame him for having no good opinion of her uncles, as they and he were of a different religion. She only wished that he would not publicly misrepresent them, without sufficient evidence upon which to ground his charges. Knox left Mary, "with a reasonable merry countenance," and some one observing it, remarked, "He is not afraid!" Knox's answer is characteristic, and does him credit, "Why should the pleasing face of a gentlewoman affray me? I have looked in the faces of many angry men, and yet have not been afraid above measure."

The third time that Knox was admitted into Mary's presence was at Loch Leven. This, as indeed every interview she had with the celebrated Reformer, and she had only four, exhibits her character in a very favourable point of view. It appears, that whilst the Queen reserved for herself the right of celebrating mass in her own chapel, it was prohibited throughout the rest of the kingdom. Some instances had occurred in which this prohibition had been disregarded; and upon these occasions the over-zealous Protestants had not scrupled to take the law into their own hands. Mary wished to convince Knox of the impropriety of this interference. He thought it necessary to defend his brethren; but his answer to the Queen's simple question,—"Will ye allow that they shall take my sword in their hands?"—though laboured, is quite inconclusive. That "the sword of justice is God's," may be a very good apophthegm, but would be a dangerous precept upon which to form a practical rule in the government of a state. Mary, however, knowing by experience that it was hopeless to attempt to change Knox's sentiments, and not wishing to enter into an argument with him, passed to other matters. Though she disliked the rudeness of his manners, she had a respect for the unbending Stoicism of his principles; and having too much good sense to hold any one responsible for the peculiarities of his belief, she could not help persuading herself, that she would finally soften the asperity of those with whom she disagreed, only upon articles of faith. With this view, she conversed with Knox upon various confidential matters, and actually did succeed in winning for the moment the personal favour of her stern adversary. "This interview," observes Dr M'Crie, "shows how far Mary was capable of dissembling, what artifice she could employ, and what condescensions she could make, when she was bent on accomplishing a favourite object." There is something very uncharitable in the construction thus put upon the Queen's conduct. She had, no doubt, a favourite object in view; but that object was mutual reconcilement, and the establishment, as far as in her lay, of reciprocal feelings of forbearance and good will among all classes of her subjects. The "artifice" she used, consisted merely in the urbanity of her manners, and her determination to avoid all violence, in return for the violence which had been exhibited towards herself.

Soon after this conference, Mary went to Edinburgh, to open in person the first Parliament which had been held since her return to Scotland. Its session continued only from the 26th of May, to the 24th of June 1563; but during that short period, business of some importance was transacted. The Queen on the first day rode to the Parliament House in her robes of state,—the Duke of Chatelherault carrying the crown, the Earl of Argyle the sceptre, and the Earl of Murray the sword.[74] She was present on three or four occasions afterwards; but on the first day she made a speech to the representatives of her people, which was received with enthusiastic applause. This applause was wormwood to Knox, who, with even more than his usual discourtesy towards a sex whom he seems to have despised, says,—"Such stinking pride of women as was seen at that Parliament, was never before seen in Scotland." He was heartily borne out in his vituperations by the rest of the preachers. The rich attire which Mary and the ladies of her court chose to wear, were abominations in their eyes. They held forth to their respective flocks against the "superfluity of their clothes," the "targeting of their tails," and "the rest of their vanity." It was enough, they said, "to draw down God's wrath not only upon these foolish women, but upon the whole realm." At this Parliament the Earldoms of Huntly and Sutherland were declared forfeited; an act was passed for preventing any one from summoning the lieges together without the Queen's consent; some judicious legislative measures of a domestic nature were established; and an act of oblivion for all acts done from the 6th of March 1558, to the first of September 1561, was unanimously carried. This act of oblivion was declared to have no reference whatever to a similar act sanctioned by the Treaty of Edinburgh, the ratification of which was expressly avoided by the Queen. Its object, how—was precisely the same,—namely, to secure the Reformers against any disagreeable consequences which might arise out of the violences they committed during the first heat of the Reformation.

An act of oblivion thus obtained as a free gift from Mary, and not as a consequence of his favourite Treaty of Edinburgh, was by no means agreeable to Knox. He assembled some of the leading Members of Parliament, and urged upon them the necessity of forcing from the Queen a ratification of this treaty. Even the Protestant Lords, however, felt how unjust such a demand would be. The Earl of Murray himself, one of Knox's oldest and staunchest friends, refused to ask Mary to take this step. Knox, in consequence, solemnly renounced Murray's friendship, and a coldness subsisted between them for nearly two years. Foiled in his object, the Reformer had recourse to his usual mode of revenge. He preached another "thundering sermon." The object of this sermon was to convince the people, that as soon as a Parliament was assembled, they had the Queen in their power to make her do what they chose. "And is this the thankfulness that ye render unto your God," said he, "to betray his cause, when ye have it in your hands to establish it as you please?" Before concluding, he adverted to the report that her Majesty would soon be married, and called upon the nobility, if they regarded the safety of their country, to prevent her from forming an alliance with a Papist.

"Protestants as well as Papists," says Knox's biographer, "were offended with the freedom of this sermon, and some who had been most familiar with the preacher, now shunned his company." There must have been something more than usually bitter and unjust in a discourse which produced such results. It was the occasion of the last and most memorable interview which the Reformer had with Mary. As soon as she was made acquainted with the manner in which he had attacked her, she summoned him to her presence. He was accompanied to the palace by Lord Ochiltree, and some other gentlemen; but John Erskine of Dun, a man of a mild and gentle temper, was the only one allowed to enter Mary's apartment along with Knox. The Reformer found his Queen in considerable agitation. She told him she did not believe any prince had ever submitted to the usage she had experienced from him. "I have borne with you," she said, "in all your rigorous manner of speaking, both against myself, and against my uncles; yea, I have sought your favour by all possible means; I offered unto ye presence and audience whensoever it pleased ye to admonish me; and yet I cannot be quit of you." She then passionately burst into tears, so that, as Knox says with apparent satisfaction, they could scarce "get handkerchiefs to hold her eyes dry; for the tears and the howling, besides womanly weeping, stayed her speech." The preacher, when he was allowed to speak, complacently assured her Majesty that when it pleased God to deliver her from that bondage of darkness and error wherein she had been nourished, she would not find the liberty of his tongue offensive. He added, that in the pulpit he was not his own master, but the servant of Him who commanded that he should speak plain, and flatter no flesh upon the face of the earth. Mary told him that she did not wish for his flattery, but begged to know what rank he held in the kingdom to entitle him to interfere with her marriage. Knox, whose self-esteem seldom forsook him, replied, that though neither an Earl, Lord, nor Baron, he was a profitable and useful member of the commonwealth, and that it became him to teach her nobility, who were too partial towards her, their duty. "Therefore, Madam," he continued, "to yourself I say that which I spake in public: whensoever the nobility of this realm shall be content, and consent that you be subject to an unlawful husband, they do as much as in them lies to remove Christ, to banish the truth, to betray the freedom of this realm, and perchance shall in the end do small comfort to yourself." Language so unwarranted and uncalled for again drew tears from Mary, and Erskine, affected by her grief, attempted to soften down its harshness. Knox looked on with an unaltered countenance, and comparing his Sovereign to his own children, when he saw occasion to chastise them, he said,—"Madam, in God's presence I speak. I never delighted in the weeping of any of God's creatures; yea, I can scarcely well abide the tears of mine own boys, when mine own hands correct them. Much less can I rejoice in your Majesty's weeping; but, seeing I have offered unto ye no just occasion to be offended, but have spoken the truth as my vocation craves of me, I must sustain your Majesty's tears, rather than dare hurt my conscience, or betray the commonwealth by silence." That he might not be longer under the necessity of sustaining tears he could so ill abide, Mary commanded him to leave her presence, and wait her pleasure in the adjoining room.

Here his friends who were expecting him, and who had overheard some of the conversation which had just taken place, perceiving how much he had excited the Queen's just indignation, would hardly acknowledge him. In his own words, "he stood as one whom men had never seen." His confidence, however, did not forsake him. Observing Mary's maids of honour seated together, and richly dressed, he took the opportunity, that he might not lose his time, of giving them also some gratuitous advice. "Fair ladies," he said with a smile, "how pleasant were this life of yours, if it should ever abide, and then in the end that we might pass to heaven with this gear: but fy upon that knave, Death, that will come whether we will or not; and when he has laid on the arrest, then foul worms will be busy with this flesh, be it never so fair and so tender; and the silly soul I fear shall be so feeble, that it can neither carry with it gold, garnishing, targeting, pearl, nor precious stones." Shortly afterwards Erskine, who had somewhat pacified the Queen, came to inform him that he was allowed to go home.[75]

As the Queen and Knox came just once more into public contact, and that only a few weeks after the date of the above interview, it may be as well to terminate our interference with the affairs of the Reformer in this place. The Queen having gone to Stirling, a disturbance took place one Sunday during her absence at the Chapel of Holyrood. Some of her domestics and Catholic retainers, had assembled for the celebration of worship, after the form of the Romish Church. The Presbyterians were at the time dispensing in Edinburgh the Sacrament of the Supper, and were consequently more zealous than usual in support of their own cause. Hearing of the Catholic practices carried on at Holyrood, they proceeded thither in a body, burst into the Chapel, and drove the priests from the altar. To quell the riot, the Comptroller of the Household was obliged to obtain the assistance of the Magistrates, and even then it was not without difficulty that the godly were prevailed upon to disperse. Two of their number, who had been more violent than the rest, had indictments served upon them for "forethought felony, hamesucken, and invasion of the Palace." Knox and his friends determined to save these two men from punishment, at whatever risk. The means they adopted to effect their purpose were of the most seditious kind. It was determined to overawe the judges by displaying the power of the accused; and with this view, Knox wrote circular letters to all the principal persons of his persuasion, requesting them to crowd to Edinburgh on the day of trial. He thus assumed to himself the prerogative of calling Mary's subjects together, in direct opposition to one of the acts of the late Parliament. When those letters were shown to the Queen, and her Privy Council, at Stirling, they were unanimously pronounced treasonable, and Knox was summoned to appear before a convention of nobles, to be held in Edinburgh a few weeks afterwards, for the purpose of trying him. It was, however, intimated to him, that as the Queen wished to be lenient, if he would acknowledge his fault, and throw himself upon her mercy, little or no punishment would be awarded. He obstinately refused to make the slightest concession, and in consequence nearly lost the friendship of Lord Herries, with whom he had been long intimate.

On the day of trial, public curiosity was much excited to know the result. The Lords assembled in the Council Chamber at Holyrood; the Queen took her seat at the head of the table, and Knox stood uncovered at the foot. The proceedings were opened by Secretary Maitland, who stated the grounds of the accusation, and explained in what manner the law had been infringed. Knox made a declamatory and very unsatisfactory reply. The substance of his defence was, that there were lawful and unlawful convocations of the people, and that, as the Act of Parliament could not apply to the assembling of his congregation every Sunday, neither could he be held to have transgressed it by writing letters to the heads of his church, calling them together upon a matter of vital importance to their religion. The sophistry of this reasoning was easily seen through. It was answered for the Queen, that his sermons were sanctioned by Government, and that their tendency was supposed to be peaceable; but that the direct purpose of the letters in question was to exasperate the minds of the lieges. One passage, in particular was read, in which Knox said, alluding to the two persons who were indicted,—"This fearful summons is directed against them, to make, no doubt, a preparative on a few, that a door may be opened to execute cruelty upon a greater multitude." "Is it not treason, my Lords," said Mary, "to accuse a Prince of cruelty? I think there be acts of Parliament against such whisperers." Knox endeavoured to evade the force of this remark by a very evident quibble. "Madam," he said, "cast up when you list the acts of your Parliament, I have offended nothing against them; for I accuse not in my letter your Grace, nor yet your nature, of cruelty. But I affirm yet again, that the pestilent Papists who have inflamed your Grace against those poor men at this present, are the sons of the Devil, and therefore must obey the desires of their father, who has been a liar and a man-slayer from the beginning." More words were spoken on both sides, but nothing further was advanced that bore directly upon the subject in hand. It is worthy of notice, however, that Knox, in the course of his defence, actually forgot himself so far as to institute a comparison between Mary and the Roman Nero. At length, having been fully heard, he was ordered to retire, and after some discussion, the vote of guilty or not guilty was put to the nobles. There being a considerable preponderance of Protestant lords at the meeting, it was carried that Knox had not committed any breach of the laws. He evinces his triumph on this occasion by remarking spitefully in his History,—"That night was neither dancing nor fiddling in the Court; for Madam was disappointed of her purpose, whilk was to have had John Knox in her will by vote of her nobility." His acquittal certainly disappointed Mary; but it only served to convince her more and more, that bigotry and justice were incompatible.

Before concluding this chapter, one of the peculiarities of the Scottish Reformer's mind deserves to be noticed. That he was a strong thinker and a bold man, cannot be denied; yet, as has been before remarked, he himself confesses that he was much addicted to superstition. This weakness, if real, lowers him considerably in the scale of intellect; and, if affected, proves that, amidst all the pretensions of his new doctrines, he still retained a taint of priestly craft. Alluding to the year of which we speak, (1563), he has incorporated into his History the following remarkable passage. "God from Heaven, and upon the face of the earth, gave declaration that he was offended at the iniquity that was committed even within this realm; for upon the 20th day of January, there fell wet in great abundance, which in the falling freezed so vehemently, that the earth was but one sheet of ice. The fowls both great and small freezed, and could not fly; many died, and some were taken and laid before the fire, that their feathers might resolve; and in that same month the sea stood still, as was clearly observed, and neither ebbed nor flowed the space of twenty-four hours. In the month of February, the fifteenth and eighteenth days thereof, were seen in the firmament battles arrayed, spears and other weapons, and as it had been the joining of two armies. These things were not only observed, but also spoken and constantly affirmed by men of judgement and credit. But the Queen and our Court made merry."[76] It would thus appear, that Knox's mind was either a strange compound of strength and

imbecility, courage and fear, sound sense and superstition, or that duplicity
was more a part of his character than is generally supposed.

CHAPTER XI.

THE DOMESTIC LIFE OF MARY, WITH SOME ANECDOTES OF ELIZABETH.

The summer and autumn of the year 1563, were spent by Mary in making various excursions through the country. She had not yet visited the west and south-west of Scotland. Shortly after the rising of Parliament, she set out for Glasgow, and from thence went on to Dumbarton and Loch-Lomond. In the neighbourhood of its romantic scenery, she spent some days, and then crossed over to Inverary, where she visited her natural sister, the Countess of Argyle, to whom she was much attached. Upon leaving Inverary, she passed over the Argyleshire hills, and came down upon the Clyde at Dunoon. Following the course of the river, she next visited Toward Castle, near the entrance of the Bay of Rothesay. Here she crossed the Frith of Clyde, and landing in Ayrshire, spent several weeks in this Arcadian district of Scotland. She then went into Galloway, and before her return to Edinburgh, visited Dumfries, and other towns in the south. Her next excursion was to Stirling, Callander, and Dumblane, in the neighbourhood of which places she remained till late in the season. The earlier part of 1564, she spent at Perth, Falkland, and St Andrews; and in the autumn of this year, she again went as far north as Inverness, and from thence into Ross-shire. "The object of that distant journey," says Chalmers, "was not then known, and cannot be completely ascertained." "She repassed through the country of the Gordons, which had once been held out as so frightful. She remained a night at Gartley, where there is still a ruined castle, and the parish whereof belongs even now to the Duke of Gordon. She rode forward to Aberdeen, without seeing Huntly's ghost, and went thence to Dunnottar, where she remained a night, and thence, proceeding along the coast road, to Dundee. She then crossed the Tay into Fife, and diverging for a few days to St Andrews, she returned to Edinburgh about the 26th of September, after an absence of two months."

As we are speedily to enter upon a new and more bustling, though not a happier period, of Mary's life, we should wish to avail ourselves of the present opportunity, to convey to the reader some notion of her domestic habits and amusements, and how, when left to herself, she best liked to fill up her time. The affability and gentleness of her manners, had endeared her even more than her personal attractions, to all who frequented her court. She had succeeded, by the firm moderation of her measures, not only in giving a more than ordinary degree of popularity to her government, but, by the polished amenity of her bearing, her powers of conversation, and varied accomplishments, she had imparted to the court of Holyrood a refinement and elegance we in vain look for under the reign of any of her predecessors. There is a vast difference between an over-degree of luxuriousness and a due attention to the graces. Under the influence of the former, a nation becomes effeminate, and addicted to every species of petty vice; under that of the latter, its characteristic virtues are called only more efficiently into action. The tree is not the less valuable divested of its rugged bark. It is to the example set by Mary, that we are to attribute, in a great degree, that improvement in the manners and feelings of Scotch society, which speedily placed this country more upon a par with the rest of civilized Europe. Had the precepts of John Knox been strictly followed, the blue bonnets of a rigid, unbending Presbyterianism would probably to this day have decorated the heads of two-thirds of the population. A scarcity which prevailed about the commencement of the year 1564, drew from this stern Reformer the assertion, that "the riotous feasting and excessive banqueting used in city and country, wheresoever the profane Court repaired, provoked God to strike the staff of bread, and to give his maledictions upon the fruits of the earth." Mary judged differently of the effects produced by these "profane banquetings,"—and so will the political economists of more modern times.

It was only, after the performance of duties of a severer kind, that Mary indulged in recreation. She sat some hours regularly every day with her Privy Council; and, with her work-table beside her and her needle in her hand, she heard and offered opinions upon the various affairs of State. To the poor of every description, she was, like her mother, exceedingly attentive; and she herself benevolently superintended the education of a number of poor children. To direct and distribute her charities, two ecclesiastics were appointed her *elcemosynars*; and they, under her authority, obtained money from the Treasurer in all cases of necessity. She gave an annual salary also to an advocate for the poor, who conducted the causes of such as were unable to bear the expenses of a lawsuit; and to secure proper attention for these causes, she not unfrequently took her seat upon the bench when they came to be heard. Her studies were extensive and regular. She was well versed in history, of which she read a great deal. Every day after dinner she devoted an hour or two to the perusal of some Latin classic, particularly Livy, under the superintendence of George Buchanan. In reward for his services, she gave him the revenue of the Abbey of Crossraguel in Ayrshire, worth about 500*l*. a year. This grant was probably made at the request of the Earl of Murray, who was Buchanan's patron, and to whom he always considered himself more indebted than to the Queen. Buchanan, whose talents for controversial writing it was foreseen might be useful, had also a pension of 100*l*. a year from

Elizabeth. Mary had a competent knowledge of astronomy and geography; and her library in the Palace of Holyrood contained, among other things, two globes, which were at that time considered curiosities in Scotland,—"the ane of the heavin, and the uther of the earth." She had, besides, several maps, and a few pictures, in particular portraits of her father, her mother, her husband Francis II., and Montmorency. Being fond of all sorts of exercises, she frequently received ambassadors and others, to whom she gave audience, in the Palace gardens. She had two of these,—the southern and the northern; and, not contented with their more limited range, she often extended her walk through the King's Park, and sometimes even along the brow of Salisbury Crags or Arthur Seat. She had gardens and parks attached to all her principal residences throughout Scotland,—at Linlithgow,—at Stirling,—at Falkland,— at Perth,—and at St Andrews. It was in one of her gardens at Holyrood that she planted a sycamore she had brought with her from France, and which, becoming in time a large and valuable tree, was an object of curiosity and admiration even in our own day. It was blown down only about ten years ago, and its wood was eagerly sought after, to be made into trinkets and costly relics.

To her female followers and friends, Mary was ever attentive and kind. For her four Maries, her companions from infancy, she retained her affection during all the vicissitudes of her fortune. At the period of which we write, she still enjoyed the society of all of them; but Mary Fleming afterwards became the wife of Secretary Maitland, and Mary Livingstone of Lord Semple. Mary Beaton and Mary Seaton remained unmarried. Madame de Pinguillon, who had come with the Queen from France, and to whom she was extremely partial, continued in her service for several years, her husband being appointed Master of the Household. They both returned to their own country when the troubles in Scotland began. There were many other ladies belonging to the court, whose names possess no interest, because unconnected with any of the events of history.

Mary's establishment was by no means expensive or extraordinary. She does not appear to have had so great a variety of dresses as Elizabeth, yet she was not ill provided either. Her common wearing gowns, as long as she continued in mourning, which was till the day of her second marriage, were made either of camlet, or damis, or serge of Florence, bordered with black velvet. Her riding-habits were mostly of serge of Florence, stiffened in the neck and body with buckram, and trimmed with lace and ribands. In the matter of shoes and stockings, she seems to have been remarkably well supplied. She had thirty-six pair of velvet shoes, laced with gold and silver; she had ten pair of hose woven of gold, silver, and silk, and three pair woven of worsted of Guernsey. Silk stockings were then a rarity. The first pair worn in England were sent as a present from France to Elizabeth. Six pair of gloves of worsted of Guernsey are also mentioned in the catalogue, still existing, of Mary's wardrobe. She was fond of tapestry, and had the walls of her chambers hung with the richest specimens of it she could bring from France. She had not much plate; but she had a profusion of rare and valuable jewels. Her cloth of gold, her Turkey carpets, her beds and coverlids, her table-cloths, her crystal, her chairs and foot-stools covered with velvet, and garnished with fringes, were all celebrated in the gossiping chronicles of the day.

The Scottish Queen's amusements were varied, but not in general sedentary. She was, however, a chess-player, and anxious to make herself a mistress of that most intellectual of all games. Archery was one of her favourite out-of-door pastimes, and she indulged in it frequently in her gardens at Holyrood. She revived the ancient chivalric exercise of riding at the ring, making her nobles contend against each other; and crowds frequently collected on the sands at Leith to witness their trials of skill. Tournaments Mary did not so much like, because they tempted the courageous to what she thought unnecessary danger; and when obliged to be present at them in France, it was remarked, that her superior delicacy of feeling always marred her enjoyment, from the anticipation that they might end in bloodshed. These sentiments were probably strengthened by the unfortunate manner in which Henry II. met his death. The now almost obsolete, but then fashionable and healthful amusement of hawking, was much esteemed by Mary. Her attachment to it was hereditary, for both her father and grandfather were passionately fond of it. James V. kept a master-falconer, who had seven others under him. In 1562, hawks of an approved kind were brought for Mary from Orkney; and in the same year, she sent a present of some of them to Elizabeth. To riding and hunting, as has been already seen, Mary had long been partial.

Within doors, Mary found an innocent gratification in dancing, masquings, and music. She was herself, as has been seen, a most graceful dancer, moving, according to Melville, "not so high, nor so disposedly," as Elizabeth; by which we may understand that she danced, as they who have been taught in France usually do, with greater ease and self-possession, or, in other words, with less effort—less consciousness that she was overcoming a difficulty in keeping time, and executing the steps and evolutions of the dance. The masques and mummeries, which were occasionally got up, were novelties in Scotland, and excited the anger of the Reformers, though it is difficult to tell why. Randolph, describing a feast at which he was present in 1564, mentions that, at the first course, some one, representing Cupid, made his appearance, and sung, with a chorus, some Italian verses; at the second, "a fair young maid" sung a few Latin verses; and at the third, a figure dressed as Time concluded the mummery, with some wholesome piece of morality. Upon other occasions, several of which will be alluded to afterwards, masques were performed upon a more extensive scale. These amusements were seldom or never allowed to degenerate into dissipation, by being protracted to untimely hours. Mary was always up before eight o'clock;—she supped at seven, and was seldom out of bed after ten.[77]

The Queen's taste in music had been cultivated from her earliest years. When almost an infant she had *minstrels* attached to her establishment. On her return to Scotland, she had a small band of about a dozen musicians—vocal and instrumental—whom she kept always near her person. Five of these were violars, or players on the viol;[78] three of them were players on the lute; one or two of them were organists, but the organs in the chapels at Stirling and Holyrood were the only ones which had been saved from the fury of the Reformers; and the rest were singers, who also acted as *chalmer-chields*, or valets-de-chambre. Mary could herself play upon the lute and virginals, and loved to hear concerted music upon all occasions. She even introduced into her religious worship a military band, in aid of the organ, consisting of trumpet, drum, fife, bagpipe, and tabor.

It was as one skilled in music that David Rizzio first recommended himself to Mary. He came to Edinburgh towards the end of the year 1561, in the train of the ambassador from Savoy. He was a Piedmontese by birth, and had received a good education. His father was a respectable professional musician in Turin, who, having a large family, had sent his two sons, David and Joseph, to push their own way in Nice, at the court of the Duke of Savoy. They were both noticed at that court, and were taken into the service of the Duke of Moretto, the ambassador already mentioned. The knowledge which David Rizzio possessed of music, says a French writer, was the least of his talents: He had a polished and ready wit, a lively imagination, full of pleasant fancies, soft and winning manners, abundance of courage, and still more assurance. "He was," says Melville, "a merry fallow, and a guid musician." He was, moreover, abundantly ugly, and past the meridian of life, as attested by all cotemporary writers of any authority. His brother, Joseph, is scarcely mentioned in history, though it appears that he also attached himself to Mary's Court. At the time of David's arrival, the Queen's three pages, or *sangsters*, who used to sing trios for her, wanted a fourth as a bass. Rizzio was recommended, and he received the appointment, together with a salary of 80*l*. Being not only by far the most scientific musician in the Queen's household, but likewise well acquainted both with French and Italian, Rizzio contrived to make himself generally useful. In 1564 he was appointed Mary's French secretary, and in this situation he continued till his death.[79]

An amusing peep into the interior of both the Scots and English Courts, afforded by Sir James Melville, will form an appropriate conclusion to this chapter. Sir James returned from the Continent to Scotland in May 1564. He found the Queen at St Johnstone; and she, aware of his fidelity, requested him to give up thoughts of going back to France, where he had been promised preferment. "She was so affable," says he, "so gracious and discreet, that she won great estimation, and the hearts of many both in England and Scotland, and mine among the rest; so that I thought her more worthy to be served for little profit, than any other prince in Europe for great commodity." But Mary had too proud a spirit to submit to be served for nothing. She was by nature liberal almost to a fault. Out of her French dowry she settled upon Melville a pension of a thousand marks, and in addition, she begged him to accept of the heritage of the lands of Auchtermuchty, near Falkland. These he refused, as he was unwilling that she should dismember, on his account, her own personal property; but they were subsequently given to some one less scrupulous. Sir James was soon afterwards sent by Mary on an embassy to Elizabeth, principally for the sake of expediting some matters connected with Mary's intended matrimonial arrangements.

The morning after his arrival in London, he was admitted to an audience by Elizabeth, whom he found pacing in an alley in her garden. The business upon which he came being arranged satisfactorily, Melville was favourably and familiarly treated by the English Queen. He remained at her Court nearly a fortnight, and conversed with her Majesty every day, sometimes thrice on the same day. Sir James, who was a shrewd observer, had thus an opportunity of remarking the many weaknesses and vanities which characterized Elizabeth. In allusion to her extreme love of power, he ventured to say to her, when she informed him she never intended to marry, "Madam, you need not tell me that; I know your stately stomach. You think, if you were married, you would be but Queen of England; and now you are King and Queen both; you may not suffer a commander." Elizabeth was fortunately not offended at this freedom. She took Sir James, upon one occasion, into her bedchamber, and opened a little case, in which were several miniature pictures. The pretence was to show him a likeness of Mary, but her real object was, that he should observe in her possession a miniature of her favourite the Earl of Leicester, upon which she had written with her own hand, "My Lord's picture." When Melville made this discovery, Elizabeth affected a little amiable confusion. "I held the candle," says Sir James, "and pressed to see my Lord's picture; albeit she was loth to let me see it; at length, I by importunity obtained the sight thereof, and asked the same to carry home with me unto the Queen; which she refused, alleging she had but that one of his." At another time, Elizabeth talked with Sir James of the different costumes of different countries. She told him she had dresses of many sorts; and she appeared in a new one every day during his continuance at Court. Sometimes she dressed after the English, sometimes after the French, and sometimes after the Italian fashion. She asked Sir James which he thought became her best. He said the Italian, "whilk pleasit her weel; for she delighted to show her golden coloured hair, wearing a kell and bonnet as they do in Italy. Her hair was redder than yellow, and apparently of nature." Elizabeth herself seems to have been quite contented with its hue, for she very complacently asked Sir James, whether she or Mary had the finer hair? Sir James having replied as politely as possible, she proceeded to inquire which he considered the more beautiful? The ambassador quaintly answered, that the beauty of either was not her worst fault. This evasion would not serve; though Melville, for many sufficient reasons, was unwilling to say any thing more definite. He told her that she was the fairest queen in England, and Mary the fairest in Scotland. Still this was not enough. Sir James ventured, therefore, one step farther. "They were baith," he said, "the fairest ladies of their courts, and that the Queen of England was whiter, but our Queen was very lusome." Elizabeth next asked which of them was of highest stature? Sir James told her the Queen of Scots. "Then she said the Queen was over heigh, and that herself was neither over heigh nor over laigh. Then she askit what kind of exercises she used. I said, that as I was dispatchit out of Scotland, the Queen was but new come back from the Highland hunting; and that when she had leisure frae the affairs of her country, she read upon guid buiks the histories of divers countries; and sometimes would play upon the lute and virginals. She spearit gin she played weel; I said, raisonably for a Queen."

This account of Mary's accomplishments piqued Elizabeth's vanity, and determined her to give Melville some display of her own. Accordingly, next day one of the Lords in waiting took him to a quiet gallery, where, as if by chance, he might hear the Queen play upon the virginals. After listening a little, Melville perceived well enough that he might take the liberty of entering the chamber whence the music came. Elizabeth coquettishly left off as soon as she saw him, and, coming forward, tapped him with her hand, and affected to feel ashamed of being caught, declaring that she never played before company, but only when alone to keep off melancholy. Melville made her a flattering speech, protesting that the music he had heard was of so exquisite a kind, that it had irresistibly drawn him into the room. Elizabeth, who does not seem to have thought as people are usually supposed to do in polite society, that "comparisons are odious," could not rest satisfied, without putting, as usual, the question, whether Mary or she played best? Melville gave the English Queen the palm. Being now in good humour, she resolved that Sir James should have a specimen of her learning, which it is well known degenerated too much into pedantry. She praised his French, asking if he could also speak Italian, which, she said, she herself spoke reasonably well. She spoke to him also in Dutch; but Sir James says it was not good. Afterwards, she insisted upon his seeing her dance; and when her performance was over, she put the old question, whether she or Mary danced best. Melville answered,—"The Queen dancit not so high and disposedly as she did." Melville returned to Scotland, "convinced in his judgment," as he says, "that in Elizabeth's conduct there was neither plain-dealing nor upright meaning, but great dissimulation, emulation, and fear that Mary's princely qualities should too soon chase her out, and displace her from the kingdom."

Sir James, by way of contrast, concludes this subject with the following interesting account of Mary's well-won popularity, prudence, modesty, and good sense. "The Queen's Majesty, as I have said, after her returning out of France to Scotland, behaved herself so princely, so honourably and discreetly, that her reputation spread in all countries; and she was determined, and also inclined to continue in that kind of comeliness even to the end of her life, desiring to hold none in her company, but such as were of the best quality and conversation, abhorring all vices and vicious persons, whether they were men or women; and she requested me to assist her in giving her my good counsel how she might use the meetest means to advance her honest intention; and in case she, being yet young, might forget herself in any unseemly gesture or behaviour, that I would warn her thereof with my admonition, to forbear and reform the same. Which commission I refused altogether; saying, that her virtuous actions, her natural judgment, and the great experience she had learned in the company of so many notable princes in the Court of France, had instructed her so well, and made her so able, as to be an example to all her subjects and servants. But she would not have it so, but said she knew that she had committed divers errors upon no evil meaning, for lack of the admonition of loving friends, because that the most part of courtiers commonly flatter princes, to win their favour, and will not tell them the verity, fearing to tine their favour; and therefore she adjured me and commanded me to accept that charge, which I said was a ruinous commission, willing her to lay that burden upon her brother, my Lord of Murray, and the Secretary Lethington; but she said that she would not take it in so good a part of them as of me. I said, I feared it would cause me, with time, to tine her favour; but she said it appeared I had an evil opinion of her constancy and discretion, which opinion, she doubted not, but I would alter, after that I had essayed the occupation of that friendly and familiar charge. In the meantime, she made me familiar with all her most urgent affairs; but chiefly in her dealing with any foreign nation. She showed unto me all her letters, and them that she received from other princes; and willed me to write unto such princes as I had acquaintance of, and to some of their counsellors; wherein I forgot not to set out her virtues, and would show her again their answers, and such occurrences as passed at the time between countries, to her great contentment. For she was of a quick spirit, and anxious to know and to get intelligence of the state of other countries; and would be sometimes sad when she was solitary, and glad of the company of them that had travelled in foreign parts."[80]

This testimony in Mary's favour, from a cotemporary author of so much respectability, is worth volumes of ordinary panegyrick.

CHAPTER XII.

MARY'S SUITORS, AND THE MACHINATIONS OF HER ENEMIES.

Mary had now continued a widow for about three years, but certainly not from a want of advantageous offers. It was in her power to have formed almost any alliance she chose. There was not a court in Europe, where the importance of a matrimonial connexion with the Queen of Scotland, and heir-apparent to the English throne, was not acknowledged. Accordingly, ambassadors had found their way to Holyrood Palace from all parts of the Continent. The three most influential suitors were, the Duke of Anjou, brother of Mary's late husband, Francis II., and afterwards King of France, on the death of his other brother, Charles IX.—the Archduke Charles of Austria, third son of the Emperor Ferdinand—and Don Carlos of Spain, heir-apparent to all the dominions of his father, Philip II. None of these personages, however, were destined to be successful. The death of the Duke of Guise, and the greater influence which consequently fell into the hands of Catharine de Medicis, made some alteration in the Duke of Anjou's prospects, and diminished his interest with Mary. Besides, it was considered dangerous to marry the brother of a late husband. The Archduke Charles found, that his proposals to the Scottish Queen excited so much the jealousy of his elder brother, Maximilian, that it became necessary for him reluctantly to quit the field. It is not improbable that Don Carlos might have been listened to, had not Mary found it necessary, for reasons which will be mentioned immediately, to give up all thoughts of a Continental alliance. Had she married Carlos, she might have saved him from the untimely fate inflicted by parental cruelty in 1568.

Of all the sovereigns who at this time watched Mary's intentions with the most jealous anxiety, none felt so deeply interested in the decision she might ultimately come to, as Elizabeth. To her, Mary's marriage was a matter of the very last importance. If she connected herself with a powerful Catholic prince, her former claims upon the English throne might be renewed; and her Scottish armies, assisted by continental forces, might ultimately deprive Elizabeth of her crown. Even though Mary did not proceed to such extremities, if she had a Catholic husband, and more especially if there were any children of the marriage, all the Catholics of Europe would rally round her, and her power would be such, that her requests would be tantamount to commands. So far as Elizabeth's own interests, and those of the kingdom over which she reigned, were involved, she was called upon to pay all due attention to the proceedings of so formidable a rival as Mary. But the English Queen's selfish and invidious policy far over-stepped the limits marked out by the laws of self-defence. Having determined against marriage herself, she could not bear to think that the Queen of Scots should be any thing but a "barren stock" also. It made her miserable to know that her power should end with her life, whilst Mary might become the mother of a long line of kings. She hoped, therefore, though she did not dare to avow her object, to be able to exert such influence with Murray and the Scottish Reformers, that Mary, by their united machinations, might find it impossible ever to form another matrimonial alliance; and with this view her first step was to inform "her good sister," that if she married without her consent, she would have little difficulty in prevailing upon the Parliament of England to set aside her succession.

Driven hither and thither by so many contrary opinions and contending interests, it was no easy matter for the Scottish Queen to come to a final determination upon this subject. Although, in her own words, "not to marry she knew could not be for her, and to defer it long many incommodities might ensue," she at the same time saw that there were insuperable reasons against a foreign alliance. The loss of her best and most powerful continental friend, the Duke of Guise, was one of these; another was, the avowed wish of Elizabeth and the English nation; and the third, and that which weighed most forcibly, the earnest entreaties of her own subjects. The great proportion of the inhabitants of Scotland were now Protestants; and to have attempted to place over them a foreign Catholic Prince, would have been to have incurred the risk of throwing them at once into the arms of Elizabeth, and of losing their allegiance for ever. Mary was therefore willing to make a virtue of necessity, and to allow herself to be guided very much by "her good sister's discretion." This concession to the English Queen was far from being agreeable to Catharine de Medicis and the French Court. It seemed to be paving the way for a cessation of that friendship which had so long existed between France and Scotland. Catharine, altering her policy, began to treat Mary with every mark of attention. She paid up the dowry she received from France, which had fallen into arrears, and requested Mary to exercise as much patronage and influence in that country as she chose. Elizabeth, however, had already suggested a husband for her; and, to the astonishment of every body, had named her favourite minion, Dudley, Earl of Leicester. Though the proposal of one of her own subjects, and one too, whom she had raised from comparative obscurity, was regarded by Mary as little else than an insult, she agreed, that two commissioners upon her part, Murray and Maitland—should meet two of Elizabeth's, the Duke of Bedford and Randolph, to discuss the expediency of the match. At the conference, which took place at Berwick, it was stated for Mary, that she could never condescend to marry a newly-created English Earl, having so long a list of princes of the blood-royal of the noblest houses of Europe among her suitors; and it was added, boldly, that Elizabeth seemed somewhat deficient even in self-respect, when she could think of recommending such a husband for a Queen, her kinswoman. It is not at all likely, that either Elizabeth, or the Earl of Leicester, expected or wished any other answer. Elizabeth could hardly have done without her favourite; and the Earl would have fallen into irretrievable disgrace, had he dared to confess a preference for any mistress over the one he already had.

It was soon after this conference that Randolph, by Elizabeth's directions, repaired to the Queen at St Andrews, to ascertain from her own lips what were her real sentiments on the subject of marriage. He found her living very quietly in a merchant's house, with a small train. She had been wearied with the state and show of a Court, and had determined to pass some weeks in her favourite retirement of St Andrews, more as a subject than a queen. She made Randolph dine and sup with her every day during his visit; and she frequently, upon these occasions, drank to the health of Elizabeth. When Randolph entered upon matters of business, Mary said to him playfully,—"I sent for you to be merry, and to see how like a bourgeoise wife I live with my little troop; and you will interrupt our pastime with your great and grave matters? I pray ye, Sir, if ye be weary here, return home to Edinburgh; and keep your gravity and great embassade until the Queen come thither; for, I assure ye, you shall not get her here, nor I know not myself where she is become. Ye see neither cloth of estate, nor such appearance that you may think that there is a Queen here; nor I would not that you should think that I am she at St Andrews, that I was at Edinburgh." Randolph was thus, for the time, fairly bantered out of his diplomatic gravity. But next day, he rode abroad with the Queen, and renewed the subject. Mary then told him, that she saw the necessity of marrying, and that she would rather be guided in her choice by England than by France, or any other country after Scotland. She frankly added, that her reason for paying this deference to Elizabeth, was to obtain an acknowledgment of her right of succession to the English crown. She was making a sacrifice, she said, in renouncing the much more splendid alliances which had been offered her; and she could not be expected to do so without a return on the part of Elizabeth. Fearful that the crafty Randolph might make a bad use of this open confession, she suddenly checked herself;—"I am a fool," she said, "thus long to talk with you; you are too subtle for me to deal with." But Randolph, finding her in a communicative mood, was unwilling that the conversation should drop so soon. Some further discourse took place, and Mary, in conclusion, gave utterance to the following sentiments, which do honour both to her head and heart. "How much better were it," said she, "that we two being queens, so near of kin and neighbours, and being in one isle, should be friends and live together like sisters, than, by strange means, divide ourselves to the hurt of us both; and to say that we may for all that live friends, we may say and prove what we will, but it will pass both our powers. You repute us poor; but yet you have found us cumbersome enough. We have had loss; ye have taken scaith. Why may it not be between my sister and me, that we, living on peace and assured friendship, may give our minds, that some as notable things may be wrought by us women, as by our predecessors have been done before. Let us seek this honour against some other, rather than fall to debate amongst ourselves."[81]

Mary, however, was by this time convinced of Elizabeth's want of sincerity, and formed, therefore, a matrimonial plan of her own, which, she flattered herself, would be considered judicious by all parties. It will be recollected, that, during the troubles which ensued soon after Mary's birth, Matthew, Earl of Lennox, having drawn upon himself the suspicion, both of the Protestant and Catholic parties in Scotland, retired into England, where Henry VIII. gave him his niece in marriage. The Lady Margaret Douglas was daughter of the eldest daughter of Henry VII., the Princess Margaret, who, upon the decease of her first husband James IV., had married the Earl of Angus, of which marriage the Lady Margaret was the issue. Lennox, belonging as he did to the house of Stuart, was himself related to the Royal Family of Scotland; and his wife, failing the children of Henry VIII., and the direct line of succession by her mother's first husband James IV., in which line Mary stood, was the legal heir to the crown of England. The first child of this marriage died in infancy. The second, afterwards known as Henry Stuart, Lord Darnley, was born in 1546, and was, consequently, about four years younger than Mary. This disparity in point of years, though unfortunate in another point of view, was not such as to preclude the possibility of an alliance between two persons, in whose veins flowed so much of the blood of the Stuarts and the Tudors.

Henry VIII. had, along with his niece, bestowed upon Lennox English lands, from which he derived a yearly revenue of fifteen hundred marks. His own estates in Scotland were forfeited, so that he thus came to be considered more an English than a Scottish subject. He had long, however, nourished the secret hope of restoring his fortunes in his native land. His wife, who was a woman of an ambitious and intriguing spirit, induced him, at an early period, to educate his son with a view to his aspiring to the hand of the Scottish Queen. On the death of Francis II. she went herself to Paris, for the purpose of ingratiating herself with Mary, and securing a favourable opinion for Darnley. Mary, probably, gave her some hope that she might, at a future date, take her proposals into serious consideration; for it appears, by some papers still preserved in the British Museum, that few rejoiced more sincerely at the Queen's safe arrival in Scotland, than Lady Lennox. She is said to have fallen on her knees, and, with uplifted hands, thanked God that the Scottish queen had escaped the English ships. For this piece of piety, and to show her the necessity of taking less interest in the affairs of Elizabeth's rival, Cecil sent Lady Lennox to prison for some months.

Seeing the difficulties which stood in the way of all her other suitors, Mary, in the year 1564, began seriously to think of Darnley. A marriage with him would unite, in the person of the heir of such marriage, the rival claims of the Stuarts and the Tudors upon the English succession, failing issue by Elizabeth; and it would give to Scotland a native prince of the old royal line. It was difficult to see what reasonable objections could be made to such an alliance; and that she might at all events have an opportunity of judging for herself, Mary granted the Earl of Lennox permission to return to Scotland, in 1564, after an exile of twenty years, and promised to assist him in reclaiming his hereditary rights. Elizabeth, who was well aware of the ultimate views with which this journey was undertaken, and had certainly no desire to forward their accomplishment, made nevertheless no opposition to it. With her usual sagacity, she calculated that much discord and jealousy would arise, out of the Earl's suit, in favour of his son. She knew that the House of Hamilton, whose claims upon the Scottish crown were publicly recognised, looked upon the Lennox family as its worst enemies; and that the haughty nobility of Scotland would ill brook to see a stripling elevated above the heads of all of them. Besides, the principal estates of Lennox now lay in England; and in the words of Robertson, "she hoped by this pledge to keep the negotiation entirely in her own hands, and to play the same game of artifice and delay which she had planned out, if her recommendation of Leicester had been more favourably received."

In the Parliament which assembled towards the end of the year 1564, Lennox was restored to his estates and honours. Such of his possessions as had passed into the hands of the Earl of Argyle, were surrendered with extreme reluctance; and the Duke of Chatelherault, dreading the marriage with Darnley, continued obstinate in his hatred. The Earl of Murray too, aware that this new connection would be a fatal blow to his influence, set his face against it from the first. Maitland, on the contrary, who felt that he had been hitherto kept too much under by the prime minister, did not anticipate with any regret the decline of his ascendancy. The Secretary, and most of the other members of the Privy Council, were assiduously courted by Lennox. He made presents both to the Queen and them of valuable jewels; but to Murray, whose enmity he knew, he gave nothing.[82] That Murray's weight in the government, however, had not yet decreased, is apparent, from his procuring an enactment, to gratify the Protestants, in the parliament of this year, making the attending of mass, except in the Queen's chapel, punishable with loss of goods, lands, and life: and the Archbishop of St Andrews having infringed this act, was imprisoned, in spite of Mary's intercession, for some months.

Early in 1565, Darnley obtained leave from Elizabeth to set out for Scotland. His ostensible purpose was to visit his father, and to see the estates to which he had been recently restored; but that his real object was to endeavour to win the good graces of Mary, was no secret. Elizabeth's wish being to involve Mary in a quarrel, as well with some of her own nobility, as with England, there was much art in the plan she laid for its accomplishment. She consented that the Earl of Lennox should go into Scotland to recover his forfeited estates, and that his son should follow him to share in his father's good fortune; she even went the length of recommending them both to the especial favour of the Scottish Queen; but of course said not a word of any suspicions she entertained of the projected alliance. As soon as it should appear that Mary's resolution was taken, she would affect the greatest indignation at the whole proceedings, and pretend that they had been cunningly devised and executed, hoping either to break off the match altogether, or to make Mary's nuptial couch, any thing but a bed of roses. Thus was the Scottish Queen to be systematically harassed, and made miserable, to gratify the splenetic jealousy, and lull the selfish terrors, of her sister of England.

Darnley, in the midst of a severe snow-storm, travelled with all expedition to Edinburgh. Upon his arrival he found that Mary was at Wemyss Castle in Fife, whither, at his father's desire, he immediately proceeded. The impression which it is said he made upon the Queen, at even his first interview, has been much exaggerated. Chalmers, alluding principally to Robertson's account of this matter, acutely remarks, "The Scottish historians would have us believe, that Mary fell desperately in love with Darnley at first sight; they would have us suppose, as simply as themselves, that the widowed Queen, at the age of twenty-two," (it should have been twenty-three), "who knew the world, and had seen the most accomplished gentlemen in Europe, was a boarding-school Miss, who had never till now seen a man." Mary received Darnley frankly, and as one whom she wished to like; but she had been too long accustomed to admiration, to be prepared to surrender her heart at the first glance. It was not Mary's character to allow herself to be won before she was wooed. She was, no doubt, glad to perceive that Darnley was one of the handsomest young men of the day. She said playfully, that "he was the lustiest and best proportioned long man she had seen." She might have said a good deal more; for all historians agree in noticing the grace of his person, the easy elegance of his carriage, the agreeable regularity of his features, and the animated expression of his countenance, lighted up, as it was, by a pair of dazzling eyes. He excelled too in all the showy and manly accomplishments so much in vogue among the young nobility. His riding and dancing were unrivalled; and to gratify Mary, he avowed, whether real or affected, a great fondness for poetry and music. Melville says quaintly, "He was of a heigh stature, lang and small, even and brent up; well instructed from his youth in all honest and comely exercises."[83]

It was not, however, Darnley's exterior in which Mary and her subjects were principally interested. The bent which nature and education had given to his mind and character, was a much more important subject of consideration. With regard to his religious sentiments, they seem to have sat loosely upon him; though his mother was a Catholic, he himself professed adherence to the Established Church of England.[84] In Scotland, he saw the necessity of ingratiating himself with the Reformers; and he went, the very first Sunday he spent in Edinburgh, to hear Knox preach. But Darnley's great misfortune was, that, before he had learned any thing in the school of experience, and in the very heat and fire of youth, he was raised to an eminence which, so far from enabling him to see over the heads of other men, only rendered him giddy, and made his inferiority the more apparent. He was naturally of a headstrong and violent temper, which might, perhaps, have been tamed down by adversity, but which only ran into wilder waste in the sunshine of prosperity. He was passionately fond of power, without the ability to make a proper use of it. It is not unlikely that, had he continued a subject for some years longer, and associated with men of sound judgment and practical knowledge, he might have divested himself of some of the follies of youth, and acquired a contempt for many of its vices. But his honours came upon him too suddenly; and the intellectual strength of his character, never very great, was crushed under the load. Conscious of his inability to cope with persons of talent, he sought to gather round him those who were willing to flatter him on account of his rank, or to join him in all kinds of dissipation, with the view of sharing his ill-regulated liberality. Of the duties of a courtier, he knew something; but of those of a politician, he was profoundly ignorant. The polish of his manners gained him friends at first; but the reckless freedom with which he gave utterance to his hasty opinions and ill-grounded prejudices, speedily converted them into enemies. He had only been a short time in Scotland, when he remarked to one of the Earl of Murray's brothers, who pointed out to him on the map the Earl's lands, "that they were too extensive." Murray was told of this; and, perceiving what he had to expect when Darnley became King, he took his measures accordingly. Mary, whose affliction it was to have husbands far inferior to herself in mental qualifications, beseeched Darnley to be more guarded in future. That he was somewhat violent and self-sufficient, she did not feel to be an insuperable objection, considering, as she did, the political advantages that might accrue from the alliance. She hoped that time would improve him; and besides, she did not yet know the full extent of his imperfections, as he had, of course, been anxious to show her only the fairer side of his character. Melville speaks of him, even when he came to be most hated, as a young prince, who failed rather for lack of good counsel than of evil will. "It appeared to be his destiny," says he, "to like better of flatterers and evil company, than of plain speakers and good men; whilk has been the wreck of many princes, who, with good company, might have produced worthy effects." Randolph himself allows, that for some weeks, his "behaviour was very well liked, and there was great promise of him." He had been about a month at Court before he ventured to propose himself as a husband to Mary; and at first she gave him but small encouragement, telling him she had not yet made up her mind, and refusing to accept of a ring, which he offered her.[85] This was not like one who had fallen in love at first sight. But the Queen invariably conducted herself with becoming self-respect towards Darnley, permitting, as Miss Benger remarks, rather than inviting, his intentions.

Darnley, thus finding that, though the ball was at his foot, the game was not already won, saw it necessary to engage with his father's assistance, as powerful a party as possible to support his pretensions. Sir James Melville was his friend, and spoke in his favour to Mary. All the Lords who hated or feared Murray did the same; among whom were, the Earls of Athol and Caithness, and the Lords Ruthven and Hume. A still more useful agent than any of these, Darnley found in David Rizzio, who, as the Queen's French Secretary, and one whose abilities she respected, had a good deal of influence with her. Rizzio knew that for this very reason he was hated by Murray, and others of the Privy Council. He was, therefore, not ill pleased to find himself sought after by her future husband, for he hoped thus to retain his place at Court, and perhaps to rise upon the ruin of some of those who wished his downfal. An accidental illness which overtook Darnley, when the Queen, with her Court, was at Stirling, about the beginning of April 1565, was another circumstance in his favour. At first, his complaint was supposed to be a common cold, but in a few days it turned out to be the measles. The natural anxiety which Mary felt for Darnley's recovery, induced her to exhibit a tenderer interest in him than she had ever done before. She paid him the most flattering attentions, and continued them unwearyingly, though her patient was provokingly attacked by an ague, almost immediately after his recovery from the measles.[86]

It is worth noticing, that while Mary was thus occupied in attending to Darnley, the Earl of Bothwell returned to Scotland from his involuntary banishment. His former misdemeanours were not yet forgotten, and he was summoned by the Queen and Murray to take his trial in Edinburgh; but not liking to trust himself in the hands of his ancient enemies, he again left the country for six months. He did not depart before giving utterance to several violent threats against Murray and Maitland, and speaking so disrespectfully of the Queen, that Randolph says she declared to him, upon her honour, that he should never receive favour at her hands.[87]

The Queen of Scots being now resolved to bestow her hand on Darnley, sent her Secretary, Maitland, to London, to intimate her intentions, and to request Elizabeth's approbation. This was the very last thing Elizabeth meant to give. The matter had now arrived exactly at the point to which she had all along wished to bring it. She had prevailed upon Mary to abandon the idea of a foreign alliance; she had induced her to throw away some valuable time in ridiculous negociations concerning the Earl of Leicester; she had consented, first that the Earl of Lennox, and then that his son Darnley, should go into Scotland; and she did not say a single syllable against it till she had allowed Mary to be persuaded, that no marriage in Christendom could be more prudent. It was now that the cloven-foot was to betray itself; that her faction was to be called upon to exert itself in Scotland; that the cup was to be dashed from Darnley's lips; and that Mary was to be involved in the vortex of civil dissension. The historian Castelnau, whom Mary at this time sent as her ambassador to France, and who there obtained their Majesties' consent to the marriage, mentions, that when he returned through England, he found the Queen much colder than formerly, complaining that Mary had subtracted her relation and subject, and that she was intending to marry him without her permission, and against her approbation. "And yet I am sure," adds Castelnau, "that these words were very far from her heart; for she used all her efforts, and spared nothing to set this marriage a-going."[88]

Elizabeth seldom did things by halves. She assembled her Privy Council, and, at the instigation of Cecil, they gave it as their unanimous opinion, that "this marriage with my Lord Darnley appeared to be unmeet, unprofitable, and directly prejudicial to the sincere amity between both the Queens."[89] Upon what reasons this sage determination was founded, the Privy Council did not condescend to state. It is not difficult, however, to do so for them, the more especially as an official paper is still preserved, drawn up by Cecil himself, in which the explanations he attempts serve to disclose more fully his own and his Queen's policy. He did not think this marriage "meet or profitable;" because, in the first place, it would have given great content to those who were anxious that Mary's succession to the English crown should not be set aside; and in the second place, because, by representing it as dangerous, a plausible pretence would be furnished to all Mary's enemies to join with Elizabeth in opposing it, and harassing the Queen of Scots. Cecil proceeds to point out explicitly how the harassing system was to be carried on. *First*, It was to be represented, that in France the houses of Guise and Lorraine, and all the other leading Catholics; and in Scotland, all who hated the Duke of Chatelherault and the Hamiltons, and Murray and the Reformers, and were devoted to the authority of Rome, approved of the marriage. *Second*, It was to be spread abroad that the Devil would stir up some of the friends of Mary and Darnley, to alienate the minds of Elizabeth's subjects, and even to attempt the life of that Sovereign; and, under the pretext of preventing such evils, the most rigorous measures might be taken against all suspected persons; and, *Third*, Tumults and rebellions in Scotland were to be fomented in all prudent and secret ways.[90]

To report to Mary the decision of her Privy Council, Elizabeth sent Sir Nicolas Throckmorton into Scotland. He arrived at Stirling on the 15th of May 1565, and, in an audience which Mary gave him, he set forth Elizabeth's disliking and disallowance of what she was pleased to term "the hasty proceeding with my Lord Darnley." Mary, with becoming dignity and unanswerable argument, replied, that she was sorry Elizabeth disliked the match, but that, as to her "disallowance," she had never asked the English Queen's permission,—she had only communicated to her, as soon as she had made up her own mind, the person whom she had chosen. She was not a little surprised, she added, at Elizabeth's opposition, since it had been expressly intimated to her, through the English resident, Randolph, that if she avoided a foreign alliance, "she might take her choice of any person within the realms of England or Scotland, without any exception." Her choice had fallen upon Lord Darnley, both from the good qualities she found in him, and because being Elizabeth's kinsman and her's, and participating of the English and Scottish blood royal, she had imagined that none would be more agreeable to her Majesty and the realm of England. Convinced, by so decided an answer to his remonstrance, that Mary's resolution was fixed, Throckmorton wrote to Elizabeth, that she could not hope to stop the marriage, unless she had recourse to violence. But Elizabeth had too much prudence to take up arms herself; all she wished was, to instigate others to this measure. Accordingly, Throckmorton, one of the wiliest of her diplomatic agents, received orders to deal with the Scottish malcontents, and especially the Earl of Murray, whom he was to assure of Elizabeth's support, should they proceed to extremities. Murray was likewise invited to enter into a correspondence with Cecil, an invitation with which he willingly complied;[91] and to give the whole affair as serious an air as possible, a fresh supply of troops was sent to the Earl of Bedford, Elizabeth's Lieutenant of the Borders; and her Wardens of the Marches were commanded to show no more favour to Mary's subjects than the bare abstaining from any breach of peace. The Earl of Northumberland, who was attached to the Lennox family, was detained in London; and Lady Lennox herself, was committed to the Tower. Lady Somerset, who pretended a sort of title to the English succession in opposition to Mary, was received very graciously at the Court of Westminster. Means were used to induce Secretary Maitland to associate himself with Murray, and the other discontents; and, all this time, that no suspicion of such insiduous enmity towards the Scottish Queen might be entertained on the Continent, the good opinion of France and Spain was carefully courted.

Elizabeth next wrote letters to Lennox and Darnley, commanding them both, as her subjects, to return to England without delay. Randolph was desired to wait upon them, to know what answer they were disposed to give. He got little satisfaction from either;—Lennox firmly, and Darnley contemptuously, refused to obey the mandate of recall. Randolph then waited upon the Queen to ascertain her mind on the subject. Mary felt keenly the contemptible jealousy and envy with which she was treated by Elizabeth; and received the English resident with greater reserve than she had ever done before, "as a man new and first come into her presence that she had never seen." Randolph asked, if she would give Lennox and Darnley permission to depart for England. Mary smiled at the question, which was an artful one, and said,—"If I would give them leave, I doubt what they would do themselves; I see no will in them to return." Randolph answered with insolence, that they must either return, or do worse; for that, if they refused, and were supported by Mary in that refusal, the Queen his mistress had the power and the will to be revenged upon both them and her. The Queen of Scots merely replied, that she hoped Elizabeth would change her mind, and so dismissed Randolph.

Satisfied of the integrity of her purpose, Mary was not to be easily driven from it. She sent Mr John Hay to the English court, to state once more her anxious wish to avoid giving any just cause of offence to Elizabeth, but at the same time to repeat, that she could not but consider as strange and vexatious, any opposition to a marriage, to which there did not seem to be one plausible objection. He was desired also to complain of the "sharp handling" which had been given to Mary's aunt, the Lady Margaret Douglas, Countess of Lennox. But her chief anxieties arose from the state of matters nearer home. The Duke of Chatelherault, and the Earls of Murray, Argyle, and Glencairn, had now openly declared themselves adverse to the marriage; and Lethington and Morton were suspected of giving it only a very doubtful support. There was, in consequence, a great change at Mary's court. They who had formerly most influence kept away from it altogether; and a new set of men, little accustomed to state duties, such as Montrose, Fleming, Cassils, Montgomery, and others, came into favour. It was now that Mary found Rizzio, who was active, and well acquainted with all the details of public business, and was, besides, liked by Darnley, of the greatest use to her; and being deserted by her more efficient, but too ambitious counsellors, she gladly availed herself of his services.

CHAPTER XIII.

MARY'S MARRIAGE WITH DARNLEY.

Murray, meanwhile, was busily organizing his scheme of rebellion. "Their chief trust," says Randolph, alluding to the Earl and his associates, "next unto God, is the Queen's Majesty, (Elizabeth,) whom they will repose themselves upon; not leaving in the meantime to provide for themselves the best they can." Elizabeth was not backward to give them every encouragement. She wrote letters to the heads of the party; means were taken to win over to their views the General Assembly, which met in June 1565, the members of which, as Randolph says, were "never more constant or more earnest;" and the nobles summoned by Mary to a convention at Perth, were all tampered with. But the great majority at this convention, gave their consent and approbation to the proposed marriage; and Murray, in despair, begged Randolph to inform his mistress, in the name of himself and those who had joined his faction, that they were "grieved to see such extreme folly in their sovereign; that they lamented the state of their country, which tended to utter ruin; and that they feared the nobility would be forced to assemble themselves together, so to provide for the state, that it should not utterly perish." In other words, they had made up their mind to rebellion; at all events, to prevent Darnley from obtaining the crown, and an ascendancy over them,—and probably, if an opportunity should offer, to put Mary in confinement, and rule the country themselves. This was exactly the state of feeling which Elizabeth had long laboured to produce in Scotland. "Some that have already heard," says Randolph, "of my Lady's Grace imprisonment," (meaning the Countess of Lennox), "like very well thereof, and wish both father and son to keep her company. The question hath been asked me, whether, if they were delivered us into Berwick, we would receive them? I answered, that we could not nor would not refuse our own, in what sort soever they came unto us."[92] But as it was felt that a plausible apology would be required for proceeding to these extremities, the Earl of Murray gave out that a conspiracy had been formed to assassinate him at the Convention at Perth. His story was, that there had been a quarrel between one of his own servants and another man, who was supported by retainers of Athol and Lennox, and that it had been arranged that they should renew their dispute at Perth, and that he himself should be slain in the affray, which was expected to ensue. But the evidence of a plot against him rests only upon Murray's own statement and when Mary asked him to transmit in writing a more particular account of it, seeing that he made it his excuse for refusing to come to Court, "it appeared to her Highness and to her

Council, that his purgation in that behalf, was not so sufficient as the matter required;" and his excuse was not sustained.[93]

The treasonable views entertained by Murray and his friends, are involved in no such doubt. In these times, the common mode of effecting a change in the government, was to seize the person of the sovereign; and all historians of credit agree in affirming, that Murray was determined on making the experiment. On Sunday, the first of July, 1565, the Queen was to ride with Darnley and a small train of friends from Perth to the seat of Lord Livingston at Callander, the baptism of one of whose children she had promised to attend. Murray knew that it would be necessary for her to pass, in the course of this journey, through several steep and wild passes, where she and her attendants might easily be overpowered. At what precise spot the attack was to be made, or whether that was not left to the chapter of accidents, does not appear. Knox, who was, of course, too staunch a Presbyterian directly to accuse the great lay-head of his church of so treasonable a design, says that the path of Dron (a rugged pass about three miles south of Perth), had been mentioned, whilst Sir James Melville and others, point out the Kirk of Beith, which stood on a solitary piece of ground, between Dumfermline and the Queensferry. But late upon the previous Saturday night, a rumour reached Mary of the contemplated plot. To prevent its execution, she ordered the Earl of Athol and Lord Ruthven, to collect immediately as strong a body of men as possible; and through their exertions, she left Perth next morning at five, accompanied by three hundred horsemen well mounted. Murray was waiting at Loch Leven, Argyle at Castle Campbell, Chatelherault at his house of Kinneil, in the neighbourhood of the Queensferry, and Lord Rothes, who had joined in the conspiracy, at a place called the Parrot Well, not far distant. The Queen, however, to their great disappointment, having passed over the ground on which they intended to intercept her, both much earlier in the day, and much more strongly guarded than they had anticipated, they were obliged to remain quiet; indeed the Earl of Argyle did not come to join Murray, till two hours after Mary had ridden through Kinross.[94]

On Mary's return to Edinburgh she found that an attempt had been made, through the conjoined influence of Knox and Murray, to stir up to sedition some of the more bigoted Presbyterians—on the plea that Darnley favoured Popery. Two or three hundred of the malcontents, or *brethren*, as Knox calls them, assembled at St Leonard's Hill, and their mutinous proceedings might have led to disagreeable consequences, had not Mary arrived just in time to disperse and overawe them.[95] Murray and his associates, keeping at a greater distance, held some secret meetings at Loch-Leven, and then assembling at Stirling on the 17th of July, openly raised the standard of rebellion. But, amidst all these troubles, Mary, conscious that she had right upon her side, remained undaunted, and, at no period of her life, did her strength of mind appear more conspicuous. To retain that confidence, which she knew the great majority of her subjects still placed in her, she issued proclamations announcing her determination to abstain, as she had hitherto done, from any interference in the matter of religion; she wrote, with her own hand, letters to many of her nobles, assuring them of the integrity of her intentions; and, she sent requisitions to all upon whom she could depend, calling on them to collect their followers, and come armed to her assistance.

The Earl of Murray, on the other hand, having thrown off his allegiance to his own Sovereign, became entirely subservient to the wishes and commands of Elizabeth. He and his friends wrote to request that she would send them, as a proof of her sincerity in the cause, the sum of three thousand pounds to meet the expenses of the current year; and they would thus be able, they imagined, to carry every thing before them, unless Mary received foreign assistance. They likewise suggested that Lord Hume, whose estates lay on the Borders, and who was one of the Scottish Queen's most faithful servants, should be harassed by some ostensibly accidental incursions;—that the Bishop of Dumblane, who was to be sent on an embassy to the Continent, should be delayed in London till "his budgets were rifled by some good slight or other;"—and that Bothwell, whom Mary was about to recall, to obtain his assistance in her present difficulties, should be "kept in good surety" for a time.[96] To all this Elizabeth replied, that if the Lords suffered any inconvenience, "they should not find lack in her to succour them." She hinted, however, that the less money they asked the better, advising them "neither to make greater expense than their security makes necessary, nor less which may bring danger." "This letter," says Keith, "is an evident demonstration of the English Queen's fomenting and supporting a rebellion in Scotland; and the rebellious Lords knew too well what they had to trust to."

One can hardly attempt to unravel, as has been done in the preceding pages, the secret causes which led to the iniquitous rebellion now organized, without feeling it almost a duty to express indignation both at the malicious interference of the English Queen, and the overweening ambition and ingratitude of the Earl of Murray. Mary's conduct, since her return from France, had been almost unexceptionable. The only fault she had committed, and the necessity of the times forced it on her, was yielding too implicitly to the counsels of her brother. These had been in some instances judicious, and in others, the natural severity of his temper had been rebuked by the mildness of Mary; so that, take it for all in all, no government had ever been more popular in Scotland than hers. Her choice of Lord Darnley for a husband, so far from diminishing the estimation in which she was held by the great body of her subjects, only contributed to raise her in their opinion. For the sake of the political advantages which would result to her country from this alliance, she was willing to forego much more splendid offers; and, though the imperfections of Darnley's character might ultimately be the means of destroying her own happiness, his birth and expectations were exactly such as gave him the best right to be the father of James VI. Nor could his religious opinions be objected to, for, whatever they were, they did not influence the Queen;—indeed, ever since she had known him, she had treated the Protestants with even more than her usual liberality. At the baptism of Lord Livingston's child, she remained and heard a Protestant sermon; and about the same time she intimated to some of the leaders of the Reformers, that though she was not persuaded of the truth of any religion except of that in which she had been brought up, she would nevertheless allow a conference and disputation on the Scriptures in her presence, and also a public preaching from the mouth of Mr Erskine of Dun, whom she regarded as "a mild and sweet-natured man, with true honesty and uprightness."[97] All these things considered, one is at a loss to conceive how, even in these restless times, any set of men dared to enter into rebellion against Mary. But the selfish and insidious policy of Elizabeth—the jealousy of the Duke of Chatelherault, in whose family rested the succession to the Scottish crown, and who had hoped that his son Arran might have obtained Mary's hand—the envy and rage of the Earl of Argyle, who had been obliged to surrender to Lennox some of his forfeited estates—and, above all, the artful and grasping spirit of Murray, solve the enigma. Whatever opinion may be entertained of Mary's subsequent proceedings it appears but too evident, that the first serious troubles of her reign were forced upon her in spite of her utmost prudence, by the intrigues of enemies who were only the more dangerous, because they had for a time assumed the disguise of friends.

Whatever the hopes or wishes of the conspirators might be, Mary resolved that they should not long have it in their power to make their desire to prevent her nuptials a pretext for continuing in arms. On Sunday, the 29th of July 1565, she celebrated her marriage with Darnley, upon whom she had previously conferred various titles, and among others that of Duke of Albany. [98] The banns of matrimony were proclaimed in the Canongate church, the palace of Holyrood being in that parish; and, as Mary and Darnley were first cousins, a Catholic dispensation had been obtained from the Pope. The ceremony was performed, according to the Catholic ritual, in the chapel of Holyrood, between five and six in the morning—an hour which appears somewhat strange to modern habits. John Sinclair, Dean of Restalrig, and Bishop of Brechin, had the honour of presiding on the occasion. It was generally remarked, that a handsomer couple had never been seen in Scotland. Mary was now twenty-three, and at the very height of her beauty, and

Darnley, though only nineteen, was of a more manly person and appearance than his age would have indicated. The festivities were certainly not such as had attended the Queen's first marriage, for the elegancies of life were not understood in Scotland as in France; and, besides, it was a time of trouble when armed men were obliged to stand round the altar. Nevertheless, all due observances and rejoicings lent a dignity to the occasion. Mary, in a flowing robe of black, with a wide mourning hood, was led into the chapel by the Earls of Lennox and Athol, who, having conducted her to the altar, retired to bring in the bridegroom. The Bishop having united them in the presence of a great attendance of Lords and Ladies, three rings were put upon the Queen's finger—the middle one a rich diamond. They then knelt together, and many prayers were said over them. At their conclusion, Darnley kissed his bride, and as he did not himself profess the Catholic faith, left her till she should hear mass. She was afterwards followed by most of the company to her own apartments, where she laid aside her sable garments, to intimate, that henceforth, as the wife of another, she would forget the grief occasioned by the loss of her first husband. In observance of an old custom, as many of the Lords as could approach near enough were permitted to assist in unrobing her, by taking out a pin. She was then committed to her ladies, who, having attired her with becoming splendour, brought her to the ball-room, where there was great cheer and dancing till dinner time. At dinner, Darnley appeared in his royal robes; and after a great flourish of trumpets, largess was proclaimed among the multitude who surrounded the palace. The Earls of Athol, Morton, and Crawfurd, attended the Queen as sewer, carver, and cup-bearer; and the Earls of Eglinton, Cassilis, and Glencairn, performed the like offices for Darnley. When dinner was over, the dancing was renewed till supper-time, soon after which the company retired for the night.[99]

The rejoicings that attended the commencement of Darnley's career as King of Scotland, were but of short duration. Randolph, expressing the sentiments of Elizabeth and the rebels, hesitated not to say, that *"God must either send the King a short end, or them a miserable life; that either he must be taken away, or they find some support, that what he intendeth to others may light upon himself."*

CHAPTER XIV.

MURRAY'S REBELLION.

Murray had now gone too far to recede, though, had he been so inclined, Mary's leniency would willingly have given him the opportunity. Mr John Hay, who had formerly acted as her ambassador in England, and who was one of her brother's personal friends, was sent to him to declare the good will which both the Earl of Lennox and Darnley bore towards him. Mary even avowed her readiness to bring to trial any one he would accuse of having conspired against his life; but he had no evidence to prove that such a conspiracy had ever existed, much less to fix the guilt upon any individual. He had made the accusation originally, only the better to conceal his own nefarious purposes; for Murray well understood the practical application of Machiavel's maxim,—"Calumniare audacter aliquid adhærebit."

Acting in concert with this nobleman, Elizabeth now sent more imperative orders than before for the return of Lennox and Darnley. But the former answered, that, considering his wife had been committed to the Tower for no fault on her part, he thought it unlikely that the climate of England would suit his constitution; and the latter said boldly and gallantly, that he now acknowledged duty and obedience to none but the Queen of Scots, whom he served and honoured; and though Elizabeth chose to be envious of his good fortune, he could not discover why he should leave a country where he found himself so comfortable. Randolph coolly replied, that he hoped to see the wreck and overthrow of as many as were of the same mind; "and so turning my back to him, without reverence or farewell, I went away."[100] The disaffected Lords, on their part, as soon as they heard of Mary's marriage, and the proclamations in which she conferred upon her husband the rank and title of King, renewed their complaints with increased bitterness. The majority of their countrymen, however, saw through their real motives; and even Knox allows it was generally alleged, that these complaints were "not for religion, but rather for hatred, envy of sudden promotion or dignity, or such worldly causes." The recalling of the Earls Bothwell and Sutherland, and the restoring Lord Gordon to the forfeited estates and honours of his father, the Earl of Huntly, was another source of exasperation. From the tried fidelity of these noblemen, Mary knew she could depend upon their services; though Bothwell, personally, as we have already seen, was far from being agreeable to her.

To put in the clearest point of view the utter worthlessness of all the grounds of offence which Elizabeth and the Scottish rebels pretended at this time to have against Mary, a short and impartial account of a message sent by the English Queen, early in August 1565, and of the answer it received, will be read here with interest. The person who brought this message was one of Elizabeth's inferior officials, of the name of Tamworth, "a forward, insolent man," says Camden, and, with marked disrespect, chosen for this very reason. He was ordered not to acknowledge Darnley as King, and to give him no title but that which he had borne in England; but Mary, "having smelt," as Camden adds "the nature both of the message, and of the animal who brought it," would not admit him into her presence. His objections were therefore committed to writing, and the answer given in similar form. On the part of Elizabeth it was stated, that her Majesty had found Mary's late proceedings, both towards herself and towards her subjects, very strange, upon diverse grounds. These, as they were brought forward, so were they replied to methodically and *seriatim*. *First*, Elizabeth took God to witness, that her offer to Mary, of any of her own subjects in marriage, was made sincerely and lovingly; and that she was grieved to hear that Mary, listening to false council, had been made to think otherwise.—To this it was answered, that the Queen of Scots did not doubt Elizabeth's sincerity and uprightness in her offer of a husband from England, and that no counsel had been given to induce her to change her opinion. *Second*, Elizabeth was much surprised, that notwithstanding the offer made by Mary to Sir Nicolas Throckmorton, to delay her marriage till the middle of August, that she might have longer time to prevail upon Elizabeth to consent to it, she had consummated that marriage without giving her Majesty any intimation, on the 29th of July, and had thereby disappointed both Elizabeth and some foreign princes, who thought as strangely of the alliance as she did.—To this it was answered, that it was true, that though Mary's resolution was fixed before Sir Nicolas Throckmorton came into Scotland, she had, nevertheless, promised to delay her marriage in the hope that the doubts entertained by Elizabeth, as to the propriety of the said marriage, might in the meantime, be removed; but that this promise was made expressly on the condition, that Commissioners should be appointed on both sides to discuss the matter, and that, as Elizabeth refused to nominate any such commissioners, Mary was relieved from her promise; that further, she had good reasons, known to herself and her own people, with which no other prince needed to interfere, for consummating her marriage at the time she did; and that, with regard to foreign princes thinking the alliance strange, she had a perfect knowledge of the opinions, and had obtained the express consent of the principal and greatest princes in Christendom. *Third*, Elizabeth was astonished how Mary, in direct opposition to the conditions of the treaty of peace, existing between England and Scotland, could detain her Majesty's subjects, Lennox and Darnley in Scotland, having allured them thither under a pretence of suits for lands, but in reality to form an alliance without her Majesty's consent and license,—an offence so unnatural, that the world spoke of it, and her Majesty could not forget it.—To this it was answered, that Mary marvelled not a little at the Queen, her good sister, insisting any further upon this head, for she did not understand how it could be found strange that she detained within her realm the person with whom she had joined herself in marriage, or a Scottish Earl, whom Elizabeth herself named by his Scottish title, the more especially as they both came to her with Elizabeth's consent and letters of recommendation; and that she had no doubt that the world spoke as sound sense would dictate, judging that her detaining of them was in no ways prejudicial to any treaty of peace, existing between the two realms, since no annoyance was intended towards Elizabeth, her kingdom, or estate. *Fourth*, Elizabeth wondered that Mary's ambassador, Mr John Hay, came to ask to be informed of her Majesty's objections to the marriage, and of what she wished to be done, but had no authority either to agree to, or refuse her requests; and she therefore supposed that he had been sent more as a piece of empty form, than for any useful purpose.—To this it was answered, that Mary, though willing to hear Elizabeth's objections, if any such existed, and to endeavour to remove them, had yet expressly declared, that she would make such endeavour only through the medium of commissioners mutually agreed on; and that she was still so convinced of the expediency of the match, that though now married, she was still willing, if Elizabeth wished it, to have its propriety discussed by such commissioners. *Fifth*, Elizabeth begged that an explanation might be given of a sentence in one of Mary's French letters, which she found somewhat obscured, and which ran thus,—"Je n'estimerois jamais que cela vienne de vous, et sans en chercher autre vengeance, j'aurois recours à tous les princes mes allies pour avec moi vous remonstrer ce que je vous suis par parentage. Vous savez assez ce que vous avez resolu sur cela."—To this it was answered, that Mary, by the whole of her letter, as well as the passage in question, meant no other thing but to express her desire to remain in perfect friendship and good intelligence with the Queen her sister, from whom she expected such treatment as reason and nature required from one princess to another, who was her cousin; and that if, as God forbid, other treatment were received, which Mary would not anticipate, she could do no less than lay her case before other princes, her friends and allies. *Sixth*, Elizabeth was grieved to see that Mary encouraged fugitives and offenders from England, and practised other devices within her Majesty's realm; and that, in her own kingdom, seduced by false counsellors and malicious information, she raised up factions among the nobility.—To this it was answered, that if the Scottish Queen really wished to offend Elizabeth, she would not be contented with such paltry practices as those she was accused of towards English subjects;—and that, with regard to her proceedings in her own realm, as she had never interfered with Elizabeth's order of government, not thinking it right that one state should have a finger in the internal policy of another, so she requested that Elizabeth would not meddle with her's, but trust to her discretion, as the person most interested, to preserve peace and quietness. *Seventh*, Elizabeth warned Mary to take good heed that she did not proceed in her intention to suppress and extirpate the religion already established in Scotland, or to effect the suppression of the Reformed faith in England, for that all such designs, consultations, intelligences, and devices, should be converted to the peril and damage of those that advised and engaged in them.—To this it was answered, that Mary could not but marvel at Elizabeth's fears for a religion upon which no innovation had ever been attempted, but for the establishment of which every arrangement had been made most agreeable to her Scottish subjects; that as to an intention to interfere with the spiritual faith of England, she never heard of it before; but that, if any practices to such effect could be condescended on, they should instantly be explained and altered; and that, with regard to her designs, consultations, intelligences and devices, such as she really engaged in, would be found no vainer or more deceitful than those of her neighbours. *Eighth* and *lastly*, Elizabeth wished that Mary would not show herself so given to change, as to conceive evil of the Earl of Murray, whose just deserts she had so long acknowledged, for that by indifference and severity, there were plenty examples to prove, that many noble men had been constrained to take such measures for their own security, as they would otherwise never have resorted to; and that these were *part* of the reasons why Elizabeth was offended with Mary.—To this it was answered, that Mary wished her good sister would not meddle with the affairs of her Scottish subjects any more than Mary meddled with the affairs of Elizabeth's English subjects; but that, if Elizabeth desired any explanation of her conduct towards Murray, it would be willingly given, as soon as Elizabeth explained her motives for committing to the Tower Lady Margaret, Countess of Lennox, mother-in-law and aunt of Mary; and that, as soon as Elizabeth stated any *other* grounds of offence, they should be answered as satisfactorily as the above had been.[101]

Having thus triumphantly replied to the English Queen's irritating message, Mary, in the true spirit of conciliation, had the magnanimity to propose that the following articles should be mutually agreed upon. On the part of the King and Queen of Scotland,—*First*, That their Majesties being satisfied of the Queen their sister's friendship, are content to assure the Queen, that during the term of her life, or that of her lawful issue, they will not, directly or indirectly, attempt any thing prejudicial to their sister's title to the Crown of England, or in any way disturb the quietness of that kingdom. *Second*, They will enter into no communication with any subject or subjects of the realm of

England, in prejudice of their said sister and her lawful issue, or receive into their protection any subjects of the realm of England, with whom their sister may have occasion to be offended. *Third*, They will not enter into any league or confederation with any foreign prince, to the hurt, damage, and displeasure of the Queen and realm of England. *Fourth*, They will enter into any such league and confederation with the Queen and realm of England, as shall be for the weal of the princes and subjects on both sides. And, *Fifth*, They will not go about to procure in any way, alteration, innovation, or change in the religion, laws, or liberties of the realm of England, though it should please God at any time hereafter to call them to the succession of that kingdom. In consideration of these offers, the three following equally reasonable articles were to be agreed to, on the part of England;—*First*, That by Act of Parliament, the succession to the Crown, failing Elizabeth and her lawful issue, shall be established first, in the person of Mary and her lawful issue, and failing them, in the person of the Countess of Lennox and her lawful issue, as by the law of God and nature, entitled to the inheritance of the said Crown. *Second*, That the second offer made by the King and Queen of Scotland be also made on the part of England; and, *Third*, That the third offer shall be likewise mutual. To have agreed to these liberal articles would not have suited Elizabeth's policy, and we consequently hear nothing farther concerning them.

On the 15th of August 1565, Murray summoned the rebellious nobles to a public meeting at Ayr, where it was resolved that they should assemble together in arms on the 24th. Mary in consequence issued proclamations, calling upon her loyal subjects to come to Edinburgh, with their kin, friends, and household, and provided for fifteen days, on the 25th of August. On that day she left Edinburgh with a numerous force, and marched to Linlithgow. Before leaving the capital, measures were taken to prevent the discontented there from turning to advantage the absence of their sovereign. The Provost, who was entirely under the management of Knox, and strongly suspected to favour the rebels, was displaced, and a more trust-worthy civic officer appointed in his stead. Knox himself, a few days before, had, been suspended from the discharge of his clerical duties, in consequence of a seditious and insulting sermon he delivered before the young King, who paid him the compliment of attending divine service in St Giles's church, a Sunday or two after his marriage. In this sermon the preacher, among other things, said, that God had raised to the throne, for the sins of the people, boys and women; adding, in the words of Scripture,—"I will give children to be their princes, and babes shall rule over them: children are their oppressors, and women rule over them." In the same style of allusions grossly personal, he remarked, that "God justly punished Ahab, because he did not correct his idolatrous wife, the harlot Jezabel." It is singular, that Knox never thought of objecting to Mary's marriage with Darnley, till he found that his patron, the Earl of Murray, to whom he was now reconciled, did not approve of it. He had said only a few months before that—"The Queen being at Stirling, order was given to Secretary Lethington to pass to the Queen of England, to declare to that Queen, Mary was minded to marry her cousin, the Lord Darnley; and the rather, because he was so near of blood to both Queens; for, by his mother, he was cousin-german to the Queen of Scotland, also of near kindred and the same name by his father;—his mother was cousin-german to the Queen of England. Here, mark God's providence: King James V., having lost his two sons, did declare his resolution to make the Earl of Lennox his heir of the crown; but he, prevented by sudden death, that design ceased. Then came the Earl of Lennox from France, with intention to marry King James's widow; but that failed also: he marries Mary Douglas; and his son, Lord Darnley, marrieth Queen Mary, King James V.'s daughter: and so the King's desire is fulfilled, viz.—the crown continueth in the name and in the family." Knox had changed his opinion (as even Knox could sometimes do), both when he preached the above-mentioned sermon, and when, towards the end of August 1565, he said, that the Castle of Edinburgh was "shooting against *the exiled for Christ Jesus' sake.*"[102]

From Linlithgow, Mary advanced with an increasing force, first to Stirling, and then to Glasgow. Here she was within a short distance of the rebel army, which, mustering about 1200 strong, had taken its position at Paisley; "a fine pleasant village," says Keith, "five miles W.S.W. from Glasgow." But Murray, not venturing to attack the Royalists, made a circuit at some distance and, by a forced march, arrived unexpectedly at Edinburgh, where he hoped to increase his force. In this hope he was grievously disappointed. Finding that the Provost, who was taken by surprise, had not sufficient strength to keep him without the walls, he entered the city by the West Port, and immediately despatched messengers for assistance in every direction, and, by beat of drum, called upon all men who wished to receive wages "for the defence of the glory of God," to join his standard. But Knox confesses, that few or none resorted to him, and that he got little or no support in Edinburgh; although the preacher himself did all he could for his patron by prayers and exhortations, in which he denominated the rebels "the best part of the nobility, and chief members of the Congregation."[103] The truth is, that the current of popular opinion ran directly in favour of Mary; for the *godly* Earl's real motives were well understood.

As soon as the Queen was made aware that she had missed her enemies, she marched back in pursuit of them, at the head of 5000 men, as far as Callender. Murray could only fly from a power which he knew he was not able to withstand. Alarmed by Mary's speedy return, he left Edinburgh, and again passing her on the road, led his followers to Lanark, and from thence to Hamilton. With indomitable perseverance, the Queen retraced her steps to Glasgow, expecting Murray would make an attempt upon that city. But finding there was no safety for him in this part of Scotland, he suddenly turned off towards the south, and with as little delay as possible, retired into Dumfries-shire. Here, being near the Borders, he expected that Elizabeth would send him succour from England, and at all events, he could at any time make good his retreat into that country. The principal noblemen with him were the Duke of Chatelherault, the Earls of Argyle, Glencairn, and Rothes, and the Lords Boyd and Ochiltree. Morton and Maitland remained with the Queen; but the fidelity of both is much to be suspected, though the command of the main body of the Royal army was intrusted to the former. The Earl of Lennox led the van, and the Queen herself rode with her officers in a suit of light armour, carrying pistols at her saddle-bow; "her courage," says Knox, "manlike, and always increasing." She did not think it worth while to follow Murray into Dumfries-shire, but preferred leading her army through Fife, to St Andrews, taking possession, on the way, of Castle Campbell, the seat of the rebel Lord, Argyle.

Elizabeth in the mean time was far from being inattentive to the interests of her servants in Scotland. Randolph wrote to Cecil, that if she would assist them with men and more money, he doubted not but one country would receive both the Queens; by which he meant, that the rebels would thus be able to fulfil their design, of sending Mary prisoner into England.[104] The Earl of Bedford informed his mistress of the arrival of her friends on the Borders, and hinted to her that their cause was evidently not very popular in Scotland, and that their force was much inferior to that of Mary. Elizabeth's letter, in answer, is as artful a piece of writing as has ever proceeded even from a female pen. Afraid that she might go too far in assisting the losing party, she resolved to make it be believed that she acted against them, whilst in truth she secretly encouraged and supported them. With this view, she wrote to Bedford, that in consequence of his representations, as well as those of Randolph and others, she sent him three thousand pounds; one thousand of which was to be paid immediately to Murray, in the most private way possible, and as if it came from Bedford himself. The remainder was to be kept till occasion required its expenditure. "And where, we perceive," she continued, "by your sundry letters, the earnest request of the said Earl of Murray and his associates, that they might have at least 300 of our soldiers to aid them, and that you also write, that though we would not command you to give them aid, yet if we would but wink at your doing herein, and seem to blame you for attempting such things, as you, with the help of others, should bring about, you doubt not but things would do well,—we are content, and do authorize you, if you shall see it necessary for their defence, to let them (as of your own adventure, and without notification that you have any direction therein from us), to have the number of 300 soldiers, wherein you shall so precisely deal with them, that they may perceive your care to be such as, if it should otherwise appear, your danger should be so great, as all the friends you have could not be able to save you towards us. And so we assure you, our conscience moveth us to charge you so to proceed with them; and yet we would not that either of these were known to be our act, but rather to be covered with your own desire and attempt." Having further mentioned, that she had written lately to Mary, to assure that princess of her esteem and good will, Elizabeth boldly affixed her signature to this memorable record of unblushing duplicity.[105]

But Mary was not to be lulled into dangerous security. All her operations during this campaign were, as Robertson has remarked, "concerted with wisdom, executed with vigour, and attended with success." At St Andrews, she issued a proclamation, exposing the hollowness of the grounds upon which arms had been taken up against her, and showing that religion was only made a cloak to cover other more ungodly designs. Alluding, in particular, to the Earl of Murray, upon whom she had bestowed so many benefits, this proclamation stated, that his insatiable ambition was not to be satisfied with heaping riches upon riches, and honour upon honour, unless he should also continue to have, as he had too long had, the Queen and the whole realm in his own hands, to be used and governed at his pleasure. "By letters sent from themselves to us," Mary says, "they make plain profession that the establishment of religion will not content them, but we must per force be governed by such council as it shall please them to appoint unto us." "The like," she adds, "was never demanded of any our most noble progenitors heretofore, yea, not even of governors or regents; but the prince, or such as occupied his place, ever chose his council of such as he thought most fit for the purpose. When we ourselves were of less age, and at our first arrival in our realm, we had free choice of our council at our pleasure; and now, when we are at our full majority, shall we be brought back to the state of pupils and minors, or be put under tutelage? So long as some of them bore the whole swing with us themselves, this matter was never called in question; but now, when they cannot be longer permitted to do and undo all things of their appetite, they will put a bridle in our mouths, and give us a council chosen after their phantasy! To speak it in plain language, they would be king themselves; or at the least, leaving to us the bare name and title, take to themselves the whole use and administration of the kingdom."[106]

After levying a small fine of two hundred marks from the town of Dundee, which had given some countenance to the malcontents, Mary and Darnley returned to Edinburgh. They there received such accounts of the increasing strength of the rebels, as induced them to determine on marching southwards. Biggar was named as the place of rendezvous for the lieges, and they flocked in such crowds to join the standard of their sovereign, that the Queen was enabled to advance towards the Borders at the head of an army of 18,000 men. Before this greatly superior force, Murray and his partisans, including his 300 English soldiers, retired to Carlisle. He was closely followed thither, upon which his troops dispersed, and he himself and his friends sought refuge by flying further into England. Mary, after visiting the castle of Lochmaben, left Bothwell, with some troops, to watch the Borders; and, on the 18th of October, returned to Edinburgh with the rest of her army.[107]

Of the rebellious nobles thus forced into exile, the Duke of Chatelherault alone was able or willing to make his peace immediately. He and his sons were pardoned, on condition of their living abroad—a degree of leniency extended to them by Mary, in opposition to the wishes of the house of Lennox, which was anxious for the entire ruin of the Hamiltons.[108] Murray and the rest, being kindly received by Bedford, fixed their residence at Newcastle, whence the Earl himself, and the Abbot of Kilwinning, were deputed to proceed to the English court, and lay the state of their affairs before Elizabeth, upon whose patronage they conceived they had peculiar claims. It was, however, no part of Elizabeth's policy to befriend in their adversity those with whom she had associated herself in more prosperous days. As soon as she heard that Murray was on his way to her court, she wrote to stop him, and to inform him that it was not meet for him to have any "open dealing" with her. But at Bedford's earnest entreaty he was allowed to continue his journey, the object of which, he said, was to make some proposals for the "common cause."[109] It was nevertheless a long while before he could obtain an audience of the Queen; and when that honour was at length conceded to him, she had the confidence to ask him, with an unruffled countenance, how he, being a rebel to her sister of Scotland, durst have the boldness to come within her realm? Murray, in reply, ventured to speak of the support he had all along received from her; but as this was betraying her policy to her continental neighbours, it exasperated her to such a degree, that she declared he and his friends should never obtain any thing from her but scorn and neglect, unless he made a public recantation of such an assertion. With this demand both the Earl and the Abbot had the meanness to comply; and though Sir Nicolas Throckmorton interfered in their behalf, and openly avowed that he had been sent into Scotland expressly to make offers of assistance to the rebel lords, he could not save them from the degradation which Elizabeth inflicted. They appeared before her when she was surrounded by the French and Spanish ambassadors, and impiously affirmed, upon their knees, that her Majesty had never moved them to any opposition or resistance against their own Queen. As soon as they had uttered this falsehood, Elizabeth said to them,—"Now ye have told the truth; for neither did I, nor any in my name, stir you up against your Queen. Your abominable treason may serve for example to my own subjects to rebel against me. Therefore, get ye out of my presence; ye are but unworthy traitors."[110]

Sir James Melville, speaking of this affair, says, with his usual quaintness, that "Mary chasit the rebel lords here and there, till at length they were compellit to flee into England for refuge, to her that had promised, by her ambassadors, to wair (expend) her Croun in their defence, in case they were driven to any strait for their opposition to the said marriage."—"But Elizabeth," he adds, "handlit the matter sae subtilly, and the other twa sae blaitly, that she triumphed both over them and the ambassadors." The deputation returned quite chop-fallen, to their friends at Newcastle, where they lived for some time in great poverty, and very wretchedly. Such were the more immediate results of this piece of juggling on the part of Elizabeth, and justly unsuccessful rebellion on that of Murray.

CHAPTER XV.

THE EARL OF MORTON'S PLOT.

Hitherto, Mary's government had been prosperous and popular. Various difficulties had, no doubt, surrounded her; but, by a prudence and perseverance, beyond her sex and age, she had so successfully encountered them, that she fixed herself more firmly than ever on the throne of her ancestors. The misfortunes, however, in which all the intrigues of her enemies vainly attempted to involve her, it was Mary's fate to bring upon herself, by an act, innocent in so far as regarded her own private feelings, and praiseworthy in its intention to increase and secure the power and happiness of her country. This act was her marriage with Darnley. From this fatal connexion, all Mary's miseries took their origin; and as the sunshine which has as yet lighted her on her course, begins to gleam upon it with a sicklier ray, they who have esteemed her in the blaze of her prosperity, will peruse the remainder of her melancholy story with a deeper and a tenderer interest. Let it at the same time be remembered, that the present Memoirs come not from the pen of a partisan, but are dictated by a sacred desire to discover and preserve the truth. Mary's weaknesses shall not be concealed; but surely, whilst the common frailties of humanity thus become the subjects of history, justice imposes the nobler and the more delightful duty of asserting the talents and vindicating the virtues of Scotland's fairest Queen.

It was evident, that public affairs could not long continue in the position in which they now stood. With the Earl of Murray and the Hamiltons, the greater number of Mary's most experienced counsellors were in a state of banishment. At the head of those who remained was the crafty Earl of Morton, who, though he affected outward allegiance, secretly longed for the return of his old allies and friends of the Protestant party. It was not indeed without some show of reason that the professors of the Reformed faith considered their religion to be exposed at the present crisis to hazard. The King now openly supported Popery; the most powerful of the Lords of the Congregation were in disgrace; several of the Catholic nobility had lately been restored to their honours; some of the Popish ecclesiastics had, by Mary's influence, been allowed to resume their place in Parliament; and above all, ambassadors arrived from the French King and her Continental friends, for the express purpose of advising the Queen to grant no terms to the expatriated nobles, and of making her acquainted, with the objects of the Holy League which had been recently formed. This was the league between Charles IX. and his sister the Queen of Spain, with the consent of her husband

Philip, and Pope Pius IV., and at the instigation of Catherine de Medicis and the Duke of Alva, to secure, at whatever cost, the suppression of the Reformation throughout Europe. So great a variety of circumstances, all seeming to favour the old superstition, alarmed the Protestants not a little; but this alarm was unnecessarily exaggerated, and Mary's intentions which were not known at the time, have been misrepresented since.

Robertson has asserted, that Mary "instantly joined" the Continental Confederacy, and was willing to go any length for the restoration of Popery. He would thus have us believe that she was a direct party to the horrible massacre of the Hugonots in France; and that she would have spared no bloodshed to re-establish in Scotland that form of worship which she herself, in conjunction with her Parliament, had expressly abrogated. Robertson goes further, and maintains, with a degree of absurdity so glaring that we are at a loss to understand why it should never before have been exposed, that "to this fatal resolution (that of joining the Anti-Protestant Confederacy) may be imputed all the subsequent calamities of Mary's life." Why a secret contract which Mary might have made with an ambassador from France, the terms or effects of which were never known or felt in any corner of Scotland, should have produced "all her subsequent calamities," must remain an enigma to those who do not possess the same remarkable facility of tracing effects to their causes which seems to have been enjoyed by Dr Robertson. But it is extremely doubtful that Mary ever gave either her consent or approbation to this League. Robertson's authorities upon the subject by no means bear him out in his assertions. He affirms, that "she allowed mass to be celebrated in different parts of the kingdom; and declared that she would have mass free for all men who would hear it." But the first part of this information is supplied by the Englishman Bedford, who was not then in Scotland, and the second rests upon the authority of the insidious Randolph. Robertson likewise mentions, that Blackwood, in his "*Martyre de Marie*," says, "that the Queen intended to have procured in the approaching Parliament, if not the re-establishment of the Catholic religion, at least something for the ease of Catholics." But this announcement of what was *intended* is so very unimportant, that even, if true, it requires no refutation; the more especially, as Blackwood goes on to say, though Robertson stops short, that this "something for the ease of Catholics" was only to be a request that the Protestants would be more tolerant.[111] Robertson however adds, that "Mary herself, in a letter to the Archbishop of Glasgow, her ambassador in France, acknowledges '*that in that Parliament she intended to have done some good with respect to restoring the old religion.*'" For this quotation from Mary's letter, Robertson refers to Keith; but upon making the reference, it will be found that he has somewhat unaccountably garbled the original. All that Mary wrote to her ambassador concerning the Parliament was, that "the spiritual estate is placed therein in the ancient manner, *tending to have done some good* anent restoring the old religion, and to have proceeded against our rebels according to their demerits."[112] The different shade of meaning which Robertson has given to this passage, is rather singular.

Having thus seen the weakness of these preliminary arguments against Mary's willingness to countenance the Reformed faith, it only remains to be inquired, whether she was a party to the confederacy formed at Bayonne. It will be recollected, that the measures concocted by this confederacy were of the most sanguinary and savage description. It was resolved, "by treachery and circumvention, by fire and the sword, utterly to exterminate the Protestants over Christendom." It might very fairly be asked, and the question would carry with it its own answer, whether such a scheme, uncertain as its results were, and sure to produce in the mean time civil war and confusion wherever its execution was attempted, was at all consistent either with Mary's established policy, or her so earnestly cherished hopes of succession to the English crown? Robertson, however, says, "she instantly joined the confederacy;" and Dr Gilbert Stuart, an historian of greater research and more impartiality, allows himself to believe the same thing. These writers ground their belief on what they have found in Sir James Melville and in Keith. But the former gives us not the slightest reason to suppose that Mary had any thing to do with the League, although he allows that the representations of the French ambassador tended to harden her heart towards the Earl of Murray and the other rebels.[113] It would even appear, by his Memoirs, that Mary was never asked to become a party to the confederacy; for Sir James simply states, that the ambassadors came "with a commission to stay the Queen in nowise to agree with the Lords Protestants that were banished." Conæus, in his Life of Mary, leaves entirely the same impression, and rather strengthens it.[114] As to Keith, he nowhere goes the length of Robertson or Stuart,—merely remarking that the letters from France tended much to hinder the cause of the banished Lords. He gives, it is true, in his Appendix, an extract of a letter from Randolph to Cecil, in which we find it stated, on the very dubious authority of the English Resident, that the "band to introduce Popery through all Christendom, was signed by Queen Mary." But if Mary had actually done so, it would have been with the utmost secrecy, and surely, above all, she would have concealed such a step from the spy of Elizabeth. This letter is given at full length by Robertson; and on perusing the whole, it expressly appears, that Randolph spoke only from hearsay; for he adds, "If the copy of his band *may be gotten*, it shall be sent as I conveniently may." In the same letter he mentions that most of the nobles had been asked to attend mass, in compliment to the foreign ambassadors, and that they had all refused;

enumerating, among others, Fleming, Livingston, Lindsay, Huntly, and Bothwell; "and of them all, Bothwell is the stoutest, but worst thought of." These Lords must have had little dread of the consequences, else they would not have ventured to refuse. The truth is, Randolph's common practice was, to convert into a fact every report which he knew would be agreeable to Cecil and his mistress; and so little reliance did they place upon the accuracy of his information, that it does not appear Elizabeth ever took any notice of his statement regarding the band, which she would eagerly have done had it been true. So much, therefore, for Robertson's declaration, that "to this fatal resolution may be imputed all the subsequent calamities of Mary's life." They would have been few, indeed, had they taken their origin in any countenance she gave to the ferocious wickedness of continental bigotry.[115]

There does not, then, exist a shadow of proof that Mary contemplated the subversion of the Reformed religion in Scotland, though it may safely be admitted that she was greatly perplexed what course to pursue towards the expatriated rebels. On the one hand, Elizabeth petitioned in their behalf, well knowing she could depend on their co-operation, as soon as they were again in power; and her petition was warmly supported by Murray's friends in Scotland,—some for the sake of religion,—many for their own private interests,—and a few because they believed his return would be for the good of the country. On the other hand, the Catholic party was delighted to be rid of such formidable adversaries, and their wishes were enforced by those of Mary's uncle, the Cardinal of Lorraine. Besides, though disposed to be lenient almost to a fault, she cannot but have felt just indignation against men who had so grossly abused her kindness, and insulted her authority. It was in the midst of these contending opinions and interests, that a Parliament was summoned, first for the 4th of February 1566, and afterwards prorogued till the 7th of March, at which it was determined that, in one way or other, the subject should be set at rest. The matter would then most probably have terminated unfavourably for Murray, had not the whole affair assumed a new feature, and been hurried on to an unexpected and violent conclusion, under influences on which it would have been difficult to have calculated.

Mary had been Darnley's wife only a few months, when a painful conviction was forced upon her of the error she had committed in so far as regarded her own happiness, in uniting her fortunes with a youth so weak, headstrong, and inexperienced. The homage, whether real or affected, which before his marriage Darnley paid to Mary,—his personal graces and accomplishments, —and the care he took to keep as much as possible in the background, the numerous defects of his character, had succeeded in securing for him a place in Mary's heart, and, what he considered of greater importance, a share of her throne. But as soon as the object of his ambition was obtained, the mask was thrown aside. He broke out into a thousand excesses,—offended almost all the nobility,—and forgetting, or misunderstanding the kind of men he had to deal with, cherished a wild and boyish desire to make his own will law. He changed from the Protestant to the Catholic religion; but the Catholics had no confidence in him, whilst John Knox and the Reformers lifted up their voices loudly against his apostasy. He was addicted to great intemperance in his pleasures; was passionately fond of his hounds and hawks, grossly licentious, and much given to drinking. Upon one occasion, his indulgence in this latter vice made him so far forget himself, that at a civic banquet where the Queen and he were present, he dared to speak to her so brutally, that she left the place in tears.[116]

But there were other causes, besides the imperfections of Darnley's character, which served to sow dissension between him and his young wife. It would be wrong to say that they were mutually jealous of each other's love of power, for this would be to put Mary on an equality with her husband, who was Queen in her own right, while Darnley had no title to any authority beyond what she chose to confer on him. In the first ardor of her affection, however, she permitted him, with the confiding generosity of sincere attachment, to carry every thing his own way; and he was too conceited and selfish to appreciate as it deserved, the value of the trust she thus reposed in him. "All honour," says Randolph, "that may be attributed unto any man by a wife, he hath it wholly and fully,—all praise that may be spoken of him, he lacketh not from herself,—all dignities that she can endow him with, are already given and granted. No man pleaseth her that contenteth not him. And what may I say more? She hath given over unto him her whole will, to be ruled and guided as himself best liketh."[117] This was nothing more than the conduct naturally to be expected from a woman who warmly loved her husband, and who, in the ingenuous integrity of her heart, believed him worthy of her love. Had this indeed been the case, no evil consequences could have resulted from the excess of kindness she lavished on him; but with all his fair exterior, Darnley was incapable of understanding or estimating aright the mind and dispositions of Mary Stuart. Had he even in part answered the expectations she had formed of him,—had he listened to the prudent councils of Sir James Melville, and others whom Mary requested he would associate near his person,—and had he continued those affectionate attentions which she had a right to expect, but had far too proud a spirit to ask, he might have obtained from her every honour he desired. But what she felt that slighted love did not call upon her to yield, it was in vain to expect to win from her by force or fear; and the consequence was, that about this time, what was technically termed the *Crown matrimonial*, became a great source of dissension between herself and her husband.

On the day that Mary gave her hand to Darnley, she conferred upon him the title of King of Scotland; and his name, in all public writs, was signed, in some before, and in others after her own. The public coin of the realm, issued subsequent to the marriage, also contained his name.[118] But though Darnley had the title, and to a certain extent the authority of a King, it was never Mary's intention to surrender to him an influence in the administration greater then her own. This was the object, however, at which his discontented and restless spirit aimed, and it was to achieve it that he demanded the *crown-matrimonial*,—a term used only by Scottish historians, by many of whom its exact import does not appear to have been understood. In its more limited acceptation, it seems to have conferred upon the husband, who married a wife of superior rank, the whole of her power and dignity, so long as their union continued. Thus, if a Countess married an Esquire, he might become, by the marriage-contract, a *matrimonial Earl*; and, during the life of the Countess, her authority was vested in her husband, as entirely as if he had been an Earl by birth. But it was in a more extended sense that Darnley was anxious for this matrimonial dignity. Knowing it to be consistent with the laws of Scotland, that a person who married an heiress, should keep possession of her estate, not only during his wife's life, but till his own death, he was desirous of having a sovereign sway secured in his own person, even though Mary died without issue. In the first warmth of her attachment to Darnley, the Queen might have been willing, with the consent of Parliament, to gratify his ambition; but as soon as his unstable and ill-regulated temper betrayed itself, she felt that she was called upon, both for her own sake, and that of the country, to refuse his request.

The more opposition Darnley experienced, the more anxious he became, as is frequently the case, to accomplish his wishes. It was now for the first time, that he found Rizzio's friendship fail him. That Italian, whom the bigotry of the Reformers, and the ignorant prejudices of more recent historians, have buried under a weight of undeserved abuse, was one of the most faithful servants Mary ever had. He approved of her marriage with Darnley for state reasons, and had, in consequence, incurred the hatred of Murray and his party, whilst Darnley, on the contrary, had courted and supported him. But Rizzio loved his mistress too well to wish to see her husband become her master. His motives, it is true, may not have been altogether disinterested. He knew he was a favourite with Mary, and that he would retain his situation at court so long as her influence was paramount; but he had not the same confidence in the wayward and vacillating Darnley, who was too conceited to submit to be ruled, and too weak to be allowed to govern. The consequence naturally was, that a coldness took place between them, and that the consideration with which Mary continued to treat Rizzio, as her foreign secretary, only served to increase Darnley's disaffection.

Such was the state of matters, when the Earl of Morton, secretly supported by Maitland, and more openly by the Lords Ruthven and Lindsay, determined on making use of Darnley's discontent to forward his own private interests, and those of some of his political friends. His object was, in the first place, to strengthen his own party in the government, by securing the return of Murray, Argyle, Rothes, and the other banished Lords; and in the second, to prevent certain enactments from being passed in the approaching Parliament, by which Mary intended to restore to her ecclesiastics a considerable portion of church lands, which he himself, and other rapacious noblemen, had unjustly appropriated. These possessions were to be retained only by saving the rebels from the threatened forfeitures, and thus securing a majority in Parliament. But Mary, with a firmness which was the result of correct views of good government, was now finally resolved not to pardon Murray and his accomplices. For offences of a far less serious nature, Elizabeth was every month sending her subjects to the block; and it would have argued imbecility and fickleness in the Queen of Scots, so soon to have forgotten the treachery of her own, and her husband's enemies. There was scarcely one of her ministers, except Rizzio, who had the courage and the good sense to confirm her in these sentiments; and he continued to retain his own opinion, both in this affair and that of the crown-matrimonial, notwithstanding the open threats of Darnley, the mysterious insinuations of Morton, and the attempt at bribery on the part of Murray. This last nobleman, who had played the hypocrite so abjectly before Elizabeth and her court, did not scruple, in his selfish humility, to offer his respects, and to send presents to one whom he had always been accustomed to call, in the language of his historian Buchanan, "an upstart fellow," "a base miscreant," "a contemptible mushroom," and to whom he had never before given any thing but "a sour look."[119]

It may therefore be said, that there were, at this time, four powerful parties connected with Scotland;—Mary was at the head of one,—Morton of another, —Darnley of a third,—and Murray of the fourth. But so long as the Queen retained her ascendency, the other three factions could have little hope of arriving at their respective objects. Mutually to strengthen each other, a coalition very naturally suggested itself, founded upon the principle of a reciprocity of benefits. The idea was soon matured, and the plan of operations concocted with a secrecy and callous cruelty, worthy of Morton. The usual expedient was adopted, of drawing up and signing a formal bond, or set of articles, which were entered into between Henry, King of Scotland, and James, Earl of Murray, Archibald, Earl of Argyle, Andrew, Earl of Rothes, Robert, Lord Boyd, Andrew, Lord Ochiltree, and certain others "remaining in England;" in which it was stipulated, on the part of the Lords, that, at the first

Parliament which should be held after their return, they should take such steps as would secure to Darnley a grant of the crown-matrimonial for all the days of his life; and that, whoever opposed this grant, they should "seek, pursue, and extirpate out of the realm of Scotland, or take and slay them,"—language, it will be observed, which had a more direct application to Mary than to any one else. On the part of Darnley, and in return for these favours, it was declared, that he should not allow, in as much as in him lay, any forfeiture to be led against them; and that, as soon as he obtained the crown-matrimonial, he should give them a free remission for all crimes,—taking every means to remove and punish any one who opposed such remission.[120] In plain language, these articles implied neither more nor less than high treason, and place Darnley's character, both as a husband and a man, in the very worst point of view, showing him as a husband to be wofully deficient in natural affection, and as a man to be destitute of honour, and incapable of gratitude.

Morton's intrigues having proceeded thus far, there seemed to be only one other step necessary to secure for him the accomplishment of his purposes. Mary, strong in the integrity of her own intentions, and in the popularity of her administration, did not suspect the secret machinations which were carried on around her; and of this over-degree of confidence in the stability of her resources, Morton determined to take advantage. He saw that a change in the government must be effected at whatever risk, though he knew that nothing but a sudden and violent measure could bring it about. It was now February; —Parliament was to meet on the 7th of March, and on the 12th the trial of the absent Lords was to come on, and after they had been forfeited, the church-lands would be restored to their rightful owners. If Mary's person, however, could be seized,—if her principal anti-protestant ministers could be removed from about her,—and if Darnley could be invested for a time with the supreme command, these disagreeable consequences might be averted, and the Parliament might be either prorogued, or intimidated into submission. But, without a shadow of justice, to have openly ventured upon putting the Queen in ward, would have been too daring and dangerous. A scheme therefore was formed, by which, under the pretence of caring for her personal safety, and protecting the best interests of the country, she was to be kept, as long as they should think necessary, from exercising her own independent authority. By this scheme it was resolved to make David Rizzio the victim and the scape-goat of the conspiracy. Morton and his accomplices well knew that Rizzio was generally hated throughout Scotland. The Reformers, in particular, exaggerating his influence with the Queen, delighted in representing him as the minion of the Pope, and the servant of Antichrist, and there were no terms of abuse too gross which they did not direct against the unfortunate Italian. It would, therefore, give a popular effect to the whole enterprise, were it to be believed that it was undertaken principally for the sake of ridding the country from so hateful an interloper. Many historians, confounding the effect with the cause, have been puzzled to explain why Rizzio's murder should have led so immediately to the return of Murray and his friends; they forget that it was, on the contrary, a determination to secure their return, and to discover a plausible pretext for retaining Mary a prisoner in her own palace, that led to the murder.

In the meantime, Rizzio was not without some apprehensions for his personal safety. The Scots, though they seldom evince much reluctance to secure their own advancement in foreign countries, are of all nations the most averse to allow strangers to interfere with their affairs at home. Aware that they have little enough for themselves, they cannot bear to see any part of what they consider their birthright given away to aliens, however deserving. Rizzio's abilities, and consequent favour with the Queen, were the means of placing in his hands so much power and wealth, that he incurred the hatred and envy of almost every one about court. In the homely but expressive language of Melville, "some of the nobility would gloom upon him, and some of them would shoulder him and shoot him by, when they entered in the chamber, and found him always speaking with her Majesty." Buchanan, that able but most prejudiced and disingenuous historian, expressing the prevalent sentiments of the day, says that, "the low birth and indigent condition of this man, placed him in a station in which he ought naturally to have remained unknown to posterity; but that which fortune called him to act and to suffer in Scotland, obliges history to descend from its dignity to record his adventures." As if "low birth and indigent condition" have ever been, or will ever be, barriers sufficient to shut out genius and talent from the road to greatness. But Rizzio was in truth far from being of that officious, conceited, and encroaching disposition, which Buchanan has ascribed to him. Sir James Melville, who knew him well, gives quite an opposite impression of his character. He mentions, that not without some fear, Rizzio lamented his state to him, and asked his council how to conduct himself. Sir James told him, that strangers ought to be cautious how they meddled too far in the affairs of foreign countries, for that, though he was her Majesty's Continental secretary, it was suspected a great deal of Scottish business also passed through his hands. "I advised him," says Melville, "when the nobility were present, to give them place, and pray the Queen's Majesty to be content therewith; and shewed him for an example, how I had been in so great favour with the Elector Palatine, that he caused set me at his own table, and the board being drawn, used to confer with me in presence of his whole Court. Whereat divers of them took great indignation against me, which, so soon as I perceived, I requested him to let me sit from his own table with the rest of his gentlemen, and no more to confer with me in their presence, but to send a page for me, any time that he had leisure, to come to him in his chamber; which I obtained, and that way made my master not to be hated, nor myself to be envied; and willed him to do the like, *which he did*, and said unto me afterwards, that the Queen would not suffer him, but would needs have him to use himself in the old manner." Melville then spoke to Mary herself upon the subject, and she expressly told him, that Signor David Rizzio "meddled no further but in her French writings and affairs, as her other French secretary had done before."[121]

Rizzio's religion was another reason why he was so very unpopular. It was confidently asserted that he was in the pay of the Pope; and that he was in close correspondence with the Cardinal of Lorraine. Be this as it may, the support he undoubtedly gave, so far as lay in his power, to the Scottish Catholics, was of itself enough, in these times of bigotry, to make his assassination be considered almost a virtue. Besides, there were some more personal and private grounds for Morton and his friends wishing to get rid of the Secretary. There is a remarkable passage in Blackwood's *Martyre de Marie*, by which it would appear, that it was not the original intention of the conspirators to assassinate Rizzio, but merely to secure the person of Mary; and that it was in consequence of Rizzio's fidelity to the Queen, and refusal to sanction such a proceeding, that they afterwards changed their plan. "The Earl of Morton," says Blackwood, "had apartments in the royal palace.[122] There lodged there also her Majesty's Secretary, David Rizzio, a Piedmontese, and a man of great experience, and well versed in affairs of state. He was much respected by his mistress, not for any beauty or external grace that was in him, being rather old, ugly, austere, and disagreeable, but for his great fidelity, wisdom, and prudence, and on account of several other good qualities which adorned his mind. But, on the other hand, his master (the King) hated him greatly, both because he had laboured to effect the re-establishment of the house of Hamilton," (the Duke of Chatelherault, it will be recollected, was the only one of the rebels who had been pardoned), "and because *he had not only refused to become a party to, but had even revealed to the Queen* a certain conspiracy that had been concluded on between his Highness and the rebels, by which it was resolved to shut up her Majesty in a castle, under good and sure guard, that Darnley might gain for himself all authority, and the entire government of the kingdom. My Lord Ruthven, the head of this conspiracy, entertained the greatest ill-will against the poor Secretary, because he had neither dared nor been able to conceal from her Majesty, that he had found Ruthven and all the conspirators assembled together in council in a small closet, and had heard her husband express himself with especial violence and chagrin. Besides, Morton, fearing greatly the foresight and penetration of this man, whom he knew to be entirely opposed to his designs, resolved to accomplish his death, and in so doing comply with the advice which had been given him by the English Court." This is a passage of much interest, and puts in a clear and strong point of view the treasonable designs of this formidable conspiracy.[123]

CHAPTER XVI.

THE ASSASSINATION OF DAVID RIZZIO.

It was on the evening of Saturday the 9th of March 1566,[124] that the conspirators determined to strike the blow, which was either to make or mar them.[125] The retainers of Morton, and the other Lords his accomplices, assembled secretly in the neighbourhood of the Palace, to the number of nearly five hundred. They were all armed, and when it became dark, Morton, who took the command, led them into the interior court of Holyroodhouse, which, in his capacity of Lord High Chancellor of the kingdom, he was able to do, without much difficulty or suspicion. It had been arranged, that he should remain to guard the entry to the palace, whilst Ruthven, with a select party, was to proceed to the Queen's chamber. Patrick Lord Ruthven was exactly the sort of person suited for a deed of cowardice and cruelty, being by nature cursed with dispositions which preferred bigotry to religion, and barbarism to refinement. He was now in the forty-sixth year of his age, and had been for some months confined to a sick-bed, by a dangerous disease.[126] Though scarcely able to walk, he nevertheless undertook to head the assassins. He wore a helmet, and a complete suit of armour concealed under a loose robe.[127]

Mary, altogether unsuspicious of the tragedy about to be performed, sat down to supper, as usual, at seven o'clock. There were with her only her illegitimate sister, the Countess of Argyle, her brother the Lord Robert Stuart, and her Foreign Secretary, David Rizzio. Beaton, her Master of the Household, Erskine, an inferior attendant, and one or two other servants of the Privy Chamber, were in waiting at a side-table; or, in the words of Stranguage, "tasting the meat taken from the Queen's table, at the cupboard, as the servants of the Privy Chamber use to do."[128] It is a curious and interesting fact, that notwithstanding all the changes which time has wrought on the Palace of Holyrood, the very cabinet in which Mary supped, on this eventful evening, as well as the adjoining rooms and passages through which the conspirators came, still exist, in nearly the same state in which they were in the year 1566. The principal staircase, in the north-west tower, leads up to the Queen's chamber of presence;—passing through this apartment, a door opens into Mary's bedroom, where her own bed yet stands, although its furniture is now almost in tatters. It was in the small closet or cabinet off her bed-room, containing one window, and only about twelve feet square, that Mary sat at supper on the 9th of March, two hundred and sixty-two years ago. Communicating with Darnley's chamber, immediately beneath, there was, and is, a private passage into Mary's bedroom, by which it could be entered, without previously passing through the presence-chamber. The approach to this passage from the Queen's room is concealed by a piece of wainscot, little more than a yard square, which hangs upon hinges in the wall, and opens on a trap-stair. It had been originally proposed to seize Rizzio in his own apartment; but this plan was abandoned, for two reasons; *first*, because it was less certain, since it was often late before Rizzio retired for the night, since he sometimes did not sleep in his own room at all, but in that of another Italian belonging to the Queen's household, named Signor Francis, and since there were back-doors and windows, through which he might have effected his escape; and, *second*, because it would not have so much intimidated Mary, and would have made it necessary to employ another party to secure her person—the chief object of the conspirators.[129]

To ascertain whether there was any thing to hinder the execution of their design, Darnley, about eight o'clock, went up the private stairs, and, entering the small room where his wife was supping, sat down familiarly beside her. He found, as he expected, his victim Rizzio in attendance, who, indeed, owing to bad health, and the little estimation in which he was held by the populace, seldom went beyond the precincts of the palace.[130] He was dressed, this evening, in a loose *robe-de-chambre* of furred damask, with a satin doublet, and a hose of russet velvet; and he wore a rich jewel about his neck, which was never heard of after his death.[131] The conspirators having allowed sufficient time to elapse, to be satisfied that all was as they wished, followed the King up the private way, which they chose in order to avoid any of the domestics who might have been in the presence-chamber, and given an alarm. They were headed by the Lord Ruthven, and George Douglas, an illegitimate son of the late Earl of Angus, and the bastard brother of Darnley's mother, the Lady Lennox; a person of the most profligate habits, and an apt instrument in the hands of the Earl of Morton. These men, followed by as many of their accomplices as could crowd into the small room where Mary sat, entered abruptly and without leave; whilst the remainder, to the number of nearly two score, collected in her bedroom. Ruthven, with his heavy armour rattling upon his lank and exhausted frame, and looking as grim and fearful as an animated corpse, stalked into the room first, and threw himself unceremoniously into a chair. The Queen, with indignant amazement, demanded the meaning of this insolent intrusion, adding, that he came with the countenance, and in the garb of one who had no good deed in his mind. Turning his hollow eyes upon Rizzio, Ruthven answered, that he intended evil only to the villain who stood near her. On hearing these words, Rizzio saw that his doom was fixed, and lost all presence of mind; but Mary, through whose veins flowed the heroic blood of James V., and his warlike ancestors, retained her self-possession. She turned to her husband, and called upon him for protection; but perceiving that he was disposed to remain a passive spectator of the scene, she ordered Ruthven to withdraw under pain of treason, promising, that if Rizzio was accused of any crime, it should be inquired into by the Parliament then assembled. Ruthven replied only by heaping upon the unfortunate Secretary a load of abuse; and, in conclusion, declared the determination of the conspirators to make themselves masters of Rizzio's person. Rizzio, scarcely knowing what he did, pressed close into the recess at the window, with his dagger drawn in one hand, and clasping the folds of Mary's gown with the other. In spite of every threat, he remained standing behind her, and continually exclaiming in his native language, and in great agitation, *Giustizia! Giustizia!* Mary's own person was thus exposed to considerable danger, and the assassins desired Darnley to take his wife in his arms and remove her out of the way. The confusion and terror of the scene now increased a hundredfold;—the master of the household, and the three or four servants of the privy-chamber, attempted to turn Lord Ruthven out of the room;—his followers rushing to his support, overturned the supper-table, threw down the dishes and the candles, and, with hideous oaths, announced their resolution to murder Rizzio. Their own impetuosity might have frustrated their design; for, had not the Countess of Argyle caught one of the candles in her hand as it was falling, they would have been involved in darkness, and their victim might have escaped.

The first man who struck Rizzio was George Douglas. Swords and daggers had been drawn, and pistols had been presented at him and at the Queen; but no blow was given, till Douglas, seizing the dirk which Darnley wore at his side, stabbed Rizzio over Mary's shoulder, though, at the moment, she was not aware of what he had done. The unhappy Italian was then forcibly dragged out into the bed-room, and through the presence-chamber, where the conspirators, gathering about him, speedily completed the bloody deed, leaving in his body no fewer than fifty-six wounds. He lay weltering in his gore at the door of the presence-chamber for some time; and a few large dusky spots, whether occasioned by his blood or not, are to this day pointed out, which stain that part of the floor. The body was afterwards thrown down the stairs, and carried from the palace to the porter's lodge, with the King's dagger still sticking in his side. He was obscurely buried next day; but, subsequently, more honourably near the Royal vault in Holyrood Chapel.[132]

Such was the unhappy end of one who, having come into Scotland poor and unbefriended, had been raised, through the Queen's penetration and his own talents, to an honourable office, the duties of which he discharged with fidelity. If his rise was sudden, his fall was more so; for, up to the very day of his assassination, many of the Scottish nobility, says Buchanan, "sought his friendship, courted him, admired his judgment, walked before his lodgings, and observed his levee." But death no sooner put an end to his influence, than the memory of the once envied Italian was calumniated upon all hands. Knox even speaks approvingly of his murder, (as he had formerly done of that of Cardinal Beaton), assuring us that he was slain by those whom "God raised up to do the same"—an error, indicating a distorted moral perception, from the reproach consequent on which, his biographer, M'Crie, has unsuccessfully endeavoured to defend him.[133] The Reformer adds to his notice of Rizzio, a story which suits well the superstitious character of the times, and which Buchanan has repeated. He mentions, that there was a certain John Daniot, a French priest, and a reputed conjuror, who told Rizzio "to beware of a bastard." Rizzio, supposing he alluded to the Earl of Murray, answered, that no bastard should have much power in Scotland, so long as he lived; but the prophecy was considered to be fulfilled, when it was known that the bastard, Douglas, was the first who stabbed him.[134]

In the meantime, the Earl of Morton, who had been left below, to guard the gates, being informed that Rizzio was slain, and that Ruthven and Darnley retained possession of the Queen's person, made an attempt to seize several of the nobility who lodged in the palace, and whom he knew to be unfavourable to his design of restoring the banished Lords. Whether it was his intention to have put them also to death, it is difficult to say; but it is at all events not likely that he would have treated them with much leniency. The noblemen in question, however, who were the Earls of Huntly, Bothwell, and Athol, the Lords Fleming and Livingston, and Sir James Balfour, contrived, not without much difficulty, to effect their escape. The two first let themselves down by ropes at a back window; Athol, who was supping in the town with Maitland, was apprised of his danger, and did not return to Holyrood that night. He, or some of the fugitives, hastened to the Provost of Edinburgh, and informed him of the treasonable proceedings at the Palace. The alarm-bell was immediately rung; and the civic authorities, attended by five or six hundred of the loyal citizens, hastened down to Holyrood, and called upon the Queen to show herself, and assure them of her safety. But Mary, who was kept a prisoner in the closet in which she had supped, was not allowed to answer this summons, the conspirators well knowing what would have been the consequences. On the contrary, as she herself afterwards wrote to her ambassador in France, she was "extremely threatened by the traitors, who, in her face, declared, that if she spoke to the town's people they would cut her in collops, and cast her over the walls." Darnley went to the window, and informed the crowd that he and the Queen were well, and did not require their assistance; and Morton and Ruthven told them, that no harm had been done, and beseeched them to return home, which, upon these assurances, they consented to do.

A scene of mutual recrimination now took place between Mary and her husband, which was prolonged by the rude and gross behaviour of Ruthven. That barbarian, returning to the Queen's apartment, after having imbrued his hands in the blood of Rizzio, called for a cup of wine, and having seated himself, drained it to the dregs, whilst Mary stood beside him. Being somewhat recovered from the extreme terror she had felt when she saw her Secretary dragged away by the assassins, she rebuked Ruthven for his unmannerly conduct; but he only added insulting language to the crimes he had already committed. Perceiving, however, that her Majesty was again growing sick and ill, (and even without considering, what the conspirators well knew, that she was in the seventh month of her pregnancy, her indisposition will excite little wonder), he proposed to the King that they should retire, taking care to station a sufficiently strong guard at the door of Mary's chamber. "All that night," says Mary, "we were detained in captivity within our chamber, and not permitted to have intercommunion scarcely with our servant-women."[135]

Next morning, although it was Sunday, the conspirators issued a proclamation in the King's name, and without asking the Queen's leave, proroguing the Parliament,—and commanding all the temporal and spiritual lords, who had come to attend it, to retire from Edinburgh. Illegal as it was, this proclamation was obeyed; for Morton, and his accomplices, had the executive power in their own hands, and Mary's more faithful subjects were taken so much by surprise, that they were unable to offer any immediate resistance. Mary herself was still kept in strict confinement; and the only attempt she could make to escape, which was through the assistance of Sir James Melville, failed. Sir James was allowed to leave the Palace early on the forenoon of Sunday; and, as he passed towards the outer gate, Mary happened to be looking over her window, and called upon him imploringly for help. "I drew near unto the window," says Melville, "and asked what help lay in my power, for that I should give. She said, 'Go to the Provost of Edinburgh, and bid him, in my name, convene the town with speed, and come and relieve me out of these traitors' hands; but run fast, for they will stay you.'" The words were scarcely spoken, before some of the guards came up, and challenged Sir James. He told them, he "was only passing to the preaching in St Giles's Kirk," and they allowed him to proceed. He went direct to the Provost, and delivered his commission from the Queen; but the Provost protested he did not know how to act, for he had received contrary commands from the King; and, besides, the people, he said, were not disposed to take up arms to revenge Rizzio's death. Sir James was, therefore, reluctantly obliged to send word to Mary, by one of her ladies, that he could not effect her release. In the course of the day, Mary was made acquainted with Rizzio's fate, and she lamented the death of her faithful servant with tears. Between seven and eight in the evening, the Earls of Murray and Rothes, with the other banished Lords, arrived from England. During the whole of the night, and all next day, the Queen was kept as close a prisoner as before.

Morton and his accomplices, however, now found themselves in a dilemma. They had succeeded in bringing home their rebel friends, in proroguing or dissolving the Parliament, in conferring upon Darnley all the power he wished, in murdering Rizzio, and in chasing from Court the nobles who had formed part of the administration along with him. But to effect these purposes, they had grossly insulted their lawful sovereign, and had turned her own palace into a prison, constituting themselves her gaolers. Having achieved all their more immediate objects, the only remaining question was— what were they to do with the Queen? If they were to set her at liberty, could they expect that she would tamely forget the indignities they had offered her, or quietly submit to the new state of things they had established? Had they, on the other hand, any sufficient grounds for proceeding to further extremities against her? Would the country allow a sovereign, whose reign had been hitherto so prosperous, to be at once deprived of her crown and her authority? [136] Daring as these men were, they could hardly venture upon a measure so odious. Besides, Darnley, always vacillating, and always contemptible, was beginning to think he had gone too far; and, influenced by something like returning affection for his beautiful consort, who was probably in a month or two to make him a father, he insisted that the matter should now be allowed to rest where it was, provided Mary would promise to receive into favour the Lords who had returned from banishment, and would grant a deed of oblivion to all who had taken a part in the recent assassination. Morton, Ruthven, Murray, and the rest, were extremely unwilling to consent to so precarious an arrangement; but Darnley overruled their objections. On Monday evening, articles were drawn up for their security, which he undertook to get subscribed by the Queen; and, trusting to his promises, all the conspirators, including the Lords who had just returned, withdrew themselves and their retainers from Holyroodhouse, and went to sup at the Earl of Morton's.[137]

As soon as Mary found herself alone with Darnley, she urged, with all the force of her superior mind, every argument she could think of, to convince him how much he erred in associating himself with the existing cabal. She was not aware of the full extent to which he was implicated in their transactions; for he had assured her, that he was not to blame for Rizzio's murder, and as yet she believed him innocent of contriving it. She spoke to him therefore, with the confidence of an affectionate wife, with the winning eloquence of a lovely woman, and with the force and dignity of an injured

Queen. She at length satisfied him, that his best hopes of advancement rested in her, and not on men who having first renounced allegiance to their lawful Queen, undertook to confer upon him a degree of power which was not their's to bestow. Darnley further learned from Mary, that Huntly, Bothwell, Athol, and others, had already risen in her behalf, and yielding to her representations and entreaties, he consented that they should immediately make their escape together. At midnight, accompanied only by the captain of the guard and two others, they left the palace, and rode to Dunbar without stopping.

In a few days, Mary having been joined by more than one half of her nobility, found herself at the head of a powerful army. The conspirators, on the other hand, seeing themselves betrayed by Darnley and little supported by the country, were hardly able to offer even the shadow of resistance to the Queen. Still farther to diminish the little strength they had, Mary resolved to make a distinction between the old and the new rebels; and, influenced by reasons on which Morton had little calculated, she consented to pardon Murray, Argyle, and others, who immediately resorted to her, and were received into favour. After remaining in Dunbar only five days, she marched back in triumph to Edinburgh, and the conspirators fled in all directions to avoid the punishment they so justly deserved. Morton, Maitland, Ruthven, and Lindsay betook themselves to Newcastle, where, for aught that is known to the contrary, they occupied the very lodgings which Murray and his accomplices had possessed a week or two before.

The whole face of affairs was now altered; and Mary, who for some days had suffered so much, was once more Queen of Scotland. "And such a change you should have seen," says Archbishop Spottiswood, "that they who, the night preceding, did vaunt of the fact (Rizzio's murder) as a godly and memorable act, affirming, some truly, some falsely, that they were present thereat,—did, on the morrow, forswear all that before they had affirmed." But it was not in Mary's nature to be cruel, and her resentments were never of long continuance. Two persons only were put to death for their share in Rizzio's slaughter, and these were men of little note. Before the end of the year, most of the principal delinquents, as will be seen in the sequel, were allowed to return to Court. Lord Ruthven, however, died at Newcastle of his old disease, a month or two after his flight thither. His death occasioned little regret, and his name lives in history only as that of a titled murderer.[138]

CHAPTER XVII.

THE BIRTH OF JAMES VI.

Mary's vigorous conduct had again put her in possession of that rightful authority of which so lawless an attempt had been made to deprive her; but though restored to power, she was far from being likewise restored to happiness. The painful conviction was now at length forced upon her, that she had not in all the world one real friend. She felt that the necessities of her situation forced her to associate in her councils men, who were the slaves of ambition, and whose heartless courtesies were offered to her, only until a prospect of higher advantages held out a temptation to transfer them to another. She had not been long in her own kingdom, before Bothwell and others contemplated seizing her person, and assassinating her prime minister, the Earl of Murray;—she had hardly succeeded in frustrating these designs, when Murray himself directed his strength against her; and now, still more recently, the husband, for whose sake she had raised armies to chase her brother from the country, had aimed at making himself independent, and, to ingratiate himself with traitors, had scrupled not to engage in a deed of wanton cruelty, personally insulting to his wife and sovereign.

Ignorant where to turn for repose and safety, Mary began to lose much of the natural vivacity and buoyancy of her temper; and to feel, that in those turbulent times, she was endowed with too little of that dissimulation, which enabled her sister Elizabeth to steer so successfully among the rocks and shoals of government. In a letter written about this period to one of her female relations in France, she says, touchingly, "It will grieve you to hear how entirely, in a very short time, I have changed my character, from that of the most easily satisfied and care-chasing of mortals, to one embroiled in constant turmoils and perplexities." "She was sad and pensive," says Sir James Melville, "for the late foul act committed in her presence so irreverently. So many great sighs she would give that it was pity to hear her, and over-few were careful to comfort her." But the perfidy of her nobles Mary could have borne;—it was the disaffection and wickedness of her husband that afflicted her most. Anxious to believe that he told her the truth, when he asserted that he was not implicated in the murder of Rizzio, she rejoiced to see him issue a proclamation, declaring that he was neither "a partaker in, nor privy to, David's slaughter." But the truth was too notorious to be kept long concealed. Randolph wrote to Cecil on the 4th of April 1566:—"The Queen hath seen all the covenants and bands that passed between the King and the Lords, and now findeth that his declaration before her and Council, of his innocency of the death of David, was false; and is grievously offended, that by their means he should seek to come to the crown matrimonial." Hence sprang the grief which, in secret, preyed so deeply upon Mary's health and spirits. Few things are more calculated to distress a generous mind, than to discover that the object of its affections is unworthy the love which has been lavished upon it. The young and graceful Darnley, laying at Mary's feet the real or pretended homage of his heart, was a very different person from the headstrong and designing King, colleaguing with her rebels, assassinating her faithful servant, and endeavouring to snatch the crown from her head. "That very power," says Robertson, "which, with liberal and unsuspicious fondness she had conferred upon him, he had employed to insult her authority, to limit her prerogative, and to endanger her person: such an outrage it was impossible any woman could bear or forgive." Yet Mary looked upon these injuries, coming as they did from the man whom she had chosen to be the future companion of her life, "more in sorrow than in anger;" and though she shed many a bitter tear over his unworthiness, she did not cease to love him.

In the midst of these anxieties, the time for the Queen's delivery drew near. After a short excursion to Stirling and the neighbourhood, in which she was accompanied by Darnley, Murray, Bothwell and others, she returned to Edinburgh, and, by the advice of her Privy Council, went to reside in the Castle, as the place of greatest security, till she should present the country with an heir to the throne. During the months of April and May, she lived there very quietly, amusing herself with her work and her books, and occasionally walking out, for she had no wheeled carriage. She occupied herself, too, in endeavouring to reconcile those of her nobility whom contrary interests and other circumstances had disunited. It cost her no little trouble to prevail upon the two most faithful of her ministers, the Earl of Huntly her Chancellor, and Bothwell her Lord High Admiral, to submit to the returning influence of their old enemy the Earl of Murray. It was especially galling to them, that Murray and Argyle were the only persons, in addition to the King, allowed to reside in the Castle with Mary. But it was her own wish to have her husband and her brothers beside her on the present occasion; and no representations made by Bothwell or Huntly could alter her resolution. Yet these two Earls went the length of assuring the Queen, that Murray had entered into a new conspiracy with Morton, and that they would probably put in ward both herself and her infant, as soon as it was born. Surrounded as Mary was by traitors, she could not know whether this information was true or not; but her returning affection for Murray prevailed over every other consideration.[139]

Elizabeth was all this time narrowly watching the progress of affairs in Scotland. Murray's restoration to favour pleased her much; and, to reconcile

Morton and his friends to the failure of their plots, she secretly countenanced and protected them. With her usual duplicity, however, she sent to Edinburgh Henry Killigrew, to congratulate Mary on her late escape, and to assure her that she would give directions to remove Morton out of England. She likewise recalled Randolph, of whose seditious practices Mary had complained; but, as if to be even with the Scottish Queen, she commanded Killigrew to demand the reason why a certain person of the name of Ruxby, a rebel and a Papist, had been protected in Scotland? It would have been better for Elizabeth had she allowed this subject to rest. Though Ruxby feigned himself a refugee from England on account of religion, he had in reality been privately sent to Scotland by Elizabeth herself, and her Secretary Cecil. The object of his mission was to find out whether Mary carried on any secret correspondence with the English Catholics. For this purpose, he was to pretend that he was a zealous supporter of her right and title to the crown of England; and that he had some influence with the English Catholics, all of whom, he was to assert, thought as he did. Having thus ingratiated himself with Mary, he was immediately to betray any discoveries he might make to Cecil. The scheme was ingeniously enough contrived; coming as an avowed enemy to Elizabeth, and she herself actually supplying credentials to that effect, no suspicion was for some time entertained of his real designs. That he was able to learn any thing which could afford the English Queen reasonable ground of offence, is not likely; for though several communications in cipher passed between him and Cecil, their contents were never made public. Shortly before Killigrew's arrival, Ruxby's real character had been accidentally discovered; and when the ambassador, more for the sake of aiding than of hindering the spy in the prosecution of his object, made a *pro forma* request that he should not be harboured any longer, Mary instantly ordered him to be apprehended, and all his writings and ciphers to be seized and examined. The indubitable evidence which they afforded of Elizabeth's systematic cunning, forced a smile from Mary, and might have brought a blush to the cheek of her rival. The Queen of Scots, however, did not condescend to give any utterance to the feelings which this affair must have inspired; and nothing further is known of Elizabeth's disgraced and detected minion.[140]

Early in June, perceiving that the time of her delivery was at hand, Mary wrote letters to her principal nobility, requiring them to come to Edinburgh during that juncture. She then made her will, which she caused to be thrice transcribed;—one copy was sent to France, a second committed to the charge of her Privy Council, and the third she kept herself. The day preceding her delivery, she wrote, with her own hand, a letter to Elizabeth, announcing the event, but leaving a blank "to be filled," says Melville, "either with a son or a daughter, as it might please God to grant unto her."

On Wednesday the 19th day of June 1566, between nine and ten in the morning, the Queen was safely delivered of a son. The intelligence was received every where, throughout Scotland, with sincere demonstrations of joy. "As the birth of a prince," says Keith, "was one of the greatest of blessings that God could bestow upon this poor divided land; so was the same most thankfully acknowledged by all ranks of people, according as the welcome news thereof reached their ears." In Edinburgh, the triumph continued for several days; and, upon the first intimation of the event, all the nobility in the town, accompanied by most of the citizens, went in solemn procession to the High Church, and offered up thanksgiving for so signal a mercy shown to the Queen and the whole realm.

When the news was conveyed to England, it was far from being heard with so much satisfaction. It was between eleven and twelve on the morning of the 19th, that the Lady Boyne came to Sir James Melville, and told him, that their prayers being granted, he must carry Mary's letter to London with all diligence. "It struck twelve hours," says Sir James, "when I took my horse, and I was at Berwick that same night. The fourth day after, I was at London,"—a degree of despatch very unusual in those times. Melville found Elizabeth at Greenwich, "where her Majesty was in great merriness, and dancing after supper. But so soon as the Secretary Cecil sounded the news in her ear of the prince's birth, all merriness was laid aside for that night; every one that was present marvelling what might move so sudden a changement. For the Queen sat down with her hand upon her haffet (cheek), and bursting out to some of her ladies, how that the Queen of Scotland was lighter of a fair son, and that she was but a barren stock." Next morning, Elizabeth gave Melville a formal audience, at which, having had time for preparation, she endeavoured to dissemble her real feelings; though, by over-acting her part, she made them only the more apparent. She told him gravely, that the joyful news he brought her, had recovered her out of a heavy sickness, which had held her for fifteen days! "Then I requested her Majesty," says Melville, "to be a gossip unto the Queen, for our *comers* are called gossips in England, which she granted gladly to be. Then, I said, her Majesty would have a fair occasion to see the Queen, which she had so oft desired. At this she smiled, and said, that she would wish that her estate and affairs might permit her; and promised to send both honourable lords and ladies to supply her room."[141]

CHAPTER XVIII.

MARY'S TREATMENT OF DARNLEY, AND ALLEGED LOVE FOR THE EARL OF BOTHWELL.

As soon as she had sufficiently recovered to be able to quit the Castle, Mary resolved on leaving the fatigues of government behind, and going for some time into the country. Her infant son was intrusted to the care of the Earl of Mar as his governor, and the Lady Mar as his governess. The time was not yet arrived to make arrangements regarding his education; but the General Assembly had already sent a deputation to the Queen, to entreat that she would allow him to be brought up in the Reformed religion. To this request Mary avoided giving any positive answer; but she condescendingly took the infant from the nurse, and put it into the arms of some of the divines. A prayer was pronounced over it; and Spottiswood assures us, that, at the conclusion, the child gave an inarticulate murmur, which the delighted Presbyterians construed to be an *Amen*.

It was the seat of the Earl of Mar at Alloa that the Queen first visited. Being not yet equal to the fatigues of horseback, she went on board a vessel at Newhaven, and sailed up the Forth. She was accompanied by Murray and others of her nobility.[142] Buchanan, whose constant malice and misrepresentation become at times almost ludicrous, says—"Not long after her delivery, on a day very early, accompanied by very few that were privy of her council, she went down to the waterside at a place called the New-haven; and while all marvelled whither she went in such haste, she suddenly entered into a ship there prepared for her. With a train of thieves, all honest men wondering at it, she betook herself to sea, taking not one other with her."— "When she was in the ship," he says elsewhere, "among pirates and thieves, she could abide at the pump, and joyed to handle the boisterous cables."[143] It is thus this trustworthy historian describes a sail of a few hours, enjoyed by Mary and her Court.

Darnley, who, though not very contented either with himself or any one else, was about this time much in the Queen's company, went to Alloa by land, and remained with Mary the greater part of the time she continued at the Earl of Mar's. The uneasiness he suffered, and the peevish complaints to which he was continually giving utterance, were occasioned by the want of deference, with which he found himself treated by all Mary's ministers. But the general odium into which he had fallen, was entirely to be attributed to his own folly. Between him and the Earl of Murray there had long existed a deadly hatred against each other; in associating himself with Morton, and plotting against Huntly and Bothwell, he had irremediably offended these noblemen; and in deserting Morton and his faction, he had forever lost the friendship of the only men who seemed willing to regard him with any favour. The distressing consciousness of neglect occasioned by his own misconduct, was thus forced upon him wherever he turned; and instead of teaching him a lesson of humility, it only served to sour his temper, and pervert his feelings. The Queen was deeply grieved to see him so universally hated; and anxiously endeavoured to make herself the connecting link between him and her incensed nobility. This was all she could do; for, even although she had wished it, she could not have dismissed, to please him, such of her ministers as he considered obnoxious; a measure so unconstitutional would have led to a second rebellion. But she hoped by treating her husband kindly, and showing him every attention herself, to make it be understood that she expected others would be equally respectful. Having spent some days together at Alloa, Mary and Darnley went to Peebles-shire to enjoy the amusement of hunting; but finding little sport, they returned on the 20th of August to Edinburgh. Thence, they went to Stirling, taking the young Prince with them, whom they established in Stirling Castle. Bothwell, in the meantime, in his capacity of Lieutenant of the Borders, was in some of the southern shires attending the duties of his charge.[144]

It is necessary to detail these facts thus minutely, as Mary's principal calumniator, Buchanan, endeavours to establish, by a tissue of falsehoods, that immediately after her delivery, or perhaps before it, she conceived a criminal attachment for Bothwell. This absurdity has gained credit with several later writers, and particularly with Robertson, whose knowledge of Mary's motions and domestic arrangements at the period of which we speak, appears to have been very superficial. Yet he may be regarded as even a more dangerous enemy than the former. Buchanan's virulence and evident party spirit, carry their own contradiction along with them; whilst Robertson, not venturing to go the same lengths, (though guided in his belief entirely by Buchanan), imparts to the authority on which he trusts a greater air of plausibility, by softening down the violence of the original, to suit the calmer tone of *professedly* unprejudiced history. In the progress of these Memoirs, it will not be difficult to show that Robertson's affected candour, or too hastily formed belief, is as little to be depended on as Buchanan's undisguised malice.

Buchanan wishes it to be believed, in the first place, that Mary entertained a guilty love for Rizzio. He then proceeds to assert, that in little more than three months after his barbarous assassination, she had fallen no less violently in love with Bothwell, although, in the meantime, she had been employed in giving birth to her first child, by a husband, whom he allows she doated on nine or ten months before. To bolster up this story, he perverts facts with the most reckless indifference. One specimen of his style we have already seen in his account of the Queen's voyage to Alloa; and proceeding with his narrative, we find him positively asserting in the sequel, that for the two or three following months, Mary was constantly in the company of Bothwell, and of Bothwell alone, knowing as he must have done all the while, that Murray and Darnley, Bothwell's principal enemies, were her chief associates, and that Bothwell spent most of the time in a distant part of the kingdom.

Robertson dates even more confidently than Buchanan, the commencement of Mary's love for Bothwell at a period prior to her delivery. But upon this hypothesis, it is surely odd, that Murray and Argyle were permitted by the Queen to reside in the Castle previous to and during her confinement, whilst the same favour was peremptorily refused to Bothwell; and it is no less odd, that shortly after her delivery, Secretary Maitland, at the intercession of the Earl of Athol, was received once more into favour, in direct opposition to the wishes of Bothwell. It is no doubt possible, that notwithstanding this presumptive evidence to the contrary, Mary may at this very time have had a violent love for Bothwell; but are we to give credit to the improbability, merely because Buchanan was the slave of party feeling, and Robertson disposed to be credulous? Are the detected fabrications of the one, entitled to any better consideration than the gratuitous suppositions of the other? "Strange and surprisingly wild," says Keith, "are the accounts given by Knox, but more especially by Buchanan, concerning the King and Queen about this time. I shall not reckon it worth while to transcribe them here; and the best and shortest confutation I could propose of them is, to leave my readers the trouble, or rather satisfaction, to compare the same with the just now mentioned abstracts (of despatches from Randolph to Cecil) and the three following authentic letters," from the French and Scottish ambassadors and the Queen's Privy Council.[145] Robertson, it is true, after having asserted, that "Bothwell all this while was the Queen's prime confident," and that he had acquired a "sway over her heart," proceeds to confess, that "such delicate transitions of passion can be discerned only by those who are admitted near the persons of the parties, and who can view the secret workings of the heart with calm and acute observation." "Neither Knox nor Buchanan," he adds, "enjoyed these advantages. Their humble station allowed them only a distant access to the Queen and her favourite; and the ardour of their zeal, and the violence of their prejudices rendered their opinions rash, precipitate, and inaccurate." This is apparently so explicit and fair, that the only wonder is, upon what grounds Robertson ventured to make *his* accusation of Mary, having thus shown how little dependence was to be placed on the only authorities which supported him in it. It appears that he came to his conclusions by a process of his own, which rendered him independent both of Knox and Buchanan. "Subsequent historians," he says, "can judge of the reality of this reciprocal passion only by its *effects*." Robertson must of course have been aware that he thus opened the gate to a flood of uncertainty, seeing that the same effects may spring from a hundred different causes. If a man be found dead, before looking for his murderer, it is always proper to inquire whether he has been murdered. Besides, if effects are to be made the criterion by which to form an opinion, the greatest care must be taken that they be not misrepresented. Mary must not be said to have been a great deal in Bothwell's company, at a time she was almost never with him, and she must not be described as being seldom with her husband, at a time they were constantly together.

Laing is another and still later writer, who has produced a very able piece of special pleading against Mary, in which a false colouring is continually given to facts. "After her delivery," he says, "she removed secretly from the Castle, and was followed by Darnley to Alloa, Stirling, Meggetland, and back again to Edinburgh, as if she were desirous to escape from the presence of her husband." That Darnley *followed* Mary, is an assumption of Mr Laing's own. Conceited as the young King was, he would rather never have stirred out of his chamber again, than have condescended to follow so perseveringly one who wished to avoid him, first to Alloa, then to Stirling, then into Peebles-shire, then back again to Edinburgh, and once more to Stirling. The only correct part of Laing's statement is, that Mary chose to go by water to Alloa, whilst Darnley preferred travelling by land; perhaps because he wished to hunt by the way, or call at the seats of some of the nobility. The distance, altogether, was only twenty miles; and the notion that Mary removed "*secretly*" from the Castle, for the important purpose of taking an excursion to Alloa, is absolutely ludicrous. In support of his assertion that Mary had lost her heart to Bothwell, Laing proceeds to mention, that, shortly after the assassination of Rizzio, the Earl, for his successful services, was loaded with favours and preferment. That Mary should have conferred some reward upon a nobleman whose power and fidelity were the chief means of preserving her on a tottering throne, is not at all unlikely; but, to make that reward appear disproportioned to the occasion, Laing *misdates* the time when most of Bothwell's offices of trust were bestowed upon him. Several of them were his by hereditary right, such as those of Lord High Admiral, and the Sheriffships of Berwick, Haddington, and Edinburgh. Part of his authority on the Borders he had acquired during the time of the late Queen-Regent, Mary's mother, having been made her Lieutenant, and keeper of Hermitage Castle, in 1558; and it was immediately after his restoration to favour, during the continuance of Murray's rebellion, that he was appointed Lieutenant of the West and Middle Marches, a situation which implied the superiority of the Abbeys of Melrose and Haddington.[146] The only *addition* made to Bothwell's possessions and titles, in consequence of his services after Rizzio's death, was that of the Castle and Lordship of Dunbar, together with a grant of some crown lands.[147]

There is another circumstance connected with Bothwell, which we omitted to mention before, but which may with propriety be stated here. At the period of which we write, when he is accused of being engaged in a criminal intercourse with Mary, he had been only two or three months married to a wife every way deserving of his love. Three weeks before the death of Rizzio, he had espoused, in the thirty-sixth year of his age, the Lady Jane Gordon, the sister of his friend, the Earl of Huntly. She was just twenty, and was possessed of an elegant and cultivated understanding. They were married at Holyrood, on the 22d of February 1566, after the manner of the Reformed persuasion, in direct opposition to Mary's wishes. She entertained them, however, at a banquet on the first day; and the feasting and rejoicings continued for a week. "The Queen desired," says Knox, "that the marriage might be made in the chapel at the mass, which the Earl Bothwell would in no ways grant."[148] Was there any love existing at this time between Mary and her minister? Robertson and Laing seem to think there was. Choosing to judge of Mary's feelings towards Bothwell by *effects*, not of effects by feelings, they quote several passages from the letters of one or two of the foreign ambassadors then in Scotland, which mention that Bothwell possessed great influence at court. That these ambassadors report no more than the truth may be very safely granted; though certainly there is no evidence to show that he enjoyed so much weight as Murray, or more than Huntly. Yet he deserved better than the former, for he had hitherto, with one exception, continued as faithful to Mary, as he had previously been to her mother. The letters alluded to, only repeat what Randolph had mentioned six months before. So early as October 1565, only two months after Mary's marriage with Darnley, and when her love for him remained at its height, Randolph wrote to Cecil; "My Lord Bothwell, for his great virtue, doth now all, next to the Earl of Athol."[149] Was Mary in love with Bothwell at this date? Or was it with the Earl of Athol? And did she postpone her attachment to Bothwell, till he should prove his for her, by becoming the husband of the Lady Jane Gordon?—We proceed with our narrative.

Having spent some time with Darnley at Stirling, Mary returned to Edinburgh, for the despatch of public business, on the 11th or 12th of September. She wished Darnley to accompany her; but as he could not, or would not, act with either Murray's or Huntly's party, he refused. On the 21st, she came again to Stirling; but was recalled once more to Edinburgh, by her Privy Council, on the 23d. She left the French ambassador, Le Croc, with the wayward Darnley, hoping that his wisdom and experience might be of benefit to him.[150] The distinction which, from this period up to the hour of his death, Darnley constantly made between his feelings for Mary herself, and for her ministers, is very striking. With Mary he was always willing to associate, and she had the same desire to be as much as she could with him; but with the conditions he exacted, and by which alone she was to purchase much of his company, it was impossible for her to comply. She might as well have given up her crown at once, as have dismissed all those officers of state with whom Darnley had quarrelled. The truth is, her husband's situation was a very unfortunate one. His own imbecility and unlawful ambition, had brought upon him general odium; but if he had possessed a stronger mind, or a greater stock of hypocrisy, he might have re-established himself in the good graces of at least a part of the Scottish nobility. But he had neither the prudence to disguise his sentiments, nor the ability to maintain them. "He had not learned," says Chalmers, "to smile, and smile, and be a villain. He was still very young, and still very inexperienced; and the Queen could not easily govern without the aid of those odious men,"—his enemies.

Mary had been only a few days in Edinburgh, when she received a letter from the Earl of Lennox, Darnley's father, which afflicted her not a little. Lennox, who resided principally at Glasgow, had gone to Stirling to visit his son; and Darnley had there communicated to him a design, his present discontents had suggested, which was to leave the country and proceed to the Continent. Both Lennox and Le Croc, "a wise aged gentleman," as Holinshed calls him, had done all they could to divert him from so mad a purpose; but his resolution seemed to be fixed. Mary immediately laid her father-in-law's letter before her Privy Council, who "took a resolution to talk with the King, that they might learn from himself the occasion of this hasty deliberation of his, if any such he had; and likewise, that they might thereby be enabled to advise her Majesty after what manner she should comport herself in this conjuncture."[151] On the evening of the very day that this resolution was adopted, (the 29th of September), Darnley himself arrived at Holyrood;—but being informed that the Earls of Argyle, Murray, and Rothes were with the Queen, he declared he would not enter the palace till they departed.[152] The Queen took this petulant behaviour as mildly as possible; and glad of his arrival, even condescended to go forth from the palace to meet her husband, and conducted him to her own apartment, where they spent the night together.[153]

Next day, Mary prevailed upon her husband to attend a meeting of her Council. They requested to be informed by the King, whether he had actually resolved to depart out of the realm, and if he had, what were the motives that influenced him, and the objects he had in view. They added, "that if he could complain of any of the subjects of the realm, be they of what quality soever, the fault should be immediately repaired to his satisfaction." Mary herself took him by the hand, and speaking affectionately to him, "besought him, for God's sake, to declare if she had given him any occasion for this resolution."[154] She had a clear conscience, she said, that in all her life she had done no action which could any ways prejudge either his or her own honour; but, nevertheless, that as she might, perhaps, have given him offence without design, she was willing to make amends, as far as he should require, —and therefore "prayed him not to dissemble the occasion of his displeasure, if any he had, nor to spare her in the least manner."[155] Darnley answered distinctly, that he had no fault to find with the Queen; but he was either unable or unwilling to explain further. With the stubborn discontent of a petted child, he would neither say one thing nor another—neither confess nor deny. Without agreeing to alter his determination, whatever it might be, and it was perhaps, after all, only a trick contrived to work upon Mary's affections, and intimidate her into his wishes, he at length took his leave. Upon going away, he said to the Queen, "Farewell, Madam; you shall not see my face for a long while." He next bade Le Croc farewell; and then turning coldly to the Lords of the Council, he said, "Gentlemen, adieu."[156]

Shortly afterwards, Mary received a letter from Darnley, in which he complained of two things. "One is," says Maitland, "that her Majesty trusts him not with so much authority, nor is at such pains to advance him, and make him be honoured in the nation, as she at first was. And the other point is, that nobody attends him, and that the nobility deserts his company. To these two points the Queen has made answer, that if the case be so, he ought to blame himself, not her; for that in the beginning she had conferred so much honour upon him, as came afterwards to render herself very uneasy, the credit and reputation wherein she had placed him having served as a shadow to those who have most heinously offended her Majesty; but, howsoever, that she has, notwithstanding this, continued to show him such respect, that although they who did perpetrate the murder of her faithful servant, had entered her chamber with his knowledge, having followed him close at the back, and had named him the chief of their enterprise,—yet would she never accuse him thereof, but did always excuse him, and was willing to appear as if she believed it not. And then as to his being not attended,—the fault thereof must be charged upon himself, since she has always made an offer to him of her own servants. And for the nobility, they come to court, and pay deference and respect, according as they have any matters to do, and as they receive a kindly countenance; but that he is at no pains to gain them, and make himself beloved by them, having gone so far as to prohibit these noblemen to enter his room, whom she had first appointed to be about his person. If the nobility abandon him, his own deportment towards them is the cause thereof; for if he desire to be followed and attended by them, he must, in the first place, make them to love him, and to this purpose must render himself amiable to them; without which, it will prove a most difficult task for her Majesty to regulate this point, especially to make the nobility consent that he shall have the management of affairs put into his hands; because she finds them utterly averse to any such matter."[157]

No answer or explanation could be more satisfactory; and the whole affair exhibits a highly favourable view of Mary's conduct and character. Le Croc accordingly says, in the letter already quoted,—"I never saw her Majesty so much beloved, esteemed, and honoured; nor so great a harmony amongst all her subjects as at present is, by her wise conduct, for I cannot perceive the smallest difference or division." That Darnley ever seriously intended to quit the country, it has been said, is extremely uncertain. It would appear, however, according to Knox, that he still harboured some chimerical design of making himself independent of Mary, and with this view he treacherously wrote to the Pope, and the Kings of Spain and France, misrepresenting the state of affairs, and offering, with their assistance, to re-establish the Catholic religion. Copies of these letters, Knox adds, fell into Mary's hands, who, of course, took steps to prevent their meeting with any attention at the Continental courts.[158] But be this matter as it may, (and its truth rests upon rather doubtful authority, since we find no mention of it, either by the Lords of Privy Council or the French Ambassador), it is certain that Darnley's determination, hastily formed, was as hastily abandoned.[159]

Shortly after her husband's departure from Edinburgh, the Queen, attended by her officers of state, set out upon a progress towards the Borders, with the view, in particular, of holding justice-courts at Jedburgh. The southern marches of Scotland were almost always in a state of insubordination. The recent encouragement which the secret practices, first of Murray and afterwards of Morton, both aided by Elizabeth, had given to the turbulent spirit of the Borderers, called loudly for the interference of the law. Mary had intended to hold assizes in Liddisdale in August, but on account of the harvest, postponed leaving Edinburgh till October. On the 6th or 7th of that month, she sent forward Bothwell, her Lieutenant, to make the necessary preparations for her arrival, and on the 8th, the Queen and her Court set out, —the noblemen and gentlemen of the southern shires having been summoned to meet her with their retainers at Melrose. On the 10th she arrived at Jedburgh. There, or it may have been on her way from Melrose, she received the disagreeable news, that on the very day she left Edinburgh, her Lieutenant's authority had been insulted by some of the unruly Borderers, and that soon after his reaching his Castle of Hermitage, a place of strength about eighteen miles from Jedburgh, he had been severely and dangerously wounded. Different historians assign different reasons for the attack made on Bothwell. Some say that Morton had bought over the tribe of Elliots, to revenge his present disgrace upon one whom he considered an enemy. Others, with greater probability, assert, that it was only a riot occasioned by thieves, whose lawless proceedings Bothwell wished to punish. But whichever statement be correct, the report of what had actually taken place was, as usual, a good deal exaggerated when it reached Mary. Being engaged, however, with public business at Jedburgh, she was prevented, for several days, from ascertaining the precise truth for herself. Finding that she had leisure on the 16th of the month, and being informed that her Lieutenant was still confined with his wounds, she paid him the compliment, or rather discharged the duty of riding across the country with some attendants, both to inquire into the state of his health, and to learn to what extent her authority had been insulted in his person. She remained with him only an hour or two, and returned to Jedburgh the same evening.[160]

The above simple statement of facts, so natural in themselves, and so completely authenticated, acquires additional interest when compared with the common version of this story which Buchanan and his follower Robertson have contrived to render prevalent. "When the news that Bothwell was in great danger of his life," says Buchanan, "was brought to the Queen *at Borthwick*, though the *winter* was very sharp, she *flew in haste*, first to Melrose, then to Jedburgh. There, though she received certain intelligence that Bothwell was alive, yet, being impatient of delay, and not able to forbear, though in such a bad time of the year, notwithstanding the difficulty of the way, and the danger of robbers, she put herself on her journey with such attendants as hardly any honest man, though he was but of a mean condition, would trust his life and fortune to. From thence she returned again to Jedburgh, and there she was mighty diligent in making great preparations for Bothwell's being brought thither."[161] The whole of this is a tissue of wilful misrepresentation. No one, unacquainted with Buchanan's character, would read the statement without supposing that Mary proceeded direct from Borthwick to Hermitage Castle, scarcely stopping an hour by the way. Now, if Mary heard of Bothwell's accident at Borthwick (which is scarcely possible), it must have been, at the latest, on the 9th of October, or more probably on the evening of the 8th; but, so far from being in a hurry in consequence, it appears, by the Privy Council Register, that she did not reach Jedburgh till the 10th, and, by the Privy Seal Register, that she did not visit Hermitage Castle till the 16th of the month.[162] Had she really ridden from Borthwick to the Hermitage and back again to Jedburgh in one day, she would have performed a journey of nearly seventy miles, which she could not have done even though she had wished it. As to her employing herself, on her return to Jedburgh, "in making great preparations for Bothwell's being brought thither," she certainly must have made extremely good use of her time, for she returned on the evening of the 16th, and next day she was taken dangerously ill. The motives which induced Buchanan to propagate falsehood concerning Mary, are sufficiently known; but, being known, Robertson ought to have been well convinced of the truth of his allegations before he drew inferences upon such authority. But the Doctor had laid down the principle, that he was to judge of Mary's love for Bothwell by its *effects*; and it became, therefore, convenient for him to assert, that her visit to Hermitage Castle was one of those effects. "Mary *instantly* flew thither," he says, "with an impatience which strongly marks the anxiety of a lover, but little suiting the dignity of a queen." Now, "instantly," must mean, that she allowed at all events six, and probably seven days to elapse; and that, too, after being informed of the danger one of the most powerful and best affectioned of her nobility had incurred in her behalf. Robertson must have thought it strange, that she staid only an hour or two at the Castle. "Upon her finding Bothwell slightly wounded," says Tytler, "was it love that made her in such a violent haste to return back the same night to Jedburgh, by the same bad roads and tedious miles? Surely, if love had in any degree possessed her heart, it must have supplied her with many plausible reasons for passing that night in her lover's company, without exposing herself to the inconveniences of an uncomfortable journey, and the inclemencies of the night air at that season." If Mary had been blamed for an over-degree of callousness and indifference, there would have been almost more justice in the censure. With honest warmth Chalmers remarks, that "the *records* and the *facts* laugh at Robertson's false dates and frothy declamation."[163]

On the 17th of October, Mary was seized with a severe and dangerous fever, and for ten days her life was esteemed in great danger; indeed, it was at one time reported at Edinburgh, that she was dead. The fever was accompanied with fainting or convulsion-fits, of an unusual and alarming description. They frequently lasted for three or four hours; and during their continuance, she was, to all appearance, lifeless. Her body was motionless; her eyes closed; her mouth fast; her feet and arms stiff and cold. Upon coming out of these, she suffered the most dreadful pain, her whole frame being collapsed, and her limbs drawn writhingly together. She was at length so much reduced, that she herself began to despair of recovery. She summoned together the noblemen who were with her, in particular Murray, Huntly, Rothes, and Bothwell, and gave them what she believed to be her dying advice and instructions. Bothwell was not at Jedburgh when the Queen was taken ill, nor did he show any greater haste to proceed thither when he heard of her sickness than she had done to visit him, it being the 24th of October before he left Hermitage Castle.[164] After requesting her council to pray for her, and professing her willingness to submit to the will of Heaven, Mary recommended her son to their especial care. She entreated that they would give every attention to his education, suffering none to approach him, whose example might pervert his manners or his mind, and studying to bring him up in all virtue and godliness. She strongly advised the same toleration to be continued in matters of religion, which she had practised; and she concluded, by requesting that suitable provision should be made for the servants of her household, to whom Mary was scrupulously attentive, and by all of whom she was much beloved. Fortunately however, after an opportunity had been thus afforded her of evincing her strength of mind, and willingness to meet death, the violence of her disease abated, and her youth and good constitution triumphed over the attack.

Darnley, who was with his father at Glasgow, probably did not hear of the Queen's illness till one or two days after its commencement; but as soon as he was made acquainted with her extreme danger, he determined on going to see her. Here again, we discover the marked distinction that characterized Darnley's conduct towards his wife and towards her nobility. With Mary herself he had no quarrel; and though his love for her was not so strong and pure as it should have been, and was easily forgotten when it stood in the way of his own selfish wishes, he never lost any opportunity of evincing his desire to continue on a friendly footing with her. When he last parted from her at Holyrood, he had said that she should not see him for a long while; but startled into better feelings by her unexpected illness, he came to visit her at Jedburgh, on the 28th of October. The Queen was, by this time, better; but her convalescence being still uncertain, Darnley's arrival was far from being agreeable to her ministers. Should Mary die, one or other of them would be appointed Regent, an office to which they knew that Darnley, as father to the young prince, had strong claims. It was their interest, therefore, to sow dissension in every possible way, between the Queen and her husband; and they trembled lest the remaining affection they entertained for each other, might be again rekindled into a more ardent flame. Mary, when cool and dispassionate, they knew they could manage easily; but Mary, when in love, chose, like most other women, to have her own way. They received Darnley, on the present occasion, so forbiddingly, and gave him so little countenance, that having spent a day and a night with Mary, he was glad again to take his departure, and leave her to carry on the business of the state, surrounded by those designing and factious men who were weaving the web of her ruin.

On the 9th of November, the Queen, with her court, left Jedburgh, and went to Kelso, where she remained two days. She proceeded thence to Berwick, attended by not fewer than 800 knights and gentlemen on horseback. From Berwick, she rode to Dunbar; and from Dunbar, by Tantallan to Craigmillar, where she arrived on the 20th of November 1566, and remained for three weeks, during which time an occurrence of importance took place.

END OF VOLUME FIRST.